Destination: Mystery!

Edited by
Andrew MacRae

DARKHOUSE BOOKS

Destination: Mystery!

These are works of fiction. Any resemblance between events, places, or characters, within them, and actual events, organizations, or people, is but happenstance.

Copyright © 2015 by Darkhouse Books
ISBN 978-0-9961828-3-6

Published August, 2015

Published in the United States of America

Darkhouse Books
160 J Street, #2223

Niles, California 94539

Mackinac Island, at the juncture of Great Lakes Huron and Michigan, and the Upper Peninsula, is the setting of our first story. Movie aficionados will recognize the island as the location for "Somewhere in Time".

Author Jack Bates grew up in Michigan. Mr. Bates is a two-time Derringer nominee. His children's book, "The Santa Spy" received the Best Holiday Book award from the Literary Classics and Book Awards Committee.

Arch Rivals

By Jack Bates

Mirabelle Odom, now in her spry sixties, energetically hiked up a paved trail. Actually, it was more of a road. The lane was wide enough for two horse drawn carriages to pass one another in opposite directions. It led up to or away from a natural formation on the eastern edge of Mackinac Island known as Arch Rock. Maribelle's nylon walking suit made a soft, whisk-whisk-whisk as the pant legs brushed against each other with every step. Behind her, Jessie Cardwell, also in her sixties though not as spry, followed along. Mirabelle could hear her one time closest friend huffing and puffing.

"Come along, Jessie," Mirabelle called over her shoulder.

"How much farther?"

"It's right up ahead."

"It's so dark. Why did we have to come at night?"

"It's the only time the Indian maiden appears."

"Are we supposed to call her that?"

"Oh, they're fine with being called Indian. You just can't say squaw or redskin when talking about them."

"How do you know?"

"I read it in a blog."

"You're always on the computer."

"Actually, this time I read it on my phone on the way to the island while you slept."

"I didn't mean to, Mirabelle. Those darn motion sickness pills tucker me out. I was afraid the waves would make me nauseous. I could still use a nap and I slept pretty much all afternoon."

"You slept through the buffet lunch at the Grand Hotel. You don't get a refund on that."

"I know."

"The dessert display was worth the extra cost alone."

"Was there apple pie?"

Mirabelle stopped walking. Her cheeks felt warm in the cool, summer evening and it wasn't from their trek up the hill. For the moment the whisk-whisk-whisking of her pant suit stayed silent. Somewhere a freighter along the Straits blew a horn. Somewhere else another freighter answered it. The moon made the Lake Huron side of the duel bodies of water sparkle. It was all very serene.

And Mirabelle was extremely pissed.

Jessie drew in a deep breath just to keep talking. "Who would have thought the island was so hilly? Or so humid? Or that there would be so many mosquitos this high up from lake level?"

Mirabelle heard the slap of palm to flesh as her friend swatted another of the pesky insects.

"The French and the British used the terrain as a natural defense," Mirabelle explained. "Up in the center is a large, natural depression they each used to defend Mackinac Island."

"How do you know so much about this place?"

"I taught middle school history for forty years."

"Teachers." The word carried the ignorance of a generation that should have known better than to buy into the idea that all teachers sucked.

Mirabelle bristled a bit at her friend's insinuation. She tried to keep her tone even the way she did when a Jeremy or a Maria smarted off in class. "Come on. We're almost there."

They really hadn't been much of friends as of late.

Two years ago Mirabelle and Jessie moved into the same condo complex. The friendship had been fast. Both had recently become widows. Both had tried living with their daughters. Both couldn't take the constant hovering of their offspring. Secretly, each had put in for a condo at Colonial Mansions, a towering, eighteenth century looking manor. Both were accepted. Within a week, they had struck up a friendship during aquatic aerobics in the complex's indoor pool. For the next year, they were nearly inseparable.

As it happens within inclusive communities like Colonial Mansions, most of the inhabitants are single. They are single because they had a spouse or a companion die on them. No one ever wants to be alone. Relationships develop. Jealousies ensue. It all becomes very middle-schoolish. Mirabelle Odom was quite familiar with this attitude. It was hard not to after witnessing it on a daily basis for over forty years.

The initial falling out with her friend Jessie began over, of all things, a slice of apple pie.

Mirabelle and Jessie had both caught the eye of one Victor Koenig, a tall, lanky man in his seventies with a full head of silvery hair. Koenig provided just the right amount of charm to court each of them. Sometimes all three ate dinner together. Sometimes Victor had lunch with one or the other on their own. The morning he had breakfast with Jessie, Mirabelle knew something was up. Especially since Victor wore the same clothes he had worn to dinner with her the night before.

Mirabelle stewed over the tete-a-tete across the room. Victor had walked Mirabelle back to her room, kissed her goodnight, and excused himself complaining of indigestion from the cafeteria lasagna.

Indigestion indeed.

The lying. The lying got to Mirabelle more than anything else. It gnawed at her. Ate away at her like one of those ridiculous television zombies that looked too weak to snap a twig but had the power to rip away flesh for a meal. That was how lies got to her. One would have thought after forty years of middle school she would just go with it.

But not Mirabelle. She knew all the signs. The eyes that dropped down and to the left. The rise in the voice. The sudden indignation of the liar. Mirabelle often wondered if she could use her talent of recognizing bull-smotch for professional development seminars.

Mirabelle didn't say anything when Jessie sat down with her at lunch the day after Jessie's peccadillo with Victor. And Jessie didn't eagerly offer any of the important details. They made small talk during which Mirabelle suggested they take advantage of one of the weekend getaways Colonial House sponsored. Perhaps if they got away, just the two of them, they could discuss how it would be better if neither of them saw Victor any longer.

And once Jessie agreed, Mirabelle would swoop in and steal him.

She was in the middle of showing Jessie the brochures for casino trips, historic tours, or romantic getaways when Victor approached their table with a tray of desserts. He popped off a wink.

"New job, Vic?" Jessie asked albeit flirtatiously even though Mirabelle wasn't one for adverbs.

"Fresh off the windowsill," Victor said. "Thought we'd try a little of each. Who wants what? I've got apple, peach, and blueberry."

Both ladies simultaneously announced they wanted apple. Victor set down the tray. He turned and walked away. At first Mirabelle thought he was going back to the kitchen for a second piece of apple but he just kept walking until he was out of the cafeteria. He wasn't about to upset his routine by giving the slice to the wrong woman. He'd been getting his pie from both of them for the last couple of months. What irked Mirabelle about the whole recent affair was it was supposed to be her night after yesterday's dinner, not Jessie's.

"Care to tell me what that was about?" Mirabelle asked. "Something about last night?"

Jessie stood. She kept her eyes down but her indignation was up. "I don't know what you're insinuating." She took the slice of apple pie on the small paper plate and carried it from the room. It was clear whose pie Victor preferred.

Mirabelle told herself not to cry. He was just a silly old man.

Of course, that made her a silly old woman.

At dinner on the night of the apple pie incident, Mirabelle arrived late. Sure enough, Jessie and Victor sat together on the patio. It was where all the Colonial Mansions couples sat. Mirabelle took an empty seat at a table of ten. She tried making conversation with her community members. They weren't much into it. During the meal, as she watched the pair on the patio, Mirabelle learned of a woman's infected gums, a man's urinary tract infection, and several other ailments that involved infections. Her meal lost all of its flavor.

Mirabelle took her empty paper cup to the refill station. Just as she was filling it with more cranberry juice, the patio door slid open. In walked Jessie and Victor sharing a private laugh that Mirabelle felt somehow involved her. Just like those snotty seventh grade girls always snickering behind her back. Without realizing it until the cool juice spilled over her hand, Mirabelle crushed the paper cup in her tightening grip choking out ice cubes that looked more like small, puffy pillows.

The inevitable engagement was announced. The envy within Mirabelle only grew. It was a mold sweeping over a brick of cheese or a slice of bread. That was how it consumed her.

One weekend, when Jessie was away at her daughter's to watch her grandchildren, Mirabelle went to Victor's room to seduce him. She still had a bounce in her step, a glint in her eyes. Push-up bras did wonders.

Victor was already occupied. She hoped he didn't contract a gum infection from his companion.

Mirabelle was unable to contain herself. So happy was she that she'd caught Victor in bed with another resident that she immediately sent a text to Jessie. The text that came back began with, 'This is Jessie's daughter. You have very much upset my mother…'

Mirabelle didn't read any more after that.

As the weekend progressed, the guilt of her actions nibbled at her. When Jessie returned on Monday, Mirabelle was there to apologize.

"Let's go away," Mirabelle said. "Just us."

"I don't know."

"There will be fellas from other floors of Colonial Mansions."

"I'm done with men."

"Don't say that. You're still very attractive."

"I'm old and spent."

"Nonsense. We're going and I'm paying."

Jessie shrugged. "What the hell. As long as you're paying."

Mirabelle was a little put-out by Jessie's quick decision go on Maribelle's dime. But the words were out and the deed was done.

The two prepared for their stay on Mackinac Island. A former college had been converted into a cozy resort. On the six hour bus ride up to Mackinaw City, where they would catch a Shepler's Rooster Tail ferry to the island, very little was said between the two. Instead of talking about the rift between them, they had watched an interesting video on island folklore.

One of the stories was of a young, native maiden who thought her lover, a British soldier, had jilted her. In fact, her father had run him off. Despondent over the loss, she went to the top of the highest hill to throw herself to the rocks below. She was visited by Pauguk, a trickster spirit who took the form of her long dead mother. The trickster talked the maiden out of leaping.

The maiden should have known better. Pauguk was an evil spirit who presided over the dead.

The soldier, having gone looking for his love, believed she had jumped when he saw what he thought was her body on the moonlit rocks below. What he didn't know was that it was Pauguk playing a trick upon him. In a show of everlasting love, the soldier jumped to his death calling out her name. The cry woke the maiden who discovered his crumpled body below on the stones. She lay down on the cliff and cried throughout the night.

The soldier was found the next morning by a patrol from Fort Henry. The princess was gone but in her place was a cairn of flat stones that had not previously been there. It rose at one end of an arch carved out of the hillside by her tears. It was said the ghost of the lost maiden returned each night looking for her lover to stop him from jumping.

It was a lovely little story even if it was a heaping pile of bulls-motch.

Why did everything have to be built upon lies? Lies always unravel. Like the time early in her career she had twenty dollars taken from her purse. Two seconds in the hall to talk to the assistant principal and when she returned, she found her purse on the floor and her wallet open and twenty dollars gone. Mirabelle knew who took it. The girl was the only one not to look up when Mirabelle asked the class why her purse was on the floor when it had been in her desk drawer. Mirabelle kept the girl after class to ask her about it and the girl lied to her face. She knew the girl was lying but she couldn't prove it. Then, when the girl graduated from high school five years later, Mirabelle received a card in her teacher's mailbox. Inside it was a note that said 'I'm sorry' and a twenty dollar bill.

After dinner and a couple of aperitifs, Mirabelle suggested they go in search of the ghosts. They were in the spirit for spirits from all of the spirits. The resort the residents of Colonial Mansions Phases One through Three stayed at was on the southeast end of the island. They took a horse drawn taxi to the island's main street where they began the two mile trek up the hill and into the woods. They passed three cemeteries and something with an historical marker called Skull Cave. At last they reached Arch Rock. Ignoring a warning sign, they went out onto a rickety, grated metal, observation deck. The metal walkway squeaked and groaned in the night.

"How long do we have to wait?" Jessie asked.

"Can't you just appreciate the beauty? Look at all those stars."

"I don't think I should have come out here. I'm feeling a little woozy."

"Have some water?" Mirabelle held out a bottle. Jessie shook her head at first. Mirabelle shook the bottle at her. Jessie took the bottle.

Jessie tipped the bottle to her lips. She leaned one hand behind her on the rail. It gave a little and Jessie jumped away from it.

"You've been a good friend, Mirabelle," Jessie said. "You paid for this trip. You looked out for me when Vic and I split."

Mirabelle said nothing. She didn't really expect to see a ghost although at that moment she felt slightly haunted.

"I thought you should know Vic and I have gotten back together."

"I was wondering when you were going to tell me."

"You know?"

"I told you, dear. I taught middle school for forty years. I knew things about my students before they did. Teacher intuition. It's how we learn to let things roll off our backs."

Her own little lie. She never let a lie go unpunished. Administrators would all the time. There was no repercussion for those dirty little liars. Never.

But Mirabelle had her own ways. Shave points here on an assignment, lose a late project, tell a parent at conferences her daughter was in no danger of failing and then punch in that LF, which didn't stand for Low F grade but Lazy Effer. Vengeance was far more satisfying than changing a loser's life.

"And will you let this roll off your back?"

"Water under the bridge. Or in this case, arch."

Jessie stumbled on the grated walkway. She looked at her feet. "Mirabelle. This water."

"Has a little something in it, yes."

Jessie dropped the bottle to the metal grate. It rolled to the drop-off side. Mirabelle heard it strike rock and then it was gone. Off into the abyss of night.

"I'm going to be sick," Jessie said. She turned to the loose and wobbly pipe railing, one of three horizontal balustrades holding up cyclone fencing in an effort to keep visitors safe.

No such luck.

Jessie bent over the rail. It broke free from its shoring. Jessie reached a hand behind her. The hand flapped and searched for Maribelle's. Instead of helping her friend, Mirabelle put her foot to Jessie's backside and pushed. There was a moment where Jessie's hand caught the nylon cuff of Maribelle's walking suit pants. Mirabelle swiftly turned and yanked her ankle free. Behind her Jessie's screams echoed through the arch.

The stars were out without a moon. The serene night cloaked her like a comfortable old coat.

Mirabelle walked back down the darkening trail to her resort. Her pants whisked softly. At some point she'd have to tell the state police about her missing friend. But she would wait until morning when an early riser jogging along the path below or a fisherman from a boat in the channel or someone at the arch spotted Jessie's crumpled and broken body below and called the police. Mirabelle would feign her ignorance. She'd ask the other Colonial Mansions travelers if they'd seen Jessie that morning. She was worried because Jessie had told her she was going for a walk last night after dinner and she hadn't seen her and she wondered if she'd been down to breakfast.

'She wasn't exactly herself,' she'd say tipping a thumb to her lips and winking playfully.

If there was one thing she learned after forty years of teaching it was that liars got away with everything.

Maybe even murder.

Copper Falls Ski Resort skiers from everywhere. But our next story demonstrates that even experienced skiers can get into trouble on the slopes, and sometimes trouble like that can be murder.

Ms Morrone's short stories appear frequently, particularly in the mystery and crime fiction genres. She has a story in Darkhouse Books' "The Anthology of Cozy-Noir", and in our science fiction collection, "Stories from the World of Tomorrow".

Death in the Crease

By Wenda Morrone

James Riggio paused at the base of Callahan lift to read the whiteboard's green magic marker scrawl: closed, avalanche risk. Callahan led to the best and riskiest terrain at Copper Falls Ski Resort, half an hour up the mountain from Copper Falls, Montana. A half dozen times a year Callahan was closed so the Ski Patrol could set off explosions on the upper slopes, triggering small slides in hopes of defanging a big one. Aside from the inevitable Dirty Harry, many ravines off Callahan had avalanche-related names: Slider, Moonwalk, Undertow. Only Dirty Harry was on the map.

Undertow got the most action. A triangle of trees at the top led to a steep, narrow gully known as the Pubic Crease, also not on the map, which made for hellishly tricky skiing. Once the Crease filled with snow it disappeared. Locals knew it was there, and tourists were warned: one careless turn and they could end up headfirst in a ten-foot drift, giving new meaning to blowjob. Nobody skied Undertow without a partner and an avalanche beacon.

James backed and skate-skied to the next lift over, MacDougal. As he boarded, he heard a boom and saw snow puff high up the mountain above Undertow. Most avies stayed more or less in the blast area, but they had been known to rumble down onto a run before they quit. This one might, too. He watched it build into a cloud, widen, and start to roll.

James kept watching as he rode up MacDougal. The avalanche poured into Undertow, wide and deep but not fast. It poured over the traverse and into Undertow like water, not snow, scouring the ravine's curves like a slow-motion flash flood. James thought if he'd been caught in front he could have outskied it. Then he realized the bobbing twigs he saw were trees. And that Undertow had already filled halfway to the brim, maybe more.

And that he had just seen a fool who must have thought he could outski it, too. Well, part of him: a leg and booted foot and a broken-off ski thrust up through the still-rolling avalanche and were borne downhill. James turned to track it, watching until it sank out of sight.

No cell phone coverage, no radio. He had to wait till the top of the lift where, thank God, a line of Ski Patrolmen waved skiers to the right, away from Undertow.

James skied off and over to them. One of them slid a step forward. "Nobody allowed this side of MacDougal, sorry."

"I spotted somebody caught in the slide on the ride up," James said. "Well, a leg. Boot. Broken ski."

"Callahan's been shut down all day."

"I know what I saw."

The patrolman gave him a searching stare. Apparently James passed the crazy cutoff, the patrolman wagged his pole at the line. Another, older man shot over to them and said, "What's up?"

"This guy says he saw somebody caught up in the avie."

The older man turned to James. "And you are?"

What difference did it make? "James Riggio."

"I'm Mark Gunderson, head of avalanche control." He hiked his goggles up, the better to stare. "What did you see and where?"

"A leg and a boot and broken ski. Sticking up, then swept under. I marked it as best I could. About opposite the third stanchion, moving with the slide."

The stare continued. "Funny nobody else spotted him."

"Maybe they didn't have as much practice in Afghanistan."

A patrolman shrugged. "Somebody could have skied over from MacDougal before we got set up."

Gunderson scowled. He turned to the line of patrolmen and wagged a ski pole at the devices each man had strapped on like a bandolier. He raised his voice. "With me. Switch your beacons to receive. We stop at the third stanchion."

An avalanche beacon sent out a continuous signal, even if its wearer was buried. Any other beacons in the immediate area could be programmed to receive—to catch and home in on that signal. It shortened the time till the victim could be found and dug out. Maybe alive.

If no one else had spotted James' man, snow and debris must be piling over him every second.

Gunderson turned down the hill, the patrolmen after him in a smooth line, only a few feet away from the edge of the ravine that had been Undertow and was now a rapidly filling river of snow and rocks and trees.

James switched his beacon to receive, too, and took out after them. Debris spewed up over the side of the ravine. Avalanche snow didn't let skis slide. It grabbed. Easy to send the best skier head over halo, and James wasn't in that category. He tried to keep the distance between them from widening, substituting brute strength for skill. Lunge, desperate save, lunge.

Gunderson pulled up opposite the third stanchion, his men swishing in just below him. "This is where Riggio thought he saw a leg," he shouted. "Start sideslipping."

The line of skiers worked down in a careful single file, snow probes piercing the rubble, edging a foot or so, probing again. Pausing frequently to listen for a transponder signal. They didn't ask James to join them—he would only slow them down—but they didn't tell him to leave. Maybe they'd forgotten he was there. He didn't remind them.

The lowest man shouted. The rest of them shot down to him. He pointed out nearly halfway across the messy expanse of snow and debris, where a gloved hand thrust up from the snow.

Far down the hill the avalanche seemed to be boiling to a stop, but the surface was obviously still unstable. Nobody said so. When they could clear their man's face quickly? While he might still breathe?

The rule on unstable snow was one man. The best man. Clearly they all knew who that was. James watched as a man nearly as tall as he but lean as a whip, shucked his skis and shuffled out onto the dirty snow. His shovel was already out.

James was no expert on snow, but he knew rubble: clear the victim's face, see if he could breathe by himself, if not clear his chest for CPR. Always dig from the downhill side: if digging triggered another avalanche, the snow would roll down and away from the victim, not bury him deeper.

The patrolmen grouped, watching. James was right there. He dared them to tell him to leave now.

The expert positioned himself downhill, cut out a wedge with the shovel and took out tiny dips so he wouldn't slash the victim's head by accident. He paused and switched to his gloved hands. The watchers understood he had found something, something vulnerable. The head.

Let him still be wearing his helmet.

The patrolman paused again, eased something away and tossed it onto the snow: a helmet. James put his cell phone's camera to zoom to confirm what his eyes had already told him. The left half of the helmet had cracked off. He tried to focus on the victim's head, but couldn't get a clear shot.

The patrolman pawed quickly at the snow—clearing the face, James' camera told him. It recorded the patrolman clearing snow quickly away from the kid's nostrils—it was a kid, not more than nineteen or twenty—then hooking a finger inside the mouth to clear it of snow. It stayed slack. He laid fingers against the throat under the chin, lifted an eyelid.

He looked over at the other men and shook his head.

Pray it had been fast, James thought, that a blow to his head had saved him from feeling anything that followed.

"Clear his chest for CPR!" Gunderson shouted.

"He's been dead too long!" the patrolman shouted back.

They didn't have to be slow or gentle now. Half a dozen men shuffled onto the slide. They used their shovels. Clumps of snow broke away and rolled, but none turned into a new slide. They uncovered the boy's shoulders and on down his body. His other arm was clamped to his side. One leg looked frozen at an odd angle, the other loose. Both jacket and pants matched the glove, the greenish blue color and sheen of a mallard's head. One ski and boot had been ripped away. They had to reach deep into the snow to free the other boot from its binding so they could lift him out of the snow and carry him off the avalanche, back to stable snow.

Once there, they heaved a collective sigh of relief.

James stepped forward with his cell.

Gunderson said, "No coverage up here, Riggio."

"I'm using the camera. Sheriff may want pictures of him before we carry him off-site."

"Sheriff?"

"Any of you know this kid?" James stared around the group. "And I don't see a lift ticket. Somebody has to ID him. They may need all the help they can get."

They stepped back. James worked from head to toe. Bloodshot eyes, irises that had once been brown already dull. Parka and shirt and pants and gloves that matched. James caught most of the watchers, too, to look at later. The camera might catch something he missed.

A toboggan arrived. The patrolmen eased the man onto it with the same care they'd give him alive, though the stiff leg made it awkward.

"I don't see how he could start freezing so fast," one man muttered.

James had his own idea. His gaze crossed Gunderson's, who said, "I'll call the sheriff as soon as we get him down," so maybe he shared it. But then he added, "We owe you, Riggio. But we'll take it from here."

James watched the patrolmen guide the toboggan down the hill, skiing slowly like a cortege. Because of James, the patrol had found a kid who might otherwise be lost till spring snowmelt, and Gunderson expected James to walk away? Of course, Gunderson didn't know him. And he must not have noticed one of the kid's gloves had ended up in James' parka pocket.

James nodded. "I'll get out of your way."

There were no restrictions on what he did next. He skied down, clapped his skis together, and headed home. With luck, he could beat everybody else back to Copper Falls.

As soon as he was clear of the Pass and could use his phone, James pulled his truck over and called Pageant, the highest-end sports shop in town. He couldn't afford to shop there, but he knew the manager pretty well.

"James? What are you doing in town on a Thursday?" Lolly had a grainy voice with a brassy edge. Now and then he could persuade her to sing jazz or country for an audience of one.

"Taking you to lunch, if you're free."

Why, yes. Yes, she was.

Lolly gave his black truck a once over before she climbed in. James knew her rule: if a truck wasn't new, it had better be clean. Today he passed muster. He drove downtown to the Hubbub Pub and paused at the bar to ask the bartender, also the owner, for two bowls of red.

"Plus French fries for me," said Lolly.

"I hope you got my vat of chili on your truck," Chili grumbled. "Because we're about scraping bottom here."

"Bubbling on my stove as we speak," James said. "I'll drop it by later."

James had a catering business, Game Chef, currently do-or-die. He hoped it was just start-up pangs. Chili was one of his specialties. The Pub was his biggest client.

"Before dinner," Chili said.

"For sure. Can you spare a booth?"

"Take your pick."

James picked the end one and slid in beside Lolly. She backed, but not to Iceland. Face it, he took up more than his share.

"Need your help, Lolly."

"Of course you do." She slid closer. "What is it this time?"

James banked on her curiosity as well as her skill. He took out his phone. "You know there was an accident up at the hill today?"

"The avalanche. I heard somebody was killed. You were there?"

"Want to show you some pictures."

"You really know how to treat a girl."

"Don't be grisly, Lolly. I thought you might know what the kid was wearing. I can't afford your stuff—"

"Tell me about it. Without duct tape you'd be skiing naked." She gave him an mmmmmmmm look.

James tried to ignore it. "—but I think this kid could."

Kid. She got serious. James thumbed the pictures slowly. He'd rather she recognize a picture than the glove in his pocket.

She only needed the first three. "River's Edge. Medium jacket, 32 pants."

"He bought them from you?"

She nodded, smug. "We outfitted him helmet to boots. And skis. Everything. The velour shirt underneath is River's Edge, too, obviously." At his uncomprehending look, "To anybody but you, sweet cheeks. Different fibers, flawless color-match. Very tricky. Means the same manufacturer."

"I'll take your word for it. You remember his name as well as the clothes?"

"I'm way ahead of you." She slipped out her own phone and pressed. "Darcy, remember that threesome the other day? Right, the odd one. Can you pull up the kid's name? Thanks."

James read over her shoulder as she typed it on her phone. "Caleb. First name or last name? Caleb Kaydross." At Kaydross, James' attention upped a few levels.

"Did the other two buy anything?" Lolly asked. "Ah. Thanks. Send his name and in-town address to my phone, will you?" She turned to James. "You heard?"

"Only his name. Could you send that stuff to my email?"

"I can do better than that." Her thumbs worked. "Now give me your phone." She pressed her screen against his smaller, cheaper one.

"That really works?"

"Don't be silly, James. I sent the address to your email. This is a preview of tonight at my place."

"I'm pretty focused on this Caleb kid right now, Lolly."

"You think you can give me a bedroom stare in the middle of the day and not follow through?" She traced the edges of his phone with a forefinger. Sloooowly. Then licked that forefinger. "Unless you don't want the address. Or anything else I heard."

"I'll try," he said hoarsely.

She took a French fry.

"I'll be there." He closed his eyes. He'd watched her with French fries before. "Now tell me what else you have."

She got serious again. A changeable woman, Lolly. Hard to keep up with.

"This Kaydross kid was with two other people, a man and a woman. They helped him shop, but they bought stuff, too. Not as high-end as his. He paid for all three of them and had everything sent to the Steele Inn. I figured him for a computer whizkid—don't they all look about fourteen? Or maybe a trustfunder. The other two were clearly his posse."

"Not computers," said James. "Highly specialized military equipment. And not him, his dad. So you could say a trustfunder."

The Kaydross Sight had seriously reduced the amount of luck James had needed to do his job in Afghanistan. A Kaydross kid would have major-league money.

"You said posse," he said. "Could they have been security?"

"Oh, no. They weren't hefty enough. Lean as greyhounds." Lolly sighed. No reason so far as James was concerned, he liked women soft, not scrawny. "Older than him, though, which made me notice when he paid."

So maybe a posse, as she said. James thumbed back to a picture of Kaydross' damaged face. And maybe not.

"I talked to Mel before I picked you up." Mel Travis, sheriff's deputy and hunting partner. "Nobody's been reported missing."

"It's only been a couple of hours, James. They probably just figure he's someplace else on the mountain."

James almost explained. Almost. Instead he said a vague, "Right. Would his clothes have ID tags anyplace?"

Lolly shook her head.

James thumbed through the pictures again with Lolly watching. "His ticket must have got ripped off. Unless it's been found—highly doubtful—and he paid with a credit card, we may be the only ones now who know who died up on the mountain this morning."

"Stop there," she commanded. "The one with his shirt."

The velour shirt, zip open at his throat as the parka had been. Not done by the ski patrol, he had been found that way.

"What's that on his throat?" Lolly pointed. "There. In the crease of his neck."

James sighed, as he had when he first saw it up on the mountain. "It continues on around his neck. It's the mark of a garrote." A line so deep it looked black on James' phone, though when he had seen it up close, it had looked like the blood it was.

Caleb Kaydross hadn't died on the mountain, at least not that morning. James wondered if he was the only one so far who knew that, too, who realized that the body was in rigor, not frozen. Maybe he'd wait and see what the kid's posse thought. Whether James was the only one who knew—scratch that, cared—that Caleb had been murdered.

"Garroting isn't a crime of impulse, Lolly. You need the weapon, you need to think of where you can use it. How to get your victim there. What to do with him afterward."

"You think somebody brought Caleb Kaydross to Copper Falls to be killed?" Lolly shivered. Always impressive.

"I do. The two he came with are most likely."

"You have to take this to the sheriff, James."

"You think I have enough to convince him to take me seriously? Before Caleb's posse leaves town?" He held out his hands like sides of an old fashioned scale. "Trustfunders versus down-at-heel chef held together by duct tape."

"But why you, James?"

"I found him. That makes him one of mine." James was more honest than he intended. "I lost too many of my guys, and nothing I could do about it. This time there is."

She thought about it. "If you convince yourself they're guilty, you promise to go to Sheriff Barnett?"

"Promise."

"Watch your step, big boy."

"If they make trouble I'll sit on them. Break them in two."

———

By the time James put finishing touches on the chili and loaded the vat into his truck, it was about three. Plenty of time for Caleb Kaydross' posse to get back from the hill. To know, or not know, he was dead.

James parked in back of the Steele Inn and asked the woman behind the desk for Kaydross' room. She had seen him there often, delivering dinners for Game Chef. She said, "First floor, the suite," and waved him toward the back.

No obvious noise from the other side of the door. Then again, the Inn was old and well built. James rapped.

A few seconds—still no noise—then, "Yes?" Female, definitely older than Caleb, edgy. All in one word.

"Got something that belongs to Caleb, ma'am."

A few more seconds before she opened the door a narrow wedge. "You said you have something for Caleb?"

"A glove, ma'am." Her eyebrows twitched. She looked mid-twenties, too young to be a ma'am. Maybe it would annoy her. He wanted to keep her on edge. "Found it up on the ski hill this morning."

"Really." Again just a word, but an impression both of tight control and of needing that control. "I wasn't aware Caleb carried ID in his gloves."

"No, ma'am. But we rode the lift together earlier in the week and I admired the color. Green, blue, whatever it is. It stands out. So when I saw his glove this morning I picked it up. Save him having to go to Lost and Found. Only I never came across him again."

It was a gamble: his only hint Caleb had skied earlier in the week was a sales slip dated over a week ago.

If he kept babbling, wouldn't they have to ask him in?

Why they? Smell? Unexplained sound?

Whatever, he was right: a masculine hand gripped the door above her head and swung it wide.

"Where are your manners, Erin? I'm sure Caleb would want us to ask Mr. Um?"

"James Riggio. Call me James."

"—to ask James in."

"Appreciate it," James said, stepping in as Erin backed reluctantly.

"Erin is Erin Padilla," said the man. "I'm Kip Daniels."

He was a few years older, she was darker, with the kind of snow tan that only came to Mediterranean skin, though her hair was blonde. He had light brown hair and eyes to match. Lolly was right: they both had a lean, greyhound look. James had learned to recognize expensive clothes. Theirs were not.

The suite had a good-sized livingroom. Fireplace at one end, overstuffed sofa and chairs with vaguely Indian upholstery, a genuine Navajo blanket thrown over the sofa back. An antler chandelier over a table, statues of horses rearing or pawing things.

Right now clothes were heaped everywhere. Two pairs of skis and poles, neatly trussed together, leaned in a corner near the fireplace.

"Please," said Daniels. "Sit. Caleb will want to thank you in person, he'll be back any minute. Drink?"

So they hadn't yet been notified. James was still at least a step ahead of the sheriff. If they had killed Caleb as James suspected, they must be strung as tight as piano wire.

The sofa looked too deep to get out of quickly. James took a chair. "Water would be fine."

Kip gave Erin a stare. She excused herself and left the room. There must be a kitchen.

"Where did you say you found the glove, James?"

Kip held out a cigarette. James shook his head but waved Go ahead.

"Over on a slope called Belvedere, about halfway down."

Another gamble: no guarantees Caleb had skied there. But Belvedere was part of the scheme James had worked out for Caleb's murder. He wanted their reaction. And his first gamble had been successful.

Kip tried to strike a match, finally tossed it aside for another. That one flamed. He stooped over it and breathed deep before he leaned back into the squashy sofa.

Something? Nothing? Pity James couldn't have timed it for when Erin was present. James waited for her to come back and put the glass down in front of him. Coke, not water. He took a healthy swallow, then dug the glove out of his cargo pants and tossed it onto the table in front of him.

Erin's gaze focused on it. "Where did you find it?"

"On a slope called Belvedere," Kip said. "Halfway down, didn't you say, James?"

James had a sense of piano wires tightening. "Near a warming hut there, people sometimes use it to picnic. Middle of winter, not my idea of fun."

But ideal for one picnicker to pass in back of another and slip a wire around his neck and pull. And a traverse led from Belvedere across the rest of the slopes, ending beyond Undertow.

"It looks like you're packing," James said. "Don't let me keep you." He made no move to rise.

"Packing?" Erin, a beat too fast, her voice too high. "Why would you think that? We're here for another week."

Kip looked around as if seeing the room with James' eyes. "This is what you might call creative mess," he said. "Caleb's not very organized. When he wanted to spend the day up at Copper Falls on his own, we decided to catch up. Laundry, cleaning, stuff like that. If you'd come an hour later it would be under control."

Did Kip always talk this much to strangers?

James put on a puzzled frown. "Your kid brother doesn't wrangle his own stuff?"

This time they both froze. Kip's voice went high tenor. "Who said we were siblings?"

"Nobody. I saw him, I'm looking at you, it's a no-brainer. Hey, none of my business. I won't pass it on."

"There's no mystery." Kip leaned forward for another cigarette. Leaned back. "Our mother liked to marry. Three marriages, three kids."

Erin's sigh of relief was a little too audible. From Kip's frown, he clearly agreed. But he was the one talking too much.

"I figured." James kept his reaction to Erin's reaction to himself. "Three different last names."

Kaydross, aka husband number three, had serious money. One and two probably didn't. Kip didn't have to point out the obvious: Kaydross must not have wanted to share with other men's kids. Maybe his son didn't either. Hard way to grow up. A big jump, though, from envy to murder.

Was this enough for the sheriff? It had to be. James stood.

"I have another stop to make, and you have your work cut out anyway, to get this place back in shape before Caleb gets back. Tell him I stopped by."

"I'll see you to the door."

Erin seemed overeager again. Kip gave her a little headshake, frowning. Get on the same page, people, conspirators were supposed to conspire.

But maybe he didn't give them enough credit, because just as he completed that thought something hit the back of his head. Much good a blow there would do, he had too much hair. He was still thinking that when his knees folded under him.

As he tipped forward, he heard Kip say something, but the words were lost in the thud when James' head hit the table. The sound seemed to echo before he felt it.

James heard Kip say, "Erin, what the hell? I had this handled."

He could see the words in block letters, all caps. He couldn't decode them.

Kip spoke again, telling Erin to get the cable.

Cable. He couldn't decode that, either, but the letters were bigger, and pulsing. He must need to do something. He took inventory. No pain, aside from his head. He tensed his legs without moving. Fine. Arms… not fine. Why? In front of him, Kip lifted them, set them down, lifted them…

"Why not behind his back?" Erin asked.

"We need his arms to drag him. Unless you'd rather use his hair."

James didn't understand what Kip was struggling to do, but his hands and wrists did. He felt them flex, stretch, thumbs at awkward angles, all to make themselves big and clumsy.

"I can't even wrap his goddam wrists twice," Kip grunted.

Like a break in the clouds, James heard the whole sentence. And he felt cord circling his wrists, only not cord, cable. Chilly. Threaded steel. Garrote-worthy.

Welcome back, James. Just in time.

"Are you sure he's out?" Erin asked. "Shall I hit him again?"

If he struggled openly, batshit Erin might well hit him again. A third blow in one night? Anything could happen.

He heard a click. "Got it," Kip panted.

Yes, he did. James' wrists were imprisoned, his arms now a single ungainly club. Maybe not as secure as Kip wanted, but more than James knew what to do with right now.

"Now what?" Erin asked.

"Search his pockets. We need his car keys. Phone, if you find it."

"Why me?"

A sharp crack of sound. James pictured it across Erin's face. No cry, no whimper. She slumped to her knees beside him and pawed through his pockets. He braced. Felt her fingers close over his keys and jerk them out.

"No phone," she reported, which made James glad his cell was in his glove box. Though he didn't know why.

"Doesn't matter," said Kip. "There won't be coverage anyway. Go out on the patio and push the unlock button so we can find his car. Though from the keys I'm betting truck. Old."

But well-maintained, James protested as if it mattered.

Whoosh of a sliding door, gush of winter air. Most welcome. Beep-beep as his truck told Erin where it was. Another whoosh and the cold air disappeared.

"An old black truck," she reported. "Only three spaces away."

"Get it as close as you can, passenger side facing our patio door. Go on the grass if you have to."

"What about other people?"

"You watch for them, dear sister. It's dark. You should have no problem."

"I've never driven a truck."

This was more than little girl helplessness. Erin might be genuinely batshit.

"Would you rather haul Yeti, here, to the railing and push him over?" Kip had more patience than James would have. Except for the slap.

"I could do the pushing-over part."

"You get to pull from the other side."

Kip caught James by his bound arms and dragged. James was a good fifty pounds heavier. He made sure it was all dead weight. He snagged any body part on any piece of furniture in their path. Kip panted. He cursed under his breath. Sweating enough to smell.

Whoosh of the doors. Out they went into the cold. Maybe it would help clear James' head. Something had better. Across slate flagstones. Cold. Kip heaved James' arms up and over a railing and manhandled him from behind.

"This better be worth it," Erin said from the other side.

"Just think about spending Caleb's money."

Have to tell the sheriff, James thought. Make a note.

A final heave took him up and across. His arms and head swung over and down, the railing dug into his gut, blood plunged down to his head… gone again.

When he came back Kip and Erin still talked. Unless he imagined it. His truck had no back seat, James was belted into the passenger seat, Kip was driving, they were on the road. Where was she?

Cell phones. They were using cell phones. Erin had to be in a car somewhere behind them.

They could talk freely because they assumed James was still out. James took care to slump over the seatbelt, muttering.

"When we reach the entrance," Kip said, "switch to parking lights only."

Entrance. They were headed to Copper Mountain, James knew without knowing why. Because it had worked to kill Caleb?

"But then where?"

"When I poked around here last year I found out where they dump the snow when they plow the parking lots."

More than James knew, as he struggled to listen. No good. He wiped out again.

The truck was crawling with no lights when James came back again. He guessed they were in a parking lot of Copper Mountain. Crawl turned to stop. He heard a second car pull up to their left. Any second there would be another What now?

Kip pulled out the keys, hopped down, and slammed the door. James flexed his wrists, pressed them tight together. Could he create wiggle room? Yes. Enough to work free if he could stay awake? Oh, and alive.

Go away, Kip. Go away, Erin. Leave me to freeze.

No. Kip jerked the passenger door open and reached past James to his seat belt. James sagged forward as far as he could, toppling against Kip as Kip pulled him out of the truck. They went hard to the ground. Kip cursed and kicked him to squirm out from under.

When Kip and Erin each took a leg and dragged James face down, he woke up for good.

He shouted. Clawed. Once he kicked free of Erin. What if she had let go only to hit him again? James twisted to kick free of Kip, but Erin seized him again before he could. He knew struggling told them he was still alive and dangerous. He couldn't stop. They wrestled him across snow, gravel, dirt. Frozen ruts.

Shouldn't that tell him where they were? He could only see where they'd been. It was a world of snow under a night sky, with occasional huge shadows that could have been anything.

There was a pause. Abruptly, James' legs took on a new, sharp angle, then the rest of his body. This was softer snow. They were dragging him up a snowbank. This was ominous. Beyond it must lie their destination. His destination. James' face dug into the bank. Snow in his nose and mouth. He tried to protect his face. No luck. No air.

Was this how Caleb felt under the avalanche?

Think, James. Caleb was dead when they dumped him.

Pause. They were sobbing for breath as much as he.

"This is it," Kip panted.

"Now I get to hit him again?"

"Sorry. My turn." He didn't sound sorry.

They dropped his legs. Briefly he was free. He twisted, trying to gather his knees under him so he could lunge downward. But then something heavy and sharp and cold, most of all cold, came down hard on the back of his head. Right where Erin had hit him, he thought, and he could think, his mind was as clear as if he were up above watching. He had no trouble telling his body to get the hell out of here. But there was no response. He felt—watched his legs dangle in space, his belly… soon enough his own weight would send him down, down to wherever they intended him to die.

A final shove to his shoulders, and he slid, first by inches, faster as his full weight came into play. His body wanted to roll. He told it to fight, to throw his arms forward, to dig in his hands. Nothing.

Think of it as an avalanche, James, ride it out. People do. But they were struggling, not watching from above.

Gravel, dirt, tree branches slid with him. His boots slammed into something with a jolt that shuddered up through feet, knees, body… his head finally stopped working, too.

When he could think again, his first thought was thanks for thinking anything at all. Other thoughts assembled slowly, like puzzle pieces. He felt cold against his face before he recognized it as snow. Maybe ice. Longer still before he could process where he was: at the bottom of a trough. Around him were walls, boulders, Godzilla-size piles: all snow. Kip's voice echoed through his head: Where they dump the snow when they plow the parking lots. Then it made sense. Plows would push the snow up and over a snowbank, they wouldn't groom it.

They had pushed him in. There had to be a way out. He attacked the nearest wall. That was when he realized his hands were oddly swollen, without feeling. Useless. All he could do was gouge snow with them, trying to support his weight long enough to dig in his elbows, then knees. Only his boots were reliable.

How long did it take to reach the top of a snowbank and peer over? Under the night sky he could see down and down, mounds and walls and banks and more mounds as far below as he could see. He rested his head on his hands and told himself not to weep. All that effort to get even farther away from where he needed to be.

It was a long time before he could bear to lift his head and look around. One of these walls had to be the way out, the place where Kip and Erin had pushed him over. He forced himself to roll back down the snowbank and start again. It took much longer to scale the next bank. It even took time to work up the courage to look over it.

Below was the parking lot. He could even see his truck. He rolled willingly down the bank and actually crawled a few more feet before it occurred to him to struggle to his feet and walk—stagger—to his truck.

He had to lean against it and sob for breath before he reached his cuffed hands up under the front fender for his spare key, cracked the driver's door and—after another timeout to breathe—stepped up into the seat.

Nine o'clock. He would have guessed four in the morning.

He stretched both hands to the right of the wheel and slid the key in the lock. The engine hummed to life.

He tried to scrape off the cable. No luck. But it stretched enough to get his hands side by side. Shifting—manual—was iffy. Park to reverse went better than reverse to drive. He kept forgetting the clutch. Luckily he was the only vehicle in sight. Plenty of room for kangaroo jumps and zigzags. By the time he reached the road back to town he was sweating like a pig.

With luck Chili and Lolly were already hounding the sheriff to search for him.

The third time he slowed for a curve and the engine cut out, he gave up, dug his cell out of his glove box and called Mel, friend and more importantly at this moment sheriff's deputy. Mel didn't recognize his voice. Maybe he hadn't been so successful at not weeping.

———————————

The door to Mel Travis' office was half-open. James sat behind it in Mel's chair. The cable still wrapped his wrists. Dried blood marked a hundred cuts and scrapes on his still-unwashed face and hands. His jacket hung in shreds.

Sheriff Barnett leaned on the wall beside the door where he could peer out. He fit what James had heard about him: shortish, stocky, with the mustache, hat, and voice of a much larger man. His attention—suspicion—seemed divided between James and conversation beyond the door, in the reception area of the sheriff's office.

Lolly's voice carried. "You're a 36L, am I right, sweetie? 34L trousers."

James pictured Mel gazing at his boots, which he did with every woman but his wife. "Yes, ma'am."

"If you want my help, sweetie, stop calling me ma'am."

Mel cleared his throat. Behind the door the sheriff echoed him, louder and deeper.

James heard a door open and straightened.

"This might be them," Mel said with relief.

Yes, it must be, James' hackles had risen. He wouldn't be surprised if his hair stood on end.

"You're the deputy who called us?" Kip's voice, light and easy. "I'm Kip Daniels."

Did he put out a hand to shake? Mel would have trouble with that.

Sheriff Barnett moved closer to the door, a hand on his pistol grip. James swiveled his chair to look, too.

"I don't understand why we couldn't deal with this on the phone." Erin, her voice barbed as wire.

"We put out some pictures a couple hours ago," Mel said. "Maybe you'd like to sit?"

"We're fine." Kip's voice had gone tenor again. "Pictures of what?"

"I don't know if you heard about an avalanche up at the ski hill today?"

Mel dragged this out like an expert. James hadn't guessed he had it in him.

"The news was full of it," Kip said. "What does it have to do with us?"

"Some ski clothes showed up, Mr. Daniels. A jacket, a helmet, and a boot. And this lady…"

"Lolly," said Lolly.

"…thought she sold them to you."

Kip had control of himself again. His voice even, he said, "You want us to look at pictures? Why not the clothes?"

"Don't want to put you to the trouble if we can avoid it, sir. And since this lady—"

"I brought in my copy of the sales slip for you to check instead," Lolly said.

Two ladies and a ma'am. Lucky for Mel all she did was interrupt.

"Want to spare you if we can," Mel mumbled.

"I recognize the sales slip. Now what?" James heard Kip's voice start to rise again.

Mel bent over the slip of paper. "Need you to go through it item by item, sir." A big forefinger moved down the list, while Kip said an impatient yes, yes, yes.

"One last time," he said. "Show us the pictures or the clothes or my sister and I leave."

"What's this here at the bottom?" Mel persevered.

Kip gave a gust of a sigh. "A ski lock."

"We always print out the combination beside it," Lolly said. "See? In case you forget, we can look it up for you."

"How thoughtful. The pictures?"

"So if you could verify the combination, sir?" Mel. Undeflected.

"Why?" Erin's voice was brittle. "Did you find that, too?"

The sheriff's stare said Move it to James. James heaved himself upright and shoved the door wide. He walked forward, hands raised enough to make the ski lock binding his wrists very visible.

Erin saw him first. She backed, mouth wide with a scream. Nothing came out.

Kip gave her a hard shake. All it did was free her to talk.

"You said the hard part was over." She sounded four years old. In a weird way she looked about four, too. "You said all we had to do now was spend Caleb's money."

"Shut up." Before James could shoulder between them, Kip's hand cracked across Erin's face.

Sheriff Barnett said sharply, "That'll do."

Kip turned, his face white as ice. Sheriff Barnett started the litany of their rights.

Then Erin screamed.

There, Caleb. Sleep soundly.

Lolly seemed to think if she put her mouth on each cut of James' she could heal them. He liked the theory and directed her toward one on his lower lip.

The sheriff interrupted. "If we could open the ski lock, Miss? Evidence. Might even be DNA from Mr. Kaydross."

Lolly gave James' cable-wrapped hands an appraising look. "I don't know, Sheriff. The idea of James bound, helpless—"

"Lolly, for God's sake—" James said.

"Tell you what, Sheriff," she said. "I'll trade. The cable for handcuffs."

Sheriff Barnett avoided James' glare, clearing his throat in a bone-rattling harrumph. "We should have a spare around somewhere."

Ireland beckons and beguiles in our next story. Ms McCracken's own adventures when a lass and loose upon the Emerald Isle, gave rise to this story.

Rosemary McCracken has published numerous stories in the crime and mystery genre. Notably, her short story, "The Sweetheart Scamster", published in the anthology, "Thirteen", was a finalist for the Derringer Award in 2014. Her novels, include "Safe Harbor" and the sequel, "Black Water".

Plastic Paddies

By Rosemary McCracken

Kevin and I decided we'd do something really special to celebrate our fortieth wedding anniversary. It was the year we were going to Ireland. Our surname was Flanagan and, before we married, I was a Connolly. It was time we visited the Ould Sod.

We boarded our very first transatlantic flight, landing at Dublin Airport on a fine Tuesday in June. We took the air coach into the city center and walked the three blocks to the Irish Heritage Inn.

Kevin and I looked at each other in the hotel lobby, feeling overwhelmed. Our kids had booked our lodgings as their anniversary present. But this hotel—with its marble floors, skylights and large floral arrangements—seemed out of our league. Our idea of luxury was a Holiday Inn.

It wasn't yet noon and our room wouldn't be ready for another hour. We stowed our luggage in the baggage room and headed over to Dublin Castle, which we could see from the hotel. What once had been a castle was a complex of government buildings, state apartments, museums and a conference center. A sign told us the next guided tour would be in the late afternoon.

We had started to fade by then. It was nine in the morning back home, and we'd been too excited to sleep on the plane. The Chester Beatty Library in the castle was open and the admission was free, so that's where we went. We collapsed at a table in the Silk Road Café.

A short, red-haired man asked if he could join us. The other tables were occupied, so we nodded our agreement.

"Americans are you?" He had a charming Irish accent.

"Canadians," Kevin said.

"We've just arrived in Ireland," I added.

"And where would you be staying?" he asked.

"The Irish Heritage Inn," I said.

He gave us a lovely smile. "I'm staying right across the street from you."

"Our room wasn't ready," I said, "so we're doing some exploring."

He held out his hand. "Desmond Leahy. Everyone calls me Des." He was about 35 with one of those faces that aren't the least bit handsome but are totally appealing. Maybe it was the smile.

"I'm Sheena Flanagan," I said, "and this is my husband Kevin." I couldn't resist adding that our great-grandparents came from Ireland. Mine from County Monaghan, Kevin's from County Clare.

"So you're full-blooded Irish. I should have known you were, Sheena, with your dark hair and green eyes."

I beamed at him. Kevin nodded his silver head.

I completely forgot how tired I was. We spent the next half-hour sipping tea and nibbling pastries filled with dates and nuts. "Ma'amoul," Des said. "Middle Eastern sweets."

"Not what I'd expected in Ireland," I said.

Des inclined his head. "Ireland is quite cosmopolitan these days."

I was enchanted. We were in Dublin eating exotic desserts with a charming leprechaun. It was beyond anything I had imagined!

"You're not from Dublin," I said.

"I live in Limerick," Des said. "I'm doing research at Trinity College this week."

"Research?" I asked.

"I teach history at the university. I'm researching a paper."

He took a sip of tea. "What do you do in Canada?"

"I was a homemaker when our kids were young," I said. "Now I'm a librarian." I was a check-out clerk at our neighborhood library, but I didn't go into that.

"And yourself?" he asked Kevin.

"I work for Canada Post."

"An important place to work."

Kevin puffed out his chest a bit. Well, mail carriers are important to a lot of people.

We left the café with Des. "You'll be wanting to see the *Book of Kells*," he said as we walked across the castle grounds. "A masterpiece of medieval art and it's in the largest library in Ireland. With your library background, Sheena, you'll want to see the Old Library."

I looked at Kevin, who's not at all interested in books or libraries. But we nodded in agreement. We weren't about to let on that we'd never heard of the *Book of Kells*.

"I'll give you a tour tomorrow," Des said. "Walk over to Trinity College, and buy two tickets to the *Book of Kells* exhibit. I'll meet you at the entrance to the Old Library at noon."

In the hotel lobby, I picked up a pamphlet on the *Book of Kells*. When we got to our room, I hung up my new traveling suit, and Kevin's new sports coat and trousers. Then I stretched out on the bed.

"Don't fall asleep," Kevin said. "We need to get in sync with this time zone. We can't sleep till evening."

"I'm exhausted but I'm far too excited to sleep."

———

Kevin and I were waiting outside the Old Library when Des arrived. We joined hundreds of people lined up to see the *Book of Kells*, but the line moved quickly. The book we were all there to see was a Bible, full of colored drawings and fancy writing. It was put together by Irish monks more than 1,000 years ago, and it's now divided into four separate books. What we saw were blowups of a few of its pages. We could look at two of the actual books under glass, but we only had a minute or so until the security staff moved us on.

"That's it?" Kevin whispered when we left the exhibit.

Des joined us, his face lit up with a smile. "I can't see the *Book of Kells* too often."

"Tourist trap," Kevin muttered when Des had gone on ahead. "Ten euros for a ticket. Could've bought a couple of rounds in a pub."

I gave him the elbow, and followed Des. He took us upstairs to the Long Room, a huge room filled with books upon books upon books. I'd never seen so many. It was like something out of the Harry Potter movies.

Des pointed to an old musical instrument in a glass box. "Brian Boru's harp, the symbol of a free Ireland. Boru united the Irish tribes against the Vikings."

Kevin and I nodded. Something else we'd never heard of.

Outside, it had started to rain. A soft, misty rain we seldom have where we live in Canada.

"I should get back to work," Des said, "but let's meet for supper. I know just the pub you'd like."

———————

O'Shea's, in the heart of downtown Dublin, was packed that night. I spotted an American flag on a wall and a large framed photo of JFK. On the stage, a woman was singing "Danny Boy."

Des handed us menus. "Authentic Irish food."

The dishes were what you'd find in any Canadian pub. Shepherd's pie, pot pie, burgers, chicken wings, even a nacho platter. The only item that stood out was the Guinness Irish stew.

I pointed to it when our server returned. "I'll have this."

"Sheena makes Irish stew on St. Paddy's Day," Kevin said when the server left. "We have it with Guinness. In our glasses and in the stew."

My Irish stew is much better than O'Shea's. The lamb was in short supply and the broth had no taste to it.

"Not bad stew," Des said, pushing away his empty bowl.

We ordered more Guinness and listened to a folk group sing "Black Velvet Band."

"Traditional Irish tune," Des said.

And one of my favorites.

When the group left the stage, Des pulled his chair closer to ours. "Would you be up for a drive in the country tomorrow?"

Kevin and I wanted to see some of the Irish countryside. We'd been looking at coach tours because we were nervous about driving on the left side of the road.

"I have business in Wicklow," Des said, "and I've booked an automobile for the day. You're welcome to come along."

I looked hopefully at Kevin. "Sure," he said.

When Des reached for the bill, Kevin put a hand on his. "This is our treat."

Des shook off his hand. "Your money's no good here. Neither is your credit card."

He put on his windbreaker. "See you at ten tomorrow morning. I'll pull up in front of your hotel." He left with the bill.

"Nice guy," Kevin said.

"Isn't he?" I took Kevin's arm. "Thoughtful of him to include us tomorrow."

Des drove up the next morning in a red Ford Fiesta. "Top of the mornin'!" he called out through the open window.

"Sure it's a grand day," he said when we were in the car. "But, as we say in Ireland, it may not last."

We hit the road with the sun shining down from a blue sky. We drove through Dalkey, a seaside village south of Dublin. Des showed us the red-brick cottage where my favorite author, Maeve Binchy, lived. Then he drove us past the big metal gates in front of rock star Bono's mansion.

The road became winding as we headed into the Wicklow Mountains. We got out of the car to stretch our legs at a crossroads called the Sally Gap. The air was crystal clear, and the view of the hills, valleys, lakes and streams was something you'd see in a movie.

"They filmed parts of *Braveheart* around here," Des said.

"Braveheart was a Scot," Kevin said. "Why would they shoot that movie here?"

"Money and tax credits." Des smiled. "That's what gets most projects off the ground these days."

Ten minutes later, we came to a stately gray-stone house on the shore of a sparkling blue lake. "Callan House Hotel," Des said.

Outside the hotel, we were greeted by a dark-haired man who looked like a young Warren Beatty. "Colm Rooney, the hotel manager," Des said. "Colm, this is Sheena and Kevin Flanagan."

"Welcome to Callan House." Colm shook our hands. "We'll have a drink in The Library, then Des will see that you have some lunch."

He led us inside and across a grand lobby to a spacious room with walls lined with shelves of books. "This is the original part of the manor house and it dates back to the 1700s," he told us when we were seated on facing leather sofas.

The men drank beer and I had a glass of sherry. Then we followed Des into the dining room. A window table facing the lake was waiting for us.

Kevin flashed me a puzzled look. I smiled, shrugged and turned my attention to the menu.

My lunch started with cream of carrot soup, followed by wild venison, which I'd never had before. Wild-tasting but… good. After a glass of wine, I was thankful we weren't driving back to Dublin on those winding roads.

Des suggested crème brûlée for dessert. While we were waiting for it, he gestured to the view from the window. "A lovely place," he said.

"It certainly is," I said.

"After we have our coffee, Colm will show us one of the rooms," Des said.

Kevin sat up straight in his chair, looking nervous. I reached over and patted his hand. I didn't think Colm had anything naughty in mind.

It wasn't a room Colm took us to—it was a suite. The sitting room was done up in shades of rose and beige with a fireplace, a corner bar and doors that opened onto a balcony. The bedroom had a king-sized bed with a silk canopy. The bathroom was almost as big as our room in Dublin.

"A cognac?" Colm said when we'd had the tour. "There's also wine and beer."

"I could get used to this," Kevin said. "A Coke, if you've got one."

"A Coke for me too," I said.

We sat on the sofas, sipping our drinks, until Des broke the silence. "Colm and I are in the final stages of purchasing Callan House."

I could see he had Kevin's interest.

"We are very excited," Colm said. "Callan is a prime property and I speak from first-hand experience. I've managed this hotel for five years. I know how much money it brings in and what it costs to operate. Callan House is a sure thing."

"You buying it with cash?" Kevin asked.

"If only we could," Colm said. "Des and I are putting our savings into it. He'll also contribute an inheritance from his grandmother."

"We're looking for a small group of investors," Des said. "Discerning individuals who appreciate Callan's history. People with ideas about how we can heighten our guests' experience. We don't want too many on the team, and we need to have our players in place before we go to the bank for a mortgage."

"Des thought you might be interested," Colm said.

Kevin glanced at me. "What size of investments are you looking for?"

I winced.

"One hundred thousand dollars," Colm said. "You'd be partners in the Callan House Property Co. and you'd be welcome to spend two weeks here every year."

"Time is a factor," Des added. "We need to have our investors in place this week."

I could see the wheels in Kevin's head turning. My husband is a sucker for "great opportunities." Five years before, he was burned by a boiler-room operation. Some guy on the phone offered him an investment deal he claimed was too good to be true. Turned out he was absolutely right. The investment didn't exist and we lost $25,000 of our hard-earned money.

That can't happen again. We'll retire in two years and we need every penny of our savings.

"We'll give it some thought." I set my glass on the coffee table and stood up. "When are we leaving for Dublin, Des?"

"I'll show you the grounds," he said. "Then we'll drive back."

———————

The next morning, we awoke to a gray Irish day. "That hotel sounds like a sure thing," Kevin said before we went down for breakfast.

"I don't trust anything that's called a sure thing," I told him. "That's what your boiler-room brokers said."

He stopped at the door to our room and turned to face me. "I'm tired of you nagging me for trying to get ahead. Trouble with you, Sheena, is you think small."

I pushed him aside and opened the door. "If we don't hurry, we'll have no breakfast."

Only a few late risers were in the breakfast room. "Top of the mornin'," I said when Angie, our pretty server, came over to the table.

She laughed and tossed her blond head. "We don't say that any more, at least not without irony. It's a traditional Irish greeting but it's been taken over by the Plastic Paddies."

"Plastic Paddies?" Kevin asked.

"Americans, Canadians, Aussies who come here to find their Oirish roots and try out their fake accents. They think we live in thatched cottages and sing sentimental songs like 'Danny Boy' and 'Galway Bay.' Right out of *The Quiet Man*."

She smiled at us. "We love to have you visit. But some tourists have no idea what Ireland is like today."

"You're a student?" She wasn't your average waitress.

"I am. I'm studying tourism management."

Kevin drank another cup of coffee while I went back to our room to powder my nose. When I returned, he introduced me to Rob and Nancy Gallagher, another Canadian couple who were exploring Ireland. Looking for their Irish roots, no doubt.

"We've asked Kevin to join us for a round of golf at Portmarnock," Rob said. "One of our foursome isn't up for it today. Kevin says you don't play, Sheena."

"Go ahead," I told Kevin. "I wouldn't mind doing some window shopping."

"Let's hope it doesn't rain," Nancy said.

I spent the morning on Grafton Street, a pedestrian mall bustling with shoppers, tourists, musicians and buskers. I passed several of the fast-food places we have back home—McDonalds, Quiznos, Burger King, Pizza Hut. Found five shops that chart Irish family trees. Bought a set of coasters with the Flanagan family crest.

I went back to the hotel to freshen up before lunch. When I got to our room, there were two phone messages from Des, neither of which I returned.

But he caught up with me in the lobby. "Sheena! What are you and Kev up to today?"

"Kevin's playing golf. I've been doing some shopping."

"A wee drop in the pub?" He took my elbow and steered me toward the lobby lounge.

Angie came over to take our orders. I asked for a pot of tea and Des ordered a Guinness.

"Have you given some thought to Callan House?" he asked when Angie had gone.

"We're talking about it."

"Colm has an appointment at the bank tomorrow. We'll need your answer by morning." He put his hand on my arm. "You can't lose, Sheena."

I said I'd talk to Kevin when he returned.

"We'd love to have you on the team," Des said.

I got up from the table.

"You haven't had your tea," he said.

"Just remembered something I have to do. I'll have Angie cancel my order."

"I have a great pub for you and Kev tonight," he called out as I walked across the room.

Back in our room, a telephone operator connected me with Callan House Hotel. To my surprise, a real person answered. I asked for the name of the hotel manager.

"Siobhan McCarthy," she said. "Shall I put you through to her office?"

"No, thank you. I'm actually looking for Colm Rooney. I thought he was the manager. What is his position at the hotel?"

"There is no one by the name of Colm Rooney here. Can someone else help you?"

"No, thank you." I hung up, my heart pounding.

I pressed a button and got our own front-desk clerk. "Where is the police station in Dublin?"

"Is there a problem, Mrs. Flanagan?" he asked.

"Not really," I said. "I'd just like to talk to a police officer."

"An Garda Síochína is our national police service. Its headquarters are in Phoenix Park. "

"Is that walking distance from here?"

"A long walk. Can I call you a taxi?"

The Morrissey Brothers had just finished their set when an attractive thirty-something couple took the table beside ours.

"You don't often hear fiddle playing like that," Des said. "Tom and Mike Morrissey are legends."

Colm signaled the server for another round.

I set my handbag on the table. "Kevin and I have given Callan House some thought." I opened my bag and passed an envelope across the table. "We want to be part of it."

Kevin stared at me, his mouth open.

Colm snatched the envelope from the table and stuffed it into the breast pocket of his jacket. He patted his jacket and smiled at Des.

The fair-haired man at the table beside us stood up. He put a hand on Des's shoulder. "Excuse me, Mr. Leahy and Mr. Rooney. Or I should say, Mr. Lennox and Mr. Reynolds."

Des started to rise. "There's some mistake."

The man pressed on Des's shoulder and he sat back down. "I think not. An Garda Síochína would like a word with both of you." He showed Colm and Des his identification card.

His partner, a brunette with a pixie haircut, motioned to four uniformed officers who had entered by the pub's back door.

Our table was surrounded by Ireland's finest.

"On your feet, Lennox and Reynolds," the woman said. "We'll talk at Garda headquarters."

The uniforms escorted Des and Colm out of the pub, the woman following behind them.

Her partner took the chair Des had vacated. "I'm Detective Sergeant Paul Fitzgerald," he said to Kevin. "Thanks to your wife, we've found the Lords of the Manor."

"Lords…?" Kevin said.

"Dennis Lennox and Chris Reynolds. They've been preying on gullible tourists. People fascinated by an Ireland that doesn't exist. Succeeded in getting a few to buy into the fairy tale."

"By investing in places like Callan House," I said to Kevin.

The woman came back to the table. Fitzgerald introduced her as Detective Maire Murphy.

She punched a fist into the air. "We've got those Plastic Paddies!"

"Plastic Paddies?" I asked.

"Lennox and Reynolds," Fitzgerald said.

"They're not…"

"They're no more Irish than you are," he said. "They're Canadians."

California's Central Valley provides a backdrop for our next tale, and a rhyming song about grammar provides the words and lyrics. But this story by JoAnne Lucas is anything but childlike.

Memories of a rhyming song from her childhood prompted the writing of this story by Ms Lucas. She lives in Clovis, California, and is a founding member of both the San Joaquin Sisters in Crime chapter, and the local Romance Writers of America chapter.

To Put The Monster in its Place

by JoAnne Lucas

Eugene, Oregon
7:30 A.M. September 4, 2012

In medieval times a crusader rode forth on his trusty steed to slay a dragon, a monster, a vicious beast. Thanks to these brave knights of old, the world is a safer place from such beings. No knight ever made it to the high desert of California, however. Thus, the Monster of Lake Elizabeth lies snug and smug in one of the two lakes that surround my hometown of Lake Hughes.

As a child I often had nightmares about the great winged entity that came out at night to grab children and animals and take them back to its cavern lair under Lake Elizabeth. It sure kept me off the street after dark. Everyone living there has heard its cry or screech. Legend has it, that it fought a rancher in the late 1800's. The rancher

55

hit it on the nose and damaged an eye with his rifle butt (bullets didn't faze it). The creature flew off to Tombstone, Arizona. Never figured out what Tombstone had to do with anything. Know-it-alls say it was a pterodactyl and it became the thunderbird of Indian lore. Far be it for me to point out the differences in time here. Whatever it was, it must have left an egg or two behind, just to ensure a continuous presence in the area. You learn to live with it.

But, the danged thing isn't even cute enough to have a name, like the famous Nessie. And who'd be scared of a beast called Elizabeth, while Lizzie just conjures up the wrong impression. Really doesn't do much as a tourist attraction, and tourists are the thin lifeblood of the town of Lake Elizabeth which resides in the middle of the town of Lake Hughes... seriously.

And so I rode forth toward my old home town. My trusty steed was an old red Toyota Carolla, but my resolve the same as those knights of old: Kill the monster.

Just call me Sir Sue Harrison.

Hughes-Elizabeth Lakes Junior High
Lake Hughes, CA–September, 1998

Line 1: *Until by into after from—*

Line 2: *Across against with toward on,*

Mr. Gregory stood tall and tan in front of my eighth grade English class. I was fourteen and I remember well the day he announced that getting a decent passing grade in his class would only be accomplished by memorizing the dreaded preposition poem, a poem consisting entirely of different prepositions, and reciting it to him.

Barbara Jean Robbins and I had been very best friends since third grade. We were really close, she practically lived in our house, but with the onset of hormones, mean changes began to manifest in her. It first hit me after we studied together for our solo English class recitations. She'd transferred the poem onto the old blackboard in our family playroom and we studied from that.

A week later I bravely announced to the teacher I was ready for my recital. I breezed through the eight lines and awaited my congratulations and A grade.

Mr. Gregory gave me an expectant look and then decided I had no more to give him. He gently told me to study some more and I felt my A plummet to a B.

Barbara Jean went next and gave a flawless recitation. She also gave Mr. Gregory a full nine lines, one more line than she had written on my blackboard.

Line 3: *Among around along of to–*

Line 4: *Beside beyond below at through.*

I was still friends with Barbara Jean. I mean, the total population was just about six hundred, so there weren't a lot of kids my age to pal around with. But from that day I no longer trusted her. Over the following years I began to notice I could not make a new close friend with anyone else. She moved in between us and pretended to be a better friend to them.

I became reticent about my school projects after she filched my ideas and handed her projects in first so that it looked as though mine were a me-too copycat.

Line 5: *Upon in for beneath between–*

Line 6: *Behind before without within,*

She was always there, determined I should be her shadow. Boyfriends? Forget about it. It wasn't to be allowed. Once I had a boyfriend she couldn't take away from me, terrible rumors circulated about us, right down to me going to an out of town abortion clinic with brave Barbara Jean by my side.

Even my family started to look sideways at me. It came down to the only way I could get away from her was to get away – far away.

Like any bright young person in Lake Hughes who had ambition, I applied for scholarships to far from home colleges. I was accepted at the University of Oregon at Eugene to study advertising and journalism. Perfect.

After graduating high school, I took a summer job at the hotel up in Yosemite Park and stayed in a cabin there provided for the help. When the season was over, I came home, packed my car and took off for Oregon a week early. I've lived in Eugene for ten years, only flying home for quick family visits and celebrations. I noticed Barbara Jean had her three acolytes of unhappy-looking women circling around her, never to become friends with one another or anyone else, yet not strong enough to leave the group. How blessed I was to get away when I did.

Eugene, Oregon
Late August, 2012

Line 7: *Up over down about—*

Line 8: *Since underneath except throughout.*

I was twenty-eight and engaged to be married. Blake Scanlon was a handsome, wealthy young attorney, and he picked me! It was almost too good to be true. I loved him so much. We planned on a November wedding. In August I received a call from my cousin Amy. She was getting married in October and wanted me to be a bridesmaid.

Being a bridesmaid involved my being in attendance for at least two weeks before the event. Blake was looking forward to this pre-nuptial mini-honeymoon in Lake Hughes. The town of Lake Hughes, where Barbara Jean Robbins still lived.

Greasy panic slid up and down my bowels. "NO!" my mind and my heart screamed in unison. She should not get a chance to practice her poison on my happiness again. Not with Blake, he'd be absolutely too irresistible for her to pass up. This would be the one thing I could never come back from.

I had to stop her.

Blake flew to Milwaukee the day after Labor Day for a week's conference. I kissed him goodbye at the airport, watched his plane take-off early in the morning, then hit the freeway heading south for the California desert near Palmdale. Because my Toyota is a little elderly, I decided to take an easy two days down and one day back. I'd disconnected my odometer earlier so the mileage wouldn't record. No sense being careless about evidence. Along the way I stopped in Modesto at a convenience store and picked up a pre-paid cell phone.

The recession had hit Lake Hughes hard. The vacation homes were closed for the season but it was more deserted than ever, with foreclosure signs defiling abandoned houses, but good for me. It meant less people to notice a car driving by. I passed our bona fide historical landmark, the old Rock Inn. Even it was subdued with only a couple of cars parked out front. Further down the road I stopped and baited the trap. I sent one message to one person:

"9:00Margarittaville@raft2nite."

I knew Barbara Jean would intercept the message.

The raft has always been my favorite place. It's located in a secluded inlet and only the locals know about it. Naturally, the area became a hangout for us kids looking for a place to swim, and later for necking and beer parties. Actually, it isn't really a raft, but a floating dock, and a long swim from shore. I could use the length of that swim as my personal growth chart. It took three years, until I was almost fifteen, before I could swim there and back and not have to float in. Of course, Barbara Jean was the stronger, better athlete and always beat everyone in a race. I could probably take her now, but I wanted more than a race win.

By eight o'clock I'd parked my car off road and hiked in, the only way to get there. The fifteen degree difference in temperature from Eugene was a killer, but I managed everything in one trip. Then I set the stage; turned on my camp lantern, laid out packaged snacks along with the contents of the cooler, and arranged a blanket and pillows into what looked like plans for a hot evening.

I was dressed in a bikini and an off the shoulder blouse. With the quiet murmuring of the lake and the soft country music from my player soothing me, I sank back among the pillows, drink in hand, and calmed myself. There was only a crescent moon to reflect on the lake's surface. It reminded me of Sinbad the Sailor and how much I had wanted to be a swashbuckling pirate when I was seven or so. Would this same symbol steer me to victory tonight?

I almost missed the stealthy approach, but was convincingly surprised when Barbara Jean suddenly stood silhouetted in front of the lantern's light. "Wha—What are you doing here?" I demanded.

"Expecting someone else? David, maybe?" she asked. "He can't be bothered and told me to let you know."

"David? Why would I be expecting David? Haven't seen him in years."

"Are those margaritas in that pitcher? His always-favorite drink of all time? Or, was. Haven't you heard, he's in the Twelve Step Program now. Not nearly so amusing."

"Amusing," I said. "Is that why you married him?"

"So you did know we were married. You snot-nosed bitch, I married him because you still wanted him. Well, you can have him back now. He got religion or something. Couldn't stand me having a drink around him. Almost went ballistic."

She moved away from the front of the light and I could see she was wearing a halter top with really short cut-offs, and flag-red toenail polish. Her summertime signature look from puberty. She was hot stuff and had been flaunting it ever since the motorcycle clubs started making regular spring and summer runs here. My parents kept us kids inside at such times. Danger could come to the innocent in more ways other than a lake monster.

But Barbara Jean relished it.

She'd been carrying her flip flops in her hand and now flung them down in the dirt near me. Of course, kinda hard to sneak in with flip flops beating out an announcement.

She poured herself a large drink from the frosty pitcher, insolently availed herself of the best pillows to lie against, and smiled. Or sniled, I should say.

Right on cue the Lake Monster let out a screech and the air around us became disturbed with the sounds like the beating of huge wings. I'd forgotten how startling it was.

"Jeeze, Sue, afraid the Lake Monster's gonna getcha?"

"No." I sat back. "I'm not scared of monsters or witches anymore."

"My, my. All grown up now, are we?" She raised her glass, "Well, here's to old times."

I raised my bottled water and countered, "Here's to the future." I thought about David Harrow, the first boy to have ever kissed me. He went from being referred to by my parents as 'That nice boy David from across the street' to 'Poor David' after his marriage. I drank a silent salute to him and his future.

She grabbed the bag of chips and didn't offer any. Fine with me. "What made you think David was meeting me?" I asked. "I have other friends here, you know."

Barbara Jean gave a low laugh. " 'Cause I kept his phone, computer and old email address. That's why. Thought you were being so smart doing the cryptic message thing, didn't you? What's the matter, Sue, guys in Oregon not good enough for you?"

I smiled and didn't say anything.

"Answer me, damn it! You think you can just waltz right in here and take over anybody you want from me? You're too late. I divorced his ass two years ago. You can have what's left."

I smiled again. "I know."

She seemed disconcerted and drank some more, pretty much chug-a-lugging her big margarita. Then she grabbed the salt and lime to coat the rim again and re-filled the glass.

I had poured a goodly amount of tequila, Grand Marnier and lime juice into the margarita mix to mask the taste of the crushed valium tablets. As the drinks hit, she went on a tour of memory lane, highlighting all the times she had upped me and refilling her glass a couple more times.

"Why did you do all that? What had I ever done to you?" I asked. I'd spent years trying to understand her.

"Because," she said.

I waited. "That's it? 'Because'?"

"Yeah. Just because. Because you got boobs before I did. Because people always liked you. Because your parents gave you nice things and you didn't live in a trailer. Because Dave Harrow never forgot you. So, yeah – a big, fat, because!"

Wow! 'Because.' Well, now I knew, but I felt off-kilter. She hated me for all those reasons and probably more.

I shivered as the depth of her malice drenched me. 'Because.' I guess if I stopped breathing she'd still hate me because. Maybe I should just leave. I could deal with Blake's being near her for Amy's wedding. I really felt empowered by what I'd learned. This poor woman shaped her whole life attacking me just because. Sick!

I stood up and started gathering things together. "What? You're not leaving yet," she said. "Don't you want to know what I plan to do for your favorite cousin's wedding?" She was slurring her words now.

I stilled my motions, but my heart raced. What nastiness did she have in mind for Amy?

"Dear little Amy is marrying Bob Harrow, Dave's oldest brother, in case you forgot. Me and Bob had quite a fling a while back. I figure he'll be fed up with Amy's totally absorbing wedding plans. She'll be much too busy to stop and give him a little nooky by then. God knows, he's probably not gettin' much now." She slurped more margarita. "I plan to give him a special little wedding present in a semi-private place where we can be discovered, and he can try to explain it away on his honeymoon. If he even gets to go on a honeymoon. Your cousin will be hurt and so will you. Dave will be hurt and so will you. And Bob? Who cares?" She giggled.

I froze. I knew she would do it. A familiar wave of nausea and helplessness threatened until I remembered why I was there.

"I'll fix it so Amy'll be watching out for you instead of me. It'll be delish—" She hic-cupped and stood up swaying. "Whoa, my head's buzzin'. Lesh go for a swim. I might even let you win – NOT!"

I relaxed and smiled to myself this time. What do you do with a monster, a witch, a horrible, terrible person? You let them go swimming, of course.

I pulled off my blouse and headed for the water. "You'd better hurry," I said over my shoulder and did a shallow dive into the cold, cold lake.

"I'll beat you like I always beat you," she staggered in after me.

I hadn't told her I'd worked on my swimming until I became captain of the university's racing team in my senior year. I just swam to the raft, pulled myself out and waited.

Barbara Jean didn't believe it at first, and when she did, she swallowed a lot of water being angry and yelling at me. Then, still angry, she swallowed a lot more water when she floundered. And finally she swallowed all the water she needed to go under.

Well, what do you know? Witches can be drowned.

I let myself back into the water and searched where she went down. I grabbed her hair and towed her to the raft. Once there, I took a deep breath and dived under it, taking Barbara Jean with me. I tangled her hair in the pilings to keep her there, and swam out for the shore.

I floated on my back part of the way in, just for old time's sake. Sometimes you need to re-visit the past and put it behind you.

On my drive home I recited the Preposition Poem as an epithet to Barbara Jean – all nine lines of it.

Line 9: *Above off during near like.*

The infamous ninth line. The line that doesn't rhyme, doesn't fit the métier, is just stuck on. The line I now like best.

Above all else, I am grateful Barbara Jean so obligingly finished all the margaritas, went off her rocker and made that swim. Near Bakersfield I decided that she really enjoyed making my life miserable during my youth. Now she has simply become the object of prepositions as in below the raft and beneath the water. I have left her behind me.

I had sent the Lake Elizabeth Monster one of its offspring to stay in Lake Hughes. Neither Barbara Jean nor the monster could scare me anymore.

Maybe Lizzie was a good name for a defeated beast.

Santa Cruz and the rocky California coast provide the location of our next story. Every writer wants an agent, but acquiring one can be murder.

Ms Hansen writes the Carol Sabala mystery series, featuring a young woman in her family's business—a detective agency. Her latest novel, "Black Beans and Venom", is now available.

Critical Mass

by Vinnie Hansen

May Knight would do anything for Hedra Zabon. Hedra represented the long sought-after prize—a New York literary agent. So May said, "Of course! Come. You will love Santa Cruz. It's a tourist destination."

"I know that, dear," Hedra rasped over the phone. "I'm thinking four days."

May swallowed. Guests, like fish, stank after three days, especially in a small condo. On the other hand, she would get to meet Hedra. She gazed at the morning newspaper spread before her, the front-page photo of a breaching humpback. "We could go out on a whale watching tour."

"I detest tours. And I don't care for the open water." Hedra coughed. "I get seasick. And I can't swim."

May sucked in her breath. Her body thrilled with tremolos. Was the woman coming just to see her? May had not told a soul the big news that she might be about to score an agent, waiting until they signed a contract. But this visit was a good omen—the woman must be traveling all the way to the West Coast so they could work out the "problematic areas" in May's manuscript.

When Hedra announced the date of her trip, May glanced at the wall calendar and chewed her lip. She'd have to cancel two appointments and maybe call in sick to work.

"I trust that will be okay with you." Hedra sniffed.

"It will be wonderful to meet you." May pumped her fist in the air.

"Will you pick me up at the airport?" Hedra asked.

What a demanding woman. But May expected nothing less from a New York literary agent.

"No problem."

* * *

Curving over the perilous Highway 17, May glimpsed the redwoods towering on the cliffs beside her and forested vistas stretching toward the Pacific. She wished Hedra would admire the view. In the leather passenger seat, Hedra made calls on her orange Apple iPhone. After six hours on a plane, the agent no doubt had urgent messages to attend to.

The woman stuck a finger in her ear. "You're breaking up!" She glared at May as though the bad reception were her fault. "Shit!" Hedra disconnected her call and punched numbers with a bronze fingernail.

"There are lots of dead zones…"

The agent thrust a palm toward May's face. "Harold! Harold, can you hear me?"

May concentrated on maneuvering her Miata past thundering oil tankers and out of the way of SUVs barreling down on her bumper. It was just as well she didn't have to converse.

"Yes, yes," Hedra screamed into the phone. "We're almost there." A pause. "Lynn Clemmons. Of course I remember the name!"

———

Frazzled after the drive, May showed Hedra into the master bedroom. All fresh linen. May had set up the office futon for herself.

The agent plopped her suitcase on top of the white bedspread. Grime and gum stuck to the rugged wheels of the case.

May cringed, but bit her lip.

Hedra scanned the room and sniffed.

"The bathroom is rather small," May said, opening the door.

After Hedra freshened up, the two women parked at the kitchen table. May served coffee from freshly ground beans.

"French roast from Santa Cruz Coffee Roasting Company."

The afternoon lay before them. Even with the jolt of caffeine, May had to dig deep to muster enthusiasm. "One of our biggest attractions is the Santa Cruz Beach Boardwalk. It's California's oldest surviving amusement park."

"A roller coaster and cotton candy?" Hedra twitched up a sandy eyebrow.

Heat crept along May's neck. What had she been thinking? From the headshot on Zabon's Agency website, May had concluded the woman was urbane. What an idiot to suggest a carnival-like place! Yet most people, even sophisticates, enjoyed the view of the bright colors spread along the beach…

Hedra tapped out a cigarette. "Do you mind?"

Resigned, May opened the kitchen window. The agent had already filled the virgin ashtray of her car with butts. "Is there any particular place you'd like to see?" She slid a small plate in front of Hedra.

Hedra jabbed a cigarette in her mouth, snicked open her gold lighter, and inhaled. She plucked a tobacco stem from her peach lipstick before jetting out smoke. She appeared pensive, crossing the legs of her tight jeans and waggling three-inch stilettos. "You have wineries, don't you?"

"Sure." May didn't sense Hedra cared about the vineyards. "We have great tasting rooms downtown."

Barring her chest with one arm, Hedra smoked and frowned at May's Banana Slugs sweatshirt.

"I'll change."

She crept into her own bedroom like an interloper, yanked off her sweatshirt, and jammed it into the hamper. She pulled on a burgundy sweater and slipped on expensive flats. All unnecessary in Santa Cruz, but she didn't want to embarrass Hedra, a woman with a gold scarf wrapped in intricate knots above a cashmere sweater, the print an array of fall colors.

As May chauffeured Hedra toward downtown, she viewed Santa Cruz through Hedra's critical eyes, the graffiti on the new freeway retaining walls and the Santa Cruz Mountains blue in the distance. At the exit, a scruffy man on the meridian thrust forward his cardboard sign: NEED MONEY FOR BEER.

Hedra pointed. "There, May, is the direct narrative you need. Straightforward honest prose. No adjectives, no unnecessary adverbs." With a sweep of her hand, Hedra eliminated May's offending words. "An element of humor."

Honest! How could a cosmopolite like Hedra be so easily suckered? Beer would hardly be the depleted man's substance of choice. Plus, May thought, the sign could benefit from well-chosen modifiers: NEED MONEY NOW FOR ARTISIAN BEER. She wiped the smirk off her face and hoped Hedra had not seen it."

The hideous blue and yellow River Street sign reared up across the intersection with "Welcome to Downtown Santa Cruz" on it. The controversial sign belonged in Bakersfield. No local resident thought of River Street as downtown.

May zoomed her gray Miata past Storr's tasting room, tucked off of River Street in an industrial complex. Hedra pursed her lips, but May wanted to show off the real downtown first, the tree and art-lined Pacific Avenue. Besides, two o'clock was early for wine.

"You can't be May Knight," Hedra pronounced with a dramatic flip of her hand. "Too monosyllabic. Audiences will mistake your name for an evening in May. Use Maybelline."

"But that's not my name."

Hedra's bony shoulders rose. She folded her arms. "That's hardly the point."

A parking spot opened right behind Bookshop Santa Cruz. They climbed from the car. "This is one of those oxymora, a thriving independent bookstore. The 1989 earthquake demolished it, but here it is—resurrected."

"For God's sake, slow up." Hedra wobbled up behind her. She halted on the sidewalk and tapped out another cigarette.

"You can't smoke here."

"Excuse me," Hedra said. "We're on the sidewalk for Christ's sake."

"We're within twenty-five feet of the entrance."

"You have to be kidding me."

"City ordinance." It was highly unlikely anyone would give a shit, but May's eyes itched from the woman's smoke, and the autumn air nipped through her sweater. She glanced longingly toward the glass double door.

Hedra lit up and puffed. "I've seen a few bookstores in my day."

An exiting customer with books crooked in her elbow scowled at Hedra and fanned her face.

"You have a problem?" Hedra growled.

The silver-haired lady shrank back and May blushed. "She's a New Yorker."

Hedra rolled her eyes and ground out the long butt on the concrete. "Well, Maybelline, it's clear where your heroine gets her cowering personality."

May ground her teeth, but the embrace of the bookstore as they entered soothed her. She turned to a shelf of New York Times best sellers with outward facing covers. Someday, she thought, especially now she had the prospect of an agent.

She startled when Hedra grasped her arm.

"What's wrong?" May followed the trajectory of Hedra's gaze to a familiar stack of gray hair atop a towering frame.

"Is that ?"

"Yes. That's Laurie King. She lives—"

May was talking to air. Hedra beelined for the author. Laurie King appeared lost in reverie over a book, her wire-rim glasses slipping down her nose.

Watching Hedra zero in on the other writer, May ducked her head in embarrassment. She had attended many of her readings and Laurie King knew her as an aspiring local mystery writer. But she would never rush the woman, assuming that between awards, Laurie King might like to lead a normal life.

Hedra yammered at the famous woman, dressed as usual in a plain blazer and sensible shoes."As Hedra thrust a business card toward King's chest, the author peered in May's direction. May wished the gaze were a bucket of water, and she could melt like the Wicked Witch of the West. She turned away from the humiliation to the comfort of the books until Hedra rejoined her. "I could use that wine now."

You and me both. May no longer desired to stroll down Pacific Avenue with this woman. She doubted the agent would admire the sculpture or boutique shops, anyway.

———————

While Hedra drank her way through the free samples, May sipped a glass of Storrs' chardonnay. The agent's tiny head lolled to the side and she didn't even fuss when the sommelier informed her she couldn't smoke. Instead she wheedled larger pours.

"Do you know Lynn Clemmons?" Hedra asked May.

"Should I?"

"She's a writer from Santa Cruz."

May wrinkled her forehead. She'd been in many writing classes and critique groups and had been featured in local publications over the years, but she couldn't recall the name Lynn Clemmons. "Is there a particular reason you're asking?"

"She had a brilliant piece in the New Yorker."

"Wow. That's prestigious." May was doubly surprised that she'd never heard of the woman. Even though Santa Cruz had over 60,000 residents and had grown together with neighboring communities, she'd lived in the area for over thirty years and ran into familiar people wherever she went.

"She's a recluse," the agent murmured. "No web presence at all."

When they returned to May's Mazda, Hedra plopped into the convertible's low seat. "Was that the best one?"

"The Christie vineyard chardonnay won a double gold medal."

Hedra shrugged. "So what's next?"

Emboldened by the wine, May said, "Maybe we should discuss my manuscript."

The woman snorted. "We could start with the title. Mojito Madness."

In the black bucket seat, May stiffened, unable to turn the key. "You don't like it?"

The woman chortled. "It's awful."

A rock dropped into the bottom of May's heart. She loved the alliterative title—had thought hard about it.

"Titles are easy to change," Hedra said breezily.

Relieved, May started the car. As she twisted around to back out, she heard the words, "But the rest of it…"

May's fingers trembled on the steering wheel. Her mouth dried to paste. "I thought you liked my book." Blinking, she turned to the agent.

"Watch where you're going!"

May slammed on her brakes. They lurched forward. A red Camaro blasted its horn as it roared by. Unsettled, May eased the car into the River Street traffic. She hit the green light and headed north on Highway 1. Driving up the hill, she pointed at a white church out her window. "Over there is Misión la Exaltacion de la Santa Cruz, founded by the Franciscans in 1791." Her voice quavered. "One of the original adobes has been restored."

Hedra sniffed. "Where are we going now?"

Certainly not there, her tone implied. May couldn't answer. Her stomach roiled with what the agent had said. It's okay, she told herself. What was another draft? With her critique group and beta readers and rejections, she had already done thirteen of them. As long as the woman would represent her…

The highway turned into Mission Street through the west side of town. A butterfly sanctuary occupied a eucalyptus meadow out this way. A walk along the cliffs of West Cliff Drive offered panoramic views of the ocean and surfers riding the waves of Steamer Lane. May felt certain none of this would captivate Hedra. When they reached the edge of town, May hit the gas pedal. The front of her car lifted.

"Take it easy," the agent said. "I can recommend a good book doctor."

A book doctor! Did that mean the woman had traveled to Santa Cruz and ensconced herself in her bedroom with no intention of becoming her agent? Maybe just cutting expenses while she tracked down Lynn Clemmons? The brilliant Lynn Clemmons!

"What do you see as the biggest problem with my book?"

Hedra drummed the dashboard. She gazed out the passenger window at rolling countryside. She could have viewed the ocean, but the bitch obviously did not want to look in May's direction.

"Everything, really," the woman said.

"Everything?" May squeaked.

"I'd start with the method. Oleander poisoning? Seriously?"

May veered onto the shoulder of the road. "It was good enough for Agatha Christie."

Hedra's head spun from side to side. "What's here?"

"A secret path to the ocean." May climbed out and slammed the door.

Hedra cracked her door. "I can't walk a dirt path in these shoes."

"You know," May said, "it occurred to me that I know a writer named Lynette. Could be Clemmons."

"Really?" Hedra struggled up onto the side of the road.

"There's a spectacular view from the cliffs." May crossed the narrow highway. "Not far."

Hobbling along the path, Hedra puffed, out of breath. "Lynette?" she asked.

"Yes," May called over her shoulder. "But I could see this woman preferring the punch of the single syllable—Lynn."

Even though chunks of earth routinely collapsed from the cliff area, May edged up to the steep drop. Raw ragged rock plunged down to the ocean. She sucked in the oxygenated sea air, big gulps as though she were drowning.

Hedra panted up beside her. "Tell me about Lynette." The agent glanced down at the surging waves, the water swirling between the rocks. She stepped back from the rugged cliff and the vista of the Pacific.

"First tell me what's so wrong with poison?"

"It's dated. Old ladyish."

"Someone might want to inform Viktor Yushchenko."

"Who?"

May moved away from the precipice to behind the agent. "You're right, Hedra." Her head nodded in agreement. "Poison is not the best vehicle for murder."

With a smug smile, the woman turned away.

"The best vehicle—" May stuck out both palms. "—is a quick push off a steep cliff."

With a raven-like caw, Hedra flew, autumn colors spread-eagled in flight. When the body bobbed in the surf, May waved goodbye. About to ease her flip phone from a pocket, May spotted the glint of Hedra's orange iPhone in the ice plant. She scooped it up and called 911.

This, she thought, dusting her hands, would make a good story. What would she call it? Agent of Death? Agent Orange?

Nah, she had it: Critical Mass.

Maine's rocky coast greets us in this story. We are social creatures and crave membership in community. But we are also creatures who fear change and difference. Alien takes place in the no-man's land between the two conflicting emotions.

Ms D'Avanzo' is well-used to residing in a netherworld between cultures, having transplanted herself to Maine on retirement. In addition to writing, she volunteers as a teacher of English to recent immigrants.

Alien

by Charlene D'Avanzo

From away, to where?

Alone in the kitchen, forehead pressed against the cool window, I silently mouthed the question. Across the channel a dying sun splashed rose over the islands, but even Maine's stunning seascape couldn't brighten my spirits.

I turned back, petted Suzanne's cat, and observed the self-named Women of Spruce Island at the far end of the living room. Bits of conversation—names of people I didn't know and places I'd never been—drifted my way.

Before I slipped out the front door, I grabbed my celebratory champagne from the frig and my parka off the mudroom hook. At seven o'clock in May, dusk would soon fade into dark. My footfall crunched gravel on the road and I nearly missed the eiders' cluck-ing from just beyond the beach-rose hedge. I stopped to listen. The ducks sounded like a bunch of old gossipy of ladies like the ones I had just left behind.

I made my way down the hill to the town dock. With my legs outstretched toward the east, I leaned against a piling and waited for the orb to rise over the horizon. When it was fully dark, the monthly show would begin. Then a generous moon would be my companion in celebration.

I followed the delicate chain circling my neck, tracing it with my fingers under my shirt, down to the gold cross on my chest. Melan-choly solace.

Finally, the ribbon of moonbeam reached my floating retreat. I opened the champagne and lifted the bottle.

"To one year, and tomorrow's new friends."

***

The next day, I turned the corner—away from Portland's chat-tering Commercial Street onto a working wharf. It was a step back in time. Turquoise, rust, and tan wooden buildings with peeling window sashes and rusted signs looked out at the cobble street. On the other side, when fishermen were in port, boats named "Endurance" and "Lilly Ann" lined up bow to stern. Good fishing was far offshore in early spring, so the pier would be peaceful until late afternoon.

I picked my way along the uneven cobbles to my destination, Harborside Fish, and stopped to read the blackboard by the front door. Wild Salmon $11.99, Mussels $5.99, Scallops $10.99, Cod $8.99, Lobster $9.99.

I stepped into a sparse little room. The air was heavy with salt and rush of seawater loud from a holding tank in the far corner.

I squinted through the gloom to see Tony Martino reach into his tank and pick up a giant lobster. The animal waved antennae and flexed its belly.

"What'd you think he weighs?"

Tony dropped the big guy back into the tank and winked. "Three pound, at least. Gina?"

"That's right."

"People want the biggest lobster." He gestured toward the tank. "I gotta know what's in there. So, what can I get you?"

I settled on a pound each of scallops and salmon, enough to keep me in seafood for most of the week.

As Tony rang up my order on his ancient cash register I said, "Can I ask you a personal question?"

"Sure."

"You've been in Maine for what, twenty years? Does it feel like home? You know, you're not from away anymore?"

"Gimme a minute."

Tony washed in a corner sink, grabbed a towel, and talked while he wiped his hands. "There's lots of Italians in Portland 'n I got brothers, sisters, cousins, and the rest. So it's home."

"What about Mainers who've been here for generations?"

"How do they treat me?"

"Yeah."

He rubbed his chin for a few seconds. "Mostly I deal with fishermen. Here 'round Portland it's more mixed than Downeast. If I was up by Bangor, say, I'd always be an outsider."

Figuring Tony had work to do, I thanked him and stepped outside. I'd just passed the ally between the fish store and the building next door when a nasty voice caught my attention. I looked around. Nobody was in sight.

I backed up and peered into the dark ally. Two men partly hidden by a couple of trash cans stood twenty feet in front of me. One loomed over the other whose back and arms were pressed against the wall.

"You're Muslim. Slimly little bastard. Go back where ya belong."

The bigger guy pulled back like he was going to land a punch.

I dropped my fish, sprinted down the ally, and hollered. "Stop! What the hell're you doing?"

The bully stepped to the side and squinted in my direction. Without thinking, I picked up a trash can, heaved it toward him, and screamed at the other one.

"Run!"

I sprinted for the street and could hear him close behind. In thirty seconds, we were inside Tony's store. Heaving, I leaned up against the door and tried to get my breath. The man fell onto rusty chair in the corner and leaned over with his head in his hands.

Tony stared at me, the stranger in his chair, back at me. "What the—?"

I gasped, "Can't... talk."

A few minutes later, I walked over to the man and held out my hand. "I'm Gina."

He stood and clasped two smooth hands around mine. "I am Abir Safar."

With chestnut eyes shaded by heavy brows, olive skin, and full lips, Abir was one of the most handsome men I'd ever seen. He looked young, maybe mid-thirties.

"Are you okay?"

If Abir was angry or embarrassed, he didn't show it. "Yes. Thank you." He turned to Tony. "And thank you, sir, for this safety."

As if he offered refuge everyday, Tony waved his hand. "Would you like some water, coffee?"

Abir declined, as did I.

"Tony, before we go outside," I said, "could you check the ally and make sure the thug who was there is gone?"

Tony returned with a plastic bag. "You dropped your fish. And I found this a wallet on the ground."

I took the bag and watched while Tony opened his prize. He whistled.

"What?"

Tony held out the billfold so we could see the ID inside.

I leaned over and read it aloud. "Police Department. Mickey O'Shea."

Tony flipped the billfold closed. "Looks like your thug's with the Portland police."

"A cop?"

"Where I come from," Abir said, "I'd expect that, but not in Portland, Maine."

I held out my hand. "I'd like to return Mickey's wallet. That way, I can talk to the bastard."

"Jus' be careful, Gina."

Abir and I thanked Tony again and stepped out onto the street.

"Would you like to go to a coffee shop?" I asked.

He shook his head. "I must go home. But I would very much like you to visit and meet my wife and children. They'll certainly want to meet you."

Abir's earnest eyes searched mine. There was no way I could decline his invitation.

"Ah, I'd love to. Give me the address and we'll pick a time."

Two days later I parked in front of a two-story house on a quiet street in an ethnic part of town. A couple of kid's bicycles lay on the cracked driveway next to an old sedan. I hadn't made it to the top step of the tiny porch when a woman pulled the door open.

"Gina? Come in. Come in"

I entered a kitchen rich with the aroma of cumin, cinnamon, and mint.

"It smells amazing in here."

"Amazing?"

Abir skirted a row of shoes and strode into the kitchen. "Gina, this is my wife, Nasim."

With thick black brows, dark honest eyes, and a shy smile, Nasim was as lovely as Abir handsome. She wore no scarf over her black hair.

She turned to Abir. "What does this mean, amazing?"

"Fantastic, wonderful. It's an American expression."

"Ah." Nasim motioned to a chair. "Please, sit while I make you coffee." She moved around the kitchen and whispered "amazing, amazing."

Abir took the chair opposite me and nodded toward his wife. "Nasim wants to improve her English."

"It sounds pretty good already."

"She's a physicist and her English-speaking colleagues were British."

"And you? Your English is perfect."

"I was a reporter in Iraq for the BBC, NPR, a few American networks."

I raised an eyebrow. "Was?"

"I'll tell you our story while you drink your coffee."

The cup and saucer Nasim placed in front of me was half the usual size and elegant —black with gold leaf trim. She poured ebony coffee that smelled of cardamom. A plate of dates, some flatbread, and a bowl of hummus sat the middle of the table.

Nasim watched while I took my first sip of her coffee.

"Do you like it?"

"Very much. It's sweeter than any I've had and much stronger. I see why the cup is small."

Abir waited until Nasim was seated with her own coffee before he began.

"Six months ago, we moved here from Baghdad. Nasim wanted to leave long before that, but the world needs to know the truth of what's happening. Then my two closest colleagues were accused of being pro-western and killed. I had Nasim and the children to protect, so we got out."

"How do you like Portland?"

"We love it, except for the cold." He laughed. "Everyone has been so generous, so kind. America is a wonderful country. We've already been granted asylum—because of my work." He turned his head. "I hear the children. They want to meet you."

I watched Abir step over the shoes. If the U.S. put him on a fast track to asylum, I thought, he must've been a prominent reporter.

Abir returned with a young girl. She held his hand, beamed at me, and in practiced English said, "I am Lulu."

A small boy peeked around the corner of the living room door and quickly pulled back.

Nasim nodded in the boy's direction. "And that is Yusef."

Abir told me a little about the children—where they were in school, that they loved and mimicked American cartoons. Then he asked, "The billfold. What will you do with it?"

"Tell me what you think about this idea. I'd like to speak with O'Shea privately but at the station so it's safe."

"What will you say?"

"He's a policeman. I'll ask why he was about to attack you."

Nasim bit her lip. "You won't tell this policeman who Abir is?"

"Not if you don't want me to. If he's hostile, I'll figure out how to report him. But there's probably more to it. I'd like to give the man a chance to explain."

"And if he does?" Abir asked.

"Perhaps he should meet you. If you agree, of course."

Nasim's eyes grew large, and she looked at Abir.

He placed his hand on hers. "We're not in Iraq, Nasim. Gina must have a reason."

"You're lovely people with two children. Abir worked with Americans to report on the Iraqi war and what happened afterward. I'd like him to—"

Abir finished my sentence. "Not see us as foreign terrorists."

"Something like that."

The next morning I slid O'Shea's billfold across the Portland Police Department's counter and explained that I wanted to return it in person.

"Oh that's not necessary," the assistant said. "I can give it to him."

I pulled the billfold back. "No, really. May I see him for a few minutes? I'd very much like to return it myself."

She narrowed her eyes and tipped her head. I smiled at her. She sighed and said, "Oh, all right. I'll go see."

She returned, opened the door beside the counter, and pointed down the corridor. "There he is."

With a buzz cut and a couple of tattoos on both arms, Mickey O'Shea looked like any other cop.

We walked toward each other.

"You have my billfold?"

I pulled it out of my purse. "Yes." I almost added "Sir".

I dropped the billfold onto his outstretched hand. He shoved it into his back pocket. "Appreciate this. Where'd you find it?"

"In the ally. I threw the trashcan at you."

O'Shea stepped back, ran his hand across his hair, and glanced to the side. We were alone.

He lowered his voice. "What do you want?"

"To know why."

"And if it's none of your business?"

"I'm dating someone here. A Sergeant," I lied.

"Who?"

"That's none of your business."

I thought I detected a hint of a grin. In any case, O'Shea must've figured he wasn't dealing with loony because he said, "Want some coffee? We can talk back there."

I followed him down the corridor to a miniscule room with a window, sink, round table, and a few chairs. It smelled of bad coffee.

"No coffee," I said.

O'Shea pulled up a chair facing the door. I sat opposite him.

He looked down at his hands, then up at me. His blue eyes gave nothing away. "You want to know why I was like that."

I nodded.

"How do I know I can trust you?"

I stuck a finger beneath my turtleneck and pulled out the large gold cross. "It was my brother's. He wore it in Iraq. You can trust me."

O'Shea regarded my brother's keepsake, nodded, sat back, crossed his arms. "I'd just come from the hospital. My brother is—was—in

Afghanistan. He's paralyzed from the waist down. I'd been hoping, but he told me it was permanent. I walked the city. Don't even know how I ended up on that pier. When I saw that guy, I just lost it."

He leaned forward, put his hands on the table, and looked directly at me. "That's the God's truth."

After more than a decade in Iraq and Afghanistan, the story wasn't unusual. But for each child, parent, sibling whose loved one was hurt or worse, that didn't matter.

We sat in silence for a long minute before I said, "I'm sorry about your brother."

O'Shea stood. "I'll walk you out."

"The man's name is Abir. Want to meet him and his family?"

"And why would I do that?"

"Because they'd like to meet you."

O'Shea stepped back, walked over to the window, and stared out. I couldn't tell what he was doing, but it looked like pulled something from beneath his shirt, fingered it, and tucked it back in.

He turned, leaned back against the windowsill, and looked at me straight on. "I'll think about it."

I put my hand on my chest. Beneath my shirt the cross felt solid, warm.

O'Shea glanced at my hand. He added, "I mean it. I'll think hard on this."

A ripped piece of paper and a pen lay in the middle of the table. I flipped the paper over, scribbled my e-mail, and slid the paper over to him. "I'll look for your message."

Back at Spruce Harbor that evening, I picked my way across boulders, down to the beach, and along the wrack line to an old, overhanging oak tree. The refuge offered a private view across salt marsh, bay, to Portland's skyline beyond. Dusk was well underway and waterfront buildings sent brilliant, drawn-out versions of themselves across the harbor.

A venerable city where people old and new were trying to make their way.

For me, there was a great deal at my feet to hold close—sloshing waves of an incoming tide, tiny periwinkles gliding across slick slabs of rock, drying seaweed pungently sweet and salty.

This was my place.

Charleston, South Carolina, home to ancient, antique churches, and where you'll meet cantankerous Abigail Grimley, a woman with a slightly anti-social hobby.

Ms Kopil is another transplant, from New Jersey suburbia to Carolina coast where she works as a graphic designer. She has had numerous stories published in a variety of publications.

Pearls of Wisdom

by Su Kopil

Abigail Grimley didn't like people, especially old people. Made no never mind that at seventy-three she was considered old herself. So when her only nephew, Everest, signed her up for a senior bus tour of historic Charleston, she was none too pleased. He owned a dinky travel agency and had been sending her hither and yon for ages. Last year, she'd told him no more. She had more important things to do like watch the dandelions grow, keep the pile of books on her armchair from teetering over, and there was her dumb cat, Clover, who insisted on being hand fed one kibble at a time.

Nope. It wasn't going to happen. Everest would just have to count her out. But then, three things happened in quick succession to change the course of Abigail's affairs.

One, her nosey neighbor Martha Ruth cut down thirty-year-old trees dividing their backyards without so much as a howdy-do. Two, her pile of books were buried beneath a heap of rubble when one of those said trees crashed into her library, and three, Clover died.

Everest's office was two towns over. The small building housing the agency was as frumpy as her nephew. Try as he might, Everest was not what you'd call a ladies man. No amount of shiny bling or designer suits could hide the fact that he took after the homely Grimley side of the family.

He handed Abigail the usual paperwork—tickets, background material, itinerary, and shooed her out the door. She stopped short in the doorway and turned to look at him. "Now, remember what I said, Everest. This is the last time. I'm only doing it because of the house repairs. And you promised to check on the workers. I don't trust that Martha Ruth as far as a horse could throw her."

She gave him a stern eye and was satisfied to see his skin pale slightly beneath the beads of sweat. No spine, that nephew of hers, which is why he always hired others to do his dirty work. More's the pity, to be saddled with the Grimley looks but not their mettle.

It rained the day Abigail met the tour bus, and as she feared, it was full of old people. The air inside was hot and sour and circulating every shade of malady that could be had. The front of the bus was packed. No matter. She preferred the back anyway. That is if she didn't break her neck tripping over the canes and umbrellas protruding into the aisle.

She was pleased as pickles, and in fact, couldn't have planned it better herself, to find an empty seat across from two of the youngest women, mid-to-late sixties by the looks of them. Seeing she was alone, they immediately introduced themselves as Pearl and Polly Platter, sisters from up Raleigh way. Their features were similar: green eyes, long noses, cleft chins. It was their demeanor and attire that set them apart.

"I've a hunch we'll become fast friends, Abigail dear." That was Pearl, decked out in a bright pink sundress, matching sandals and a big floppy hat. On her neck hung the largest strand of pearls Abigail had ever seen, so large that the woman had a permanent hunch from the weight of them. "After all strangers are just friends waiting to happen. Isn't that what I always say, Polly?"

"Friends waiting to happen." Polly dutiful parroted.

At first, Abigail thought Polly merely sat in her sister's shadow, but on closer inspection, she realized it was the woman's clothes that were gray, like an unadorned statue. Her eyes were the liveliest thing about her, constantly darting towards her sister and away.

"Let's get a move on." A man with a hearing aid yelled from the middle of the bus.

"Everything comes to those who wait," Pearl sang back, one hand fluttering over her pearls.

"Everything comes…" mimicked Polly.

Abigail soon discovered this was their habit. Pearl would spout some wise saying or other and Polly would echo it in a drab monotone.

"A hard beginning maketh a good ending." This said when the bus took a wrong turn.

"A hard beginning…"

"Patience is bitter, but the fruit is sweet." Spoken when they detoured for gas.

"Patience is bitter…"

"Slow and steady wins the race." When they finally arrived in Charleston.

"Slow and steady…"

The sun beat back the rain by the time they reached the hotel. Everyone checked in and then split up into groups, brochures and canes in hand, to take to the streets. With a little nudging from Abigail, Pearl and her sister took her under their wing.

"Do you know why Charleston is called the Holy City?" Pearl quizzed as they strolled along Meeting Street. "Because of the church steeples. There are so many, ship captains used them as landmarks. It's all in how you look at things."

"Look at things…" Polly dutifully repeated.

Abigail no longer bothered to reply.

They'd already been to White Pointe Gardens, Rainbow Row, the Old Exchange and Provost Dungeon. At each stop Pearl took it upon herself to lecture them on its history—facts they could easily have read for themselves.

Abigail wasn't used to so much walking and couldn't wait to get back home to her weeds and books, though it was true it wouldn't be the same without old Clover. Right now she'd settle for a nap at the hotel, but Pearl was pulling her and Polly into A.W. Shucks.

"I hear the she-crab soup is to die for," said Pearl.

So they dutifully ordered three, and while they tucked in, Abigail made the mistake of asking Pearl where she'd gotten her necklace.

Pearl's eyes grew misty as she stroked the gems. "They were a wedding gift from our dear Mama. An investment for my future. Isn't that right, Polly?"

Polly stared at her soup and for once didn't reply, but Pearl didn't seem to notice.

"Of course, Mama had warned me about men. 'Pearl, she said, men only want one thing from a woman.' And she was right you know. It only lasted two years before that lowdown, cheating husband of mine wandered off into the arms of a tramp. But I got a good alimony, so I didn't need to sell the necklace. Not yet anyway." Her laughter teetered off-key. "But I learned my lesson. As I always tell Polly, all are not saints, who go to church."

Abigail waited for the echo, but Polly remained mute.

"In fact, I saved my sister from a similar fate and brought her to live with me. The best revenge is happiness, and we've been happy together ever since."

Polly seemed anything but happy. In fact, she was starting to look down-right mutinous.

———••———

They returned to the hotel to nap, but Abigail's mind wouldn't let her rest. The Charleston City Market was a short walk from the hotel. The heat and crowds were a bit daunting, but the smell of fudge and fresh baked bread did much to fortify her. She passed stalls of artwork and sweet grass baskets, pausing to watch a Gullah woman weave her magic.

Then someone bumped her. She turned. The miscreant was gone but what she did see surprised her. Polly, alone, at a fashion stall leaning over a display case, with a colorful scarf in one hand. Intrigued, Abigail walked up beside her and peered at the display case of costume jewelry. "Quite real looking, aren't they?"

Polly jumped and let out a squeak, not unlike the mice Clover used to love cornering. "Abigail, I thought you were napping," she said.

"I guess neither of us could sleep."

"Oh, I was just looking for something for Pearl's birthday tomorrow." She handed the scarf to the cashier.

"I'm sure your sister will appreciate the effort." The scowl Polly gave was fleeting, but it was enough to prompt Abigail to ask, "Coffee? I could use a jolt. How about you?"

They found a vendor, bought two coffees, and settled on an out of the way bench. Even in the heat the hot liquid was refreshing.

"You know," Abigail said, "I had a sister, a bit high-maintenance, a bit above everyone else. Yet, she could never quite manage on her own. She always needed me for this or that, especially, when it came to my nephew. Yet, she never said thank you or appreciated the things

I did for her. The life I gave up for her. Never once." Abigail sniffed and stared into her coffee.

"I've lived in my sister's shadow my whole life," Polly said. "Pearl got the new clothes; I got the hand-me-downs. Pearl went to college; our parents couldn't afford to send me. I learned by helping Pearl with her homework. Even now I follow her around listening to her stupid pearls of wisdom. I'm just a doormat, gathering the crumbs she leaves behind."

Abigail nodded.

"You know, when she married I thought, here's my chance." Polly warmed to her story as the caffeine kicked in. "I even met a boy. I was happy. Then Pearl's husband cheated on her, and they divorced. She was done with men, she said. She begged me to move in with her. Just temporarily. Ivan, my fiancé, understood, but then Pearl told me she'd seen Ivan with another man. I was heartbroken."

"Years after I broke if off, I ran into an old co-worker who knew Ivan. That got me wondering, so I looked him up and found his daughter. She told me Ivan had loved me until the day he died." Polly stared into her coffee, her lips tight.

"Such a shame." Abigail drained her cup. "Some people never change. My sister didn't, so I moved on without her. These decisions are hard, but things do get better, my dear. You'll see."

The two split up after that, Polly to return to the hotel, and Abigail to finish her shopping. She was heading back when her phone buzzed. Everest.

She fumbled with the dratted cell-phone. She hated the things but Everest insisted she have it. She answered the call and cut right to the chase. "How's the house coming along? Have the workers finished yet? And what about Martha Ruth? Has she been nosing about?"

"Hello to you too, Aunt."

"Hello Everest. What about the house?"

"The workers haven't finished yet. There was significant damage you know. The money for which should be coming out of Martha Ruth's pocket."

"Throw money at lawyers, you mean. No thank you." The last thing Abigail wanted was high-falutin' lawyers crawling all over her property. "I've always paid my own way. Just make sure those workers are done when I get home. It's why I took this infernal trip, after all."

"Speaking of which, have you completed the itinerary?" He lowered his voice, and she wondered if he had company, and if so, of what persuasion.

"The ghost tour is tonight then back home tomorrow. Everything's on schedule."

"Good. I'll see you tomorrow then. Oh, I almost forgot. I found Martha Ruth in your backyard when I went to check on the house."

"What was she doing there?" Abigail demanded. "I hope you told her to leave."

"I don't know. She had a shovel. Said something about you letting her dig up daffodil bulbs."

"I never—"

"Don't worry," Everest cut in. "I sent her on her way with a stern warning to keep off your property.

"That witch killed my Clover."

"Now Aunt, you can't prove that. You don't even have a body. Besides the cat was old. He probably got lost."

"Don't you go taking her side," Abigail fumed.

"I'm not. You just worry about yourself, and I'll handle things here."

Abigail hung up and stuffed the phone in her bag. The blasted trip couldn't end soon enough for her.

It was with some reluctance as night fell, that Abigail dragged herself away from her hotel room to meet up with Polly, Pearl, and seven others from the bus for a haunted tour of the Holy City's historic district.

A few of the cane-wielders actually clung to each other as they tromped from one haunted place to another. At the Battery Carriage House Inn, one woman reported seeing a glowing orb while another said she saw a headless man. To which Pearl responded, "He who fears something gives it power over him."

"He who fears…" Polly's echo was just above a whisper.

By the time they reached the Owen T. Faunhall residence, half of their party remained downstairs with the tour guide while the rest explored the second story bedrooms where a woman in red purportedly roamed the halls looking for her lost husband. The wooden stairs creaked loudly at their ascent. At the top of the landing, the group split up to explore the antique furnishing and paintings.

Abigail trailed Polly and Pearl in and out of rooms. Ahead of them, came the occasional hushed whisper or nervous giggle. In a darkly paneled room, Polly discovered a rocking horse collection. In the corridor, Abigail paused to study a landscape watercolor by Charles Fraser. The house grew quiet until a floorboard creaked, followed by a scattering of tiny pop, pop, pops. Someone gasped. Abigail looked up. One minute Pearl hovered in front of her, the next she was tumbling down the steep staircase in a series of crashes that ended in silence. The sharp clack of heels on wood faded away, and a chorus of screams began.

Later, when they were all huddled outside on the sidewalk talking with the police, Abigail hesitantly told them she heard someone walking in high heels just before Pearl fell, only none of the women had been wearing heels. The tour guide was quick to affirm that there was indeed a woman ghost in residency at the Faunhall estate and that Abigail was not the first to hear her roaming the halls.

"All I know, officer," Abigail said for the tenth time, "is that five of us went up those stairs, Pearl, Polly, those two gray-haired ladies and myself and only four of us walked down. I don't remember who came down in what order. It was all very confusing. But I'll never forget the sound of Pearl crashing down those stairs." Here she dabbed at her eyes with a damp tissue.

When the police asked if Pearl had been wearing a necklace and then produced a broken strand of pearls, both Abigail and Polly nodded.

The tour guide looked disappointed when ghostly shenanigans were ruled out. The cause of death—an accident. A twist of fate that led to the necklace breaking, the pearls scattering on the landing, causing Pearl to slip and fall to her death.

Abigail arrived home the following day, exhausted, and half expecting an annoyed Clover to greet her at the door until she remembered—Clover was dead. She deposited her suitcase in the hallway and sighed. Still, it was good to be home. Back to her weeds and her books, which reminded her of the hole in her library ceiling. She hurried back to the converted spare bedroom and opened the door.

The tree that had been poking through her ceiling was gone. The plaster patched and painted. Her books teetered in odd piles here and there just as they had done before the crash. The repairs had bit heavily into her savings, but the results were worth it. Something in the window overlooking the backyard caught her attention. She hurried outside.

"Martha Ruth!"

Her neighbor jumped and dropped her shovel, her flimsy straw hat floated to the ground. "Abigail, I—I didn't expect you home until tomorrow."

"Of course, you didn't," Abigail snapped. "How else could I catch you snooping?"

Martha Ruth's brows furrowed. "You mean you deliberately had Everest tell me the wrong date of your return?"

Abigail smiled. "You're not the only one who can be sneaky. Now just what is it you think you're digging for on my property?"

"Oh, well." Martha Ruth retrieved her hat from the ground and squeezed it onto her head. "You have such nice peonies, I thought you wouldn't mind if I dug some up."

"I thought it was daffodils you were after. Isn't that what you told Everest? Besides, the peonies are over there." Abigail pointed to a corner bed against the house. "Or perhaps you've come to bury my dear Clover. Is that it?"

"I told you, I didn't kill your mangy cat. If he knew what was good for him, he up and left of his own accord."

"How dare you. Get off my property." Abigail flapped her arms.

"How dare I?" Martha Ruth picked up her shovel and held it sideways in both hands as if to shield herself. "I know what you're up to Abigail Grimley, and one day I'm going to prove it."

"I think you've been at the spiked lemonade again, is what I think." Abigail took a step closer.

Martha Ruth backed away, her shovel in front of her. "A woman died on your Charleston trip. It was in the papers this morning, ghostly encounter sends woman to her death. What is that? The third trip you've taken where someone mysteriously dies?"

Abigail looked at Martha Ruth sweating beneath her straw hat, her knuckles white where they clasped the shovel. "So you've taken it upon yourself to dig up my backyard looking for what? Bodies?" she asked.

"Well…" Martha Ruth's fingers loosened their grip. "Well, I suppose that does sound silly."

"Yes, it does." Abigail shielded her eyes from the sun and looked at the disturbed patch of earth then back at Martha Ruth. In a softer voice, she said, "Maybe it's my fault your imagination has run off with your mind. Our bickering has gotten out of hand. I'm sorry I accused you of killing Clover. It's just that the house is so lonely without him. It was easier to blame somebody than to think he'd run off."

Martha Ruth let the shovel fall to her side. "I guess I can understand that. And I guess I should have asked you before cutting down the trees. I'm sorry about the hole in your roof."

Abigail waved it off like it was nothing. "And I'm sorry I never invited you over more after your husband left. I should have been more… neighborly."

"You know, that's all I ever wanted—was for us to be friends." Martha Ruth smiled.

"Here," Abigail held out her hand. "Why don't you let me dig up some of those peonies for you? They came from my sister's garden, you know."

"Really? That would be wonderful." Martha Ruth handed Abigail the shovel. For a moment, they both held it, then Martha Ruth let go, and she fell into step beside Abigail.

They chatted away about the flowers, the weather, and the neighborhood until the peonies were dug up and carried over to Martha Ruth's yard. By the time they had them replanted they were talking like old friends.

"Those earrings really are beautiful," Abigail said. "Sapphires, aren't they?"

Martha Ruth's hand touched her ear. "Yes. I treated myself after the divorce. Cost more than that stupid boat Sam bought."

"Well, I really must get to my unpacking now." Abigail started back across the grass to her own yard.

"I'll bring over that tuna casserole recipe you asked for." Martha Ruth waved. "Better yet, I'll bring a dish over so you can try it first."

Abigail waved back, remembering how Clover had loved digging through Martha Ruth's dinner trash. She bet that tuna casserole recipe had a lot to do with it.

She entered the house after one last wave to her neighbor, grabbed her cell phone off the hall table, scrolled through her address book, and hit call when she found the right number. Next, she picked up her suitcase and carried it into the bedroom. Setting it on the bed, she unzipped it and flipped the top over.

"Hello Everest," she said, and then waited while the taped message finished playing. How that man ran a business when he never answered his phone was beyond her. "Everest, it's your Aunt Abigail. Looks like I'm not quite ready for retirement yet. I have one more job to do. I need you to book me a tour for two, maybe Savannah this time." Yes, Martha Ruth would love Savannah. "Bring me the details tomorrow when you drop off my payment for this last job. See you then."

She tossed her phone on the bed and pulled out the baggie from the bottom of her suitcase. The polished pearls were heavy in her hand, nothing like the fake strand she'd bought at the Charleston market. She couldn't help but smile a little as she carried them to the library. She went to the corner bookshelf and pulled down Jane Austen's Pride and Prejudice. Long ago, she'd ripped the cover off the book and pasted it onto a wooden box. She lifted the lid and placed the pearls inside next to her sister's engagement ring, and a few other trinkets she'd picked up along the way.

Through the window, she watched Martha Rose shooing the birds out of her garden.

"There's no fool like an old fool," Abigail whispered.

She patted the pearls one last time, then closed the box and tucked it back onto the bookshelf.

Revenge — among the oldest of human motivations — drives the plot of our next story. Its Caribbean setting conjures images of lazy days and steamy nights at the hacienda. But things are never what they seem to be, nor people.

Mr. Palumbo is a writer and licensed psychotherapist in private practice, specializing in creative issues. His newest crime novel, PHANTOM LIMB, is on sale now from Poisoned Pen Press. The book is the fourth in the series featuring psychologist and trauma expert Daniel Rinaldi.

Blood Lines

by Dennis Palumbo

1.

The old man blinked awake, roused from his nap by the drone of a bush plane overhead. He glanced up, just catching its locust's-wing shadow as it skimmed the edge of the jungle, banking toward the south. More tourists, he thought sourly, on their way to the ruins at Palenque or Bonampak.

He managed to sit up straighter in the cane chair and with out-stretched fingers grasped the slippery railing, pulling himself closer. He gasped once, from the effort, and peered expectantly down at the lake.

There she was, waist deep in the water, waving up at the disappearing plane. Her long brown hair fanned her shoulders in wet ringlets.

She turned suddenly, wholly naked, and he saw the swell of her breasts as she bent to slip below the surface. She swam with graceful, even strokes, moving through the haze that hung over the water, until she vanished amid the drooping foliage at the far edge of the shore.

The old man sighed gratefully, chin resting on the rail. A sudden rain had come up, misty and warm, and behind it a gentle gust that blew through the open spaces of the verandah. Across the lake, through the haze, the breadnut trees shimmered like ghosts.

The estate, originally built by a Belgian merchant at the turn of the century, lay deep in the jungle's marrow, the shallow lake long since reclaimed by riotous vegetation. Even now, there was just one dirt access road, the nearest village a hard half-day's journey away. Since coming here nearly ten years ago, the man had done nothing to disturb the somber dignity of the great house, the heavy stillness of the foliage embracing it.

It was perfect, his life here. For him, and for her…

Then he remembered, and his face grew pale as chalk. The violation she'd endured, the horrible pain—

And yet, ironically, it was because of this outrage, this sin, that the girl was finally back in his life, here at his side, after the long years of estrangement.

Here, where he'd gone into hiding after being hounded by the Feds; here, in seclusion, where his legendary status as the Boss of Bosses had only grown among the crime families on the East Coast; here, where he'd at last found the isolation in which he could prepare his soul for its Final Destination.

But not before he'd performed one last task. Not before he'd extended his hand one last time into the affairs of men. Not before one last, and most important, judgment had been rendered…

"Carlos!" The old don's voice rattled in his throat. He felt numb, half-asleep; embalmed by age and illness. He pushed up from the chair with his elbows, bony points in the loose-fitting white suit. Everything ached, pinched, conspired.

"Carlos!" he called again, squinting down the length of the veran-dah. "Where the hell are you?"

The soft padding of sandaled feet, an urgent whisper of motion, made him turn his head. Carlos stood just beyond him on the tiled floor, hands in the pockets of his crisp valet's uniform, head tilted quizzically. He smiled.

"Good afternoon, sir," he said.

The old don let out a long breath. "Where have you been?"

"The radio room. We've heard from San Cristobal."

"And…?"

"Everything's arranged." Carlos took a sheaf of faxes from his pocket, handed them over one at a time.

The old man studied them carefully, for a full five minutes. He could almost feel the young Indian's impatience. Good, he thought. These new ones were impudent, impulsive. They knew too much of the outside world, and precious little of the traditions of their own.

He glanced up at Carlos. A pity, really. He had the proper features, the mahogany-dark skin tones, but the eyes were wrong. The old man could read the ambition in them, the greed. It seemed inconceivable that Carlos, like the other Lacandon Indians in Chiapas, was a direct descendant of the Mayans.

"Well…?" Carlos failed to keep the irritation out of his voice. Behind him, on the other side of the lake, a chicle tree shook as a howler monkey scrambled atop it, shrieking up at the continuing rain.

"I'm satisfied," the old man said at last, handing the faxes back to him. He swiveled in his chair, gazing past Carlos toward the lake below. "That's all."

Carlos stayed where he was, slowly folding the sheaf of papers and slipping them back in his pocket. He turned at the railing, looked with the old man into the mists of shore-line.

"I said you could leave now, Carlos."

Carlos nodded, but didn't stir. "I've seen her before, sir…"

The old man didn't take his eyes from the lake, the rain pock-marking the glistening surface. Any moment now she would come gliding through the water, from the other side of the lake.

She liked the rain, this golden girl, this pride of his seed…

His daughter liked the rain.

"I even talked to her once," Carlos was saying, matter-of-factly. "She was coming out the water, and I called to her."

The old don leaned back, long thin fingers clutching the chair-arms. He looked up at Carlos as though for the first time.

"If you speak to her again," he said evenly, "I will have you killed. Slowly."

For a few moments, there was only the sound of the rain in the trees, spraying the clapboards of the house, dripping from the gutters to the ancient tiles.

Then there was a hurried slap of footsteps on the wet floor, as Carlos sped down the verandah and vanished into the house.

The old don sat forward, hands folded on his lap. He scanned the mists below. Waiting.

And thought about the plans he'd made, the lengths to which he had gone. The privilege of wealth, and obsession.

He allowed himself a grave smile. It would all be over soon. For himself and the girl. The gulf between them would close, and things would be as they should.

They would be father and daughter once more.

The old man let his head drop, his shoulders hunched against a sudden chill behind the rain. He told himself he could afford to close his eyes, to rest for a few minutes. Just a few minutes, before her return to his sight.

While in the trees above, unnoticed by the old man, the howler monkey flitted from branch to branch, looking for something, anything, on which to feed.

2.

Father Thomas Hobart looked down at his hands gripping the hoe, its wooden handle as coarse as shaved stone, and as hard. But he held it fiercely, digging its gray metal scoop into the earth.

Scraping the dirt. Doing the day's work.

All around were the sounds of other tools at work, the labored breathing of the men using them. There were only eight, not counting himself, but after all this time Hobart could only put a few names and faces together.

Not that it mattered, he reminded himself. They were all the same.

All the same. Broken men, failed vocations. Doing the penance of the fields. Working in the afternoon sun, sweating into their ludicrous sandals or sneakers, tending the gardens like medieval monks. Striving for their grace, he thought murkily, or at least a semblance of their ruthless piety.

He looked up at last, to see Vincent leaning on his hoe, wiping his nose with a handkerchief. Vincent was the closest thing to a friend Hobart had in the place. He gave Hobart a nod.

Hobart nodded back, straightening. He held the hoe with two hands overhead, like a barbell, and stretched. The sweat, mixed with grime, came down his forearms. The pale whiteness that had once circled his wrist, from his watch-band, was now as tanned as the rest of his arm.

The watch had been a gift from a parishioner, many years before. He remembered giving it to the Abbot when he first came here. He smiled grimly. He'd always suspected the son-of-a-bitch sold it to help buy the new wine press.

Hobart stood over a row of tomatoes, allowing himself another moment's rest. Above, the sun was pulling new colors out of the

Mediterranean sky. It was just spring, but a hot one, and already he'd caught the scent of early blossoms.

And it was then, just then, that Father Hobart realized he had no idea what day it was.

He shook his head, tried to clear his thoughts. There were still many furrows to be cut, new seeds to be planted.

Bending to work again, he felt dizzy. The heat, probably. Or lack of sleep. His head throbbed, and instinctively—an instinct reborn a thousand times—he felt near the top of his skull with anxious fingers, felt for the still-tender surgical scar, where the bullet had gone in…

It was later, Hobart had worked his way over to the stone wall that ran along the east face. Ivy sprouted, mixed with spurts of hastily-applied cement. Beyond, in the high Apennine valley, the trees were a thick tangle of greens and browns, as unkempt as a drunk's beard, and about as spiritual.

Hobart leaned against the wall, yawning. Vincent whistled over at him suddenly, making him glance up. Vincent tossed his hoe into the dirt, looked about at the others with comic-opera scorn, and gave Hobart the universal sign for jerking off.

Hobart smiled. Speaking during daylight hours was forbidden, but Vincent always managed to get his feelings across. The little man looked up at the sun, shook his head, then strode purposefully across the field toward the main house. His broken sandal strap, unmended for days, flapped softly in the dirt.

Hobart didn't follow. He simply stood where he was at the wall, hoe held upright against his shoulder, like a guard on duty.

One by one, the other men made their way back to the house. But Hobart stayed where he was, almost motionless, concentrating on the rivulets of sweat now drying on his cheeks.

The idea, he told himself, was not to go crazy. To find something to focus on, and stay focused. It was the only way to endure the ceaseless work, the silent monotony. It was the only path that led to forgetting.

He'd only been here for a number of months, but already he felt part of the place, caught up in its numbing sameness. A stone among a field of stones.

The sun was going down. There was a slight wind now, and he could feel its welcome touch on his face and arms. He wanted suddenly to stand out there forever, until all the shadows came.

But the dinner bell was ringing. There, at the door of the dining hall, stood the Abbot, his robes rustling in the breeze.

Father Hobart pushed away from the wall reluctantly, carrying his hoe toward the main house. As he did every evening, at this exact time, he'd place it against the shed wall with the other tools. As he did every evening, he'd come in the side entrance to the house and shower in the common facilities.

It was the sameness—the inescapable sameness—that was supposed to do it, rub your prickly demons into smooth dead stones. Stones in a field of stones.

He had to trust in that, he knew. It was the only sure path to forgetting. And perhaps, one day, forgiveness.

He left the hoe standing with its brothers on the shed wall, and headed over to the house.

3.

Carlos switched off the radio, then leaned back in his chair, taking a last grateful drag on his cigarette.

That's it, he thought. The final transmission.

He rose, stretched, rubbed his neck. He glanced around the small, cramped radio room and sighed. At least it was cooler after midnight, when he stole down with a bottle of tequila and listened to rock music from the pirate station up north.

On his way back to the house, along the unlit mud path, he decided to wait until morning to give his last report. The old man had gone to sleep soon after dinner, and it didn't seem wise to disturb him.

Carlos lit another cigarette, stood smoking it just beyond the east porch. From this vantage point, he could make out the two guards trudging along the perimeter. When one of them looked in his direction, Carlos waved. The guard moved on.

Carlos shook his head. Such a place. He was glad the old man's ill health forced him to spend so much time in his bed. Ever since the other day on the verandah, their contact had been reduced to curt exchanges of information, orders given and received.

Not that it had been exactly warm and familiar before that. Five years of near-slavish service, five years of the crazy old gringo's insults and threats. Five long years, and now…

He glanced up at the moon, floating like a pearl in oil over the mists of the rain forest. The clouds were heavy and somber, and even the sacred monkeys hid from his eyes and kept their voices still.

Five long years.

It was better not to think about it too much, he told himself. Still—

He let the cigarette drop to the earth, and stepped on it.

He went quietly through the main corridor of the dark house, guiding himself as much by memory as by the pale glow of the lamps in their niches. The faces of martyred saints looked down from their portraits on the high walls, and his careful footsteps on the polished floors sounded to him like the rhythmic throbbing of a sleeping heart.

He paused in a doorway. Though he knew himself to be a modern man, he also felt that, during the shank of the night when even the macaws outside the window were silent, the house revealed itself to be a living thing, its silence merely the mute echo of its spirit at rest.

Idiot, he thought bitterly. Still the village Indian boy, frightened by the white man's patriarchal wealth.

Beyond, in the dimness, stood the massive dining table, the four-hundred-year-old centerpiece of the room. Its wide mahogany grain meandered across its surface like dry riverbeds, shining dully in the moonlight. Carlos frowned uneasily. It was here that they ate dinner every night, the old man and that spooky daughter of his, sitting at either end of the long table and saying practically nothing.

So they're both crazy, he thought, suddenly anxious to get on with his business. By the time he'd reached the end of the hall, and headed down the steps toward the cellar, he was even chuckling dryly to himself, so confident he was that he'd left the last of his foolish indios fears behind.

Besides, he'd had an idea.

4.

It had been so easy...

The girl, standing at the leaded-glass window, watched the mist outside begin to rise. A pale light filtered the trees. The rain had finally ebbed.

Still, the humidity made the thick robe she'd worn from the lake cling like a shroud. She turned away from the window and shrugged it off.

Roberta crossed the bedroom—she thought of it now as her room—and pulled a simple print dress from the walk-in closet.

So easy...

She tossed her thick brown hair, still wet from her regular morning's swim. Pushing it back from her face, she headed briskly for the door, without a glance at the floor-length mirror.

As always, she walked more slowly once in the common halls, slowly and deliberately, as if encircled by heavy chains that only she could see.

Standing at the door to the library, she caught sight of Carlos. Spying on her, as usual. He quickly looked away, made a show of wiping a speck of dust from a brass wall lamp.

That's Carlos, she thought. Always making a show. Like last night, at dinner, whisking her emptied wine glass onto his tray, wearing those ridiculous white gloves the old man insisted on when Carlos served dinner. How he must despise the old man… how he must despise us…

Yet she couldn't help but notice his good looks, the erotic promise in his banked rage. Roberta smiled. Maybe…

But such thoughts would have to wait. For now.

She went into the library, closing the huge double doors behind her. Hundreds of leather-bound books loomed over her like dark angels from high, shadowed shelves. Roberta went to her usual table by the bay window. She sat in the overstuffed chair, sunlight splintered into dusty streams by the thick blinds.

Finally, she pulled an old book down from a shelf, and began idly flipping the pages.

So easy…

Of course, she'd hated the old man for as long as she could remember. Despite the family's wealth, the mansion in upstate New York, the trips to Europe when she was young, the gifts.

But how he'd mistreated her mother. Beat her, and humiliated her in front of his cronies, the other family bosses. Those large and dangerous men who always seemed to be in their house. And he'd cheated on her, openly, with "actresses" and "models."

Roberta had felt his hand, the sting of his belt, all her young life. Even at the party for her First Holy Communion, when he'd caught her eavesdropping on a whispered conversation with that Congressman. She hadn't understood a word, not one word, but he'd slapped her anyway, repeatedly, her tears staining her brand new white Communion dress…

He was a tyrant at home, as well as a monster in life. Even in private school in Switzerland, she'd read in the papers about the attempts by the U.S. Attorney to bring him to trial. One time they thought they had a case, the court date was set—but the witness soon "disappeared."

How she'd hated growing up in that house. Hated seeing her mother wither before her time. And she'd been such a beauty when she'd married the old man; Roberta had seen the pictures.

The only fatherly presence in her life, and the only solace for her mother, had been the parish priest. He knew how they suffered, and hovered about as much as possible—drinking tea in the afternoons with her mother, taking them both to the parish Carnival, and the Christmas pageant. He was always so attentive, so kind…

A sound behind her made her start. The maid, Maria, had just come in to clean. Roberta, willing herself not to turn, could just see her out of the corner of her eye.

Maria, head bent, muttered a quick apology and exited. Roberta guessed the maid's thoughts. Poor sad girl. Sits all day with the dead books, turning pages…

Just as Roberta had pitied her own mother, who'd grown old and ill in the don's house. More and more, Roberta stayed away, finally choosing to live and go to college in Paris.

Until that day the overseas call came, and she flew back to sit at her mother's bedside, as she lay dying. The old man had fled the country years before, hours ahead of a Grand Jury indictment. It was just the two of them now.

"Should I send for Father Tom?" Roberta had asked, clasping her mother's hand.

But the dying woman had shaken her head. No, there wasn't time. Besides, there was something she needed to tell Roberta. Something she must know…

How hard it had been, watching her mother die. But harder still hearing her last words. Because, in those final moments, Roberta's world turned upside-down.

Thomas… Father Hobart… he was her real father. Her mother and Hobart had had an affair, many years before. He was a new priest, torn by desires he couldn't control; she a dangerous man's lonely young wife.

Then, when her mother had become pregnant, they knew they had to end. Never suspecting, the old don thought the baby was his. A miracle from God, a child in his advancing years…

Even now, six months after laying her mother to rest, Roberta could feel the pain that had engulfed her. All those years, the priest as a kind of uncle, a refuge… nothing but a lie.

How could he have denied her like that? Let her grow up believing she was the daughter of that man, that monster…?

After the funeral, she'd confronted Hobart, lashed out at him. No matter how he begged, how much he castigated himself for his weakness, she wouldn't forgive him. He was weeping piteously as she slammed the door on her way out.

It wasn't until she'd returned to school in France the following week that she learned of his failed suicide attempt. The bullet he'd tried to put in his brain. The gun in a trembling hand.

Of course, the Diocese had no choice but to remove him from the parish. On the advice of his superiors, he was sent on retreat to a monastery overseas.

Leaving Roberta with two fathers, she thought bitterly, and yet with none.

It was then that something darkened within her, that her soul turned. Her pain cauterized into rage, and a desire for revenge. When she'd catch sight of herself in the mirror, it was only her eyes she'd see, and how they'd hardened into marble chips.

Soon, she found herself unable to look into mirrors.

As a plan began to grow, like a cancer, in her mind…

At the end of the semester, she took a plane back to the States. There was a man she had to see.

His name was Alphonse Tonelli, but in certain circles he was known as "the Hammer." The old don's most trusted lieutenant, fanatic in his loyalty, familiar to her since she was a little girl. Standing with the other large and dangerous men who attended the old man, yet standing apart. Huge and silent, with hooded eyes, he'd occupy a quiet corner of the kitchen or the dining room, slowly sipping a beer. Listening. Watching.

Roberta was terrified of him, especially when he smiled at her.

"Hey, little girl," he'd say in that flat, gravelly voice, before bowing to the old man and heading out the side door. Often, the next day, the news would arrive that another enemy of her father's had been found dead, brutally bludgeoned with a claw hammer.

It was strange to see him now, years later; older, coarser somehow. As though time had thickened him, weathered him like any other monument from the past. The hooded eyes, blinking in the afternoon sun, regarded her warily.

Roberta sat opposite him on the screened-in porch of his old tract house in New Jersey. Pungent smells of garlic and onion wafted in from the kitchen.

She argued her case before him, tearfully, beseeching him. She wanted to reconcile with her father, she explained. While there was still time. The Prodigal Daughter, returning.

"You're the only one who knows where he is," she went on. "You've got to tell me… please… so I can go to him…"

Tonelli cared nothing for the girl, of course. His loyalty—his devotion—was to the old man. Years of faithful service, bathed in blood. Yet those glory days were all gone now. Things had changed so much. There was no place anymore for the likes of him, for the Hammer…

He shifted uneasily in his chair. No, he cared nothing for her… But think of the old man's joy, his happiness at the girl's return. How his last days might be brightened. Tonelli could not deny him this.

He told her where the old man was.

———————

Then she was standing, dusted by the journey, faded like a drying leaf, at the old man's door. His eyes shone. Mother of God, could it be? The prodigal, returned…

But she seemed crushed, bruised. So young and beautiful, yet so sad. When she spoke, her words came out slowly, haltingly… like a code he couldn't break.

The old man sat across from her in the evenings at the dining table, the fetid jungle air thick as a blanket about the great house. Why was she so guarded, afraid?

Then one night, not so long after her arrival, she told him about Hobart, the priest. Not that he'd had an affair with her mother, nor that he'd been her actual biological father.

No, she told the old man that the priest had done something else, something far, far worse…

And the old man's eyes had turned to marble chips, points hard and deep in his wrinkled face.

Ironic, she'd thought, recognizing what she saw there.

Not his flesh, not his blood, and yet how like him I am.

5.

On another night, not too long after, alone in his room on the other side of the world, Thomas Hobart woke up in a cold sweat. He found himself clutching his stomach, the pain doubling him into a fetal crouch. He tried to form words, to call out. He was choking on his own bile.

Hobart managed to roll off the bed and start crawling toward the door. But with every second his strength was fading, and with it his will. What was happening?

His head was spinning. Then it came to him, with a supernal clarity. The old man… he knows… he knows…

The door was opening, a hushed sigh in the blackness. There, in a flicker of moonlight, a figure coming toward him…

Hobart, gasping, brought his eyes up, squinted against the darkness.

A face, looming over him. So familiar, so—

Hobart collapsed to the floor. Struggling to stay conscious, he caught a glimpse of something in the half-light, an image that seemed to explode in his brain—

A sandal with a broken strap.

Then he was on his back, the room swirling around him, shapes moving in and out of focus. Then there was the upraised hand, the gleam of a knife-blade. He couldn't move, couldn't—

It became unspeakable.

6.

The old don was resting now, in his bed, Roberta sitting at his side. It was almost time for his pills, she thought, taking the vial from the side-table drawer and pouring a glass of water from the pitcher. In the past week, she'd begun assuming more and more of the nursing duties Carlos usually performed.

She put her cool hand on the old man's forehead. The skin was hot, clammy. He'd been looking worse these last few days, weaker, spending most of his time in bed.

How strange, she thought as she wiped the spittle from his chin as he half-dozed. Just like I did with Mother, I'm sitting at his death-bed, waiting…

He stirred, peered up at her with watery eyes. His thin lips formed an ugly, satisfied smile. He seemed… peaceful. God, how she hated him.

Maria, the maid, stood at the end of the bed, making a sign of the cross. Then she went back to straightening up the room. Roberta shook her head. Christ.

Suddenly, Carlos was standing behind her, having slipped so silently up to the bed that she hadn't even heard him.

"Sir," he said to the old man, as if she weren't even there.

"Carlos… I didn't call for you," the old man said, voice cracking. "I have my daughter now… my own blood, not some worthless—" His body jerked, as he coughed violently.

Carlos leaned forward, his shoulder just touching Roberta's. He stared into the old don's face.

"I have news," he said. "It is done."

The old man blinked, twice, then strained to push himself up on his elbows. He turned to Roberta.

"Did you hear that, Roberta?" His arms trembled with the effort of supporting him. "It is as I promised. Your tormentor is dead. Your honor is returned."

"Then I am yours again," she said, resting her forehead against his shoulder. Her arms went around his skeletal frame, easing him back down on the sheets. "I am yours."

"It is the blood," the old man said. "And, blood to blood, all that I have will be yours. I will inform the other families, I will make it known that—" He broke into a hacking cough again.

Instinctively, Roberta took a pill from the vial. "Carlos!" she snapped. "Help me."

Carlos bent and helped calm the old man, as Roberta placed a pill on his tongue and offered the water glass. The old man gulped it, gasping. He lay back on the bed.

Suddenly, he cried out, hands twisting the sheets.

Roberta grasped his arm. "What is it?"

The old man's eyes bore into hers. "You—you…" His words were choked, pain-wracked.

She looked up at the impassive, silent Carlos, then back at the old man.

He mouthed more words. No sound came out. She felt the life leave his body, felt it slip away under her clutching fingers.

The old man was dead.

Maria, from across the room, screamed. As she came slowly toward the bed, Carlos whispered urgently to her in Spanish. She stared, wide-eyed, then bolted out of the room.

But Roberta hardly noticed. She leaned down to hear the old man's heart, listen for any tell-tale rattle of breath. It's over. He's dead. Face hidden from Carlos, she permitted herself a brief smile.

Then, contorting her face into grief, she looked up at Carlos. To her shock, the young man was smiling. He also held a revolver, leveled at her.

She sat up in her chair, found her voice. "What the hell are you doing?"

"The old man was poisoned," he said calmly. "Killed by his own daughter, who's always hated him. So that all that he had would be hers."

"But I didn't—"

"I know, you stupid bitch." His smile faded. "I did. With the arsenic in that pill you just gave him. I switched them earlier, and made sure Maria was here at his regular pill-time. As a witness. Or should I say, another witness, in addition to myself."

All she could do was stare at him.

"Don't tell me you're sorry he's dead," Carlos went on. "That you haven't been waiting like a vulture for this day to come? You think I didn't see you for what you are? Don't insult me!"

He looked past her at the old man, lying motionless on the bed. "Did you think I would accept nothing after my years of servitude to that… that thing?"

Carlos turned back to her, fingers tightening on the gun. "Since you arrived, I saw his hopes rise… that you would tend to him in his last days. I saw that I should have nothing…"

Finally, Roberta spoke, her own voice oddly calm. "Will you call the local police now? Is that it?"

"You mean, what passes for the law in this place?" He gave a hollow chuckle. "No, I had a better idea. A few days ago I contacted some people in the States…" He nodded toward the old man. "His people. Told them my suspicions about you. I have been promised a great reward."

"His people…?"

Carlos nodded again, enjoying this. "One of them flew down here just yesterday. I've already told Maria to send someone to the village to bring him." He leaned back against a large bureau, watching her carefully. "We'll just wait here, together. I believe it's someone you know."

Later, when Tonelli's heavy tread in the doorway made her turn, she was struck not so much by his size, and the labored movements of his body as he lurched toward her, but by those hooded eyes. How they were even more cold, more dead, than she'd remembered.

"Hey, little girl," said the Hammer.

And in the trees above the great house, that same howler monkey flitted from branch to branch, looking for something, anything, on which to feed.

We leave the sunny Caribbean and return to the Carolina coast, just in time for Christmas. With most of her community fled to warmer places, one resident does her best to keep an eye on things.

The burglary of a beach house near her own gave Ms Taylor the prompt for this story. In addition to short stories, she has two novels out from Five Star – Cengage, "What are Friends For?" and Jewelry from a Grave".

'Tis the Season

by Caroline Taylor

I'm taking my morning constitutional the day Sam nearly knocks me into a ditch. He comes flying around the corner, siren blaring and lights flashing, headed into the cul-de-sac at the end of the next block. I dust myself off a bit and follow him.

He's parked in front of that new house that the Ropers—Bill and Sandra—bought last summer. They're standing there, looking a little peaked, if you ask me. But you wouldn't be feeling too terrific if you'd just been robbed, either. Especially this time of year.

Took everything they had—and most of it fairly new. Not just your garden-variety burglars, it seems. In addition to the TV and microwave and DVD player and the sorts of things you expect thieves to take, they also grabbed sheets, towels, pots and pans, dishes and flatware, spices from the kitchen cabinet, everything. Even the stuff Bill and Sandra had in their bathroom medicine cabinet. Oh. And did I mention their Christmas tree?

I remember Sandra showing it to me. A darling little tabletop confection all decked out in ornaments and tiny little lights that you could just plug in and—voilà! Christmas. They'd bought it up the road at the Country Store, along with a live wreath (the tree was ersatz, but I understand, this being only their beach house). For some reason, the thieves didn't take the wreath.

Once Sam finishes talking, I offer them my spare bedroom.

"Oh, that's real kind of you," says Sandra with a distracted air. "But we'll probably just head on back to Baltimore."

"I suppose the insurance will cover it," says Bill, trying to shrug off the shock. "Looks like we're not going to be spending Christmas at the beach."

I could swear I hear her mutter "or any other day," as she paws through her handbag, looking for a cigarette.

The Ropers are at the top of that list. Instead of investing in a small trashcan with a lid, they keep putting their garbage in a plastic bag. By the time the garbage truck gets there on trash pickup day, the bag's been torn open by some critters—raccoons or possums—and food wrappers, empty cans, and other trash are scattered all over the street. I've warned them about it. Twice. Which is why I find myself hoping Sandra Roper will, indeed, decide she's had enough and won't be wasting her time restocking their beach house. It's not that I don't like the Ropers; but, really, I'm getting awfully tired of finding soggy paper towels and other icky stuff lodged in the bushes near my home.

The Ropers spend a while with Sam, going over the place, with them trying to remember exactly what was taken and Sam dutifully scribbling away in his little notebook. Feeling sort of useless, I take a look around the front yard. I'm no detective or anything, but they say I have pretty sharp eyes for a woman my age. Of course, I don't find a thing, and neither does Sam.

In a quiet little beach town like Seabreeze Shores, a big crime like this tends to make the off-season a bit more interesting. So when Sam stops by for his regular cup next morning, naturally I ask him what he knows.

"Strangest thing I ever saw," he remarks, leaning his chair back on two legs and making me wonder when he's going to fall flat on his back and crack his skull open. To look at Sam, you'd think he was army, given the gung-ho physique and buzz cut, but he's always been a cop. His blue eyes are the skeptical kind, making you think he doesn't believe a thing you're saying. Of course, that doesn't apply to me. "This was not your ordinary burglar," he adds.

"Because of what they took?"

"Yeah." He scratches his head. "Why would anybody steal cinnamon and garlic salt?"

I shrug. "When do you suppose they did it?"

"Don't know for certain. The Ropers say they were down on Labor Day weekend and then on Columbus Day and haven't been back till yesterday when they bought the tree and all."

"Any clues?"

"Nope." He tips the chair forward and shoves his empty mug across the table so I can see he needs a refill. (I do make a mean cuppa, if I say so myself.)

"'Course, you living here on the corner like you do, maybe you saw something?"

"Like what?"

"I don't know. Strange cars, maybe?"

"SUVs it'd have to be. Or a truck with one of those camper things to cover the bed. They took a lot of stuff."

"Unless they made several trips."

"Now that I'd have noticed," I assure him. "Of course, I don't spend a whole lot of time at the window, watching cars go by." Or, anyway, I try not to spend too much time at it, nor do I want Sam thinking I'm nosy.

"Well, won't hurt keeping your eyes peeled."

I give him a mock salute. "Seeing as how the horse has left the barn."

As soon as Sam's gone, I take a look around the neighborhood. During the week, the place is as quiet as a Carmelite convent, but some folks come down on weekends, all the way through December, until the weather turns really cold and those Nor'Easters pay us a call. A few hardy souls come here on weekends all year round. They like the clean sharp air and the desolate beaches of winter with the shorebirds scavenging for crabs and seagulls screaming overhead.

Then there's me and a few other retired folks who live here permanent. We all know each other, probably better than we'd really like to. We play the occasional round of social bridge, and of course I see them whenever I'm running errands or at church on Sundays. Oh, and the kid across the street. He's a lifeguard during the summer. Rents the place year round, though. He has a part-time job doing trash collection during the off season, but I doubt it pays enough to put food on the table. I do what I can to make sure he doesn't starve.

I'm walking back from St. Jerome's on Sunday when I find a pill bottle in the Gerards' front yard. They built the yellow house across the street from me, next door to the kid. The bottle is one of those white things with the child-safety cap, lying right there on the gravel parking strip in front of their house. The label is torn, and all I can read is

PER

DAILY

N TABS

The Gerards aren't at home, or I'd just march up to their door and return it. It probably fell out of a grocery bag. Only the "PER" bothers me, as in Roper, not Gerard? What if it somehow fell out of the Gerard's Cadillac Escalade when they were unloading the loot they ripped off from the Ropers? I'd take a peek inside the house to see if I can spy any signs of stolen goods, but the blinds are shut tight.

I'm also getting ahead of myself, but I can't help it. I take the bottle home and put it in the middle of my kitchen table so Sam will see it in case I forget to tell him about it between now and tomorrow. I can't help wondering what's in it, though, so I take a peek. It's halfway full of a white powder, which is strange. Doesn't the word "TABS" mean tablets?

Naturally, I do a lot of thinking about things as I tend to my chores and fix supper. Did the Gerards rob the Ropers? What would their motive be? Then I remember how they spent the entire spring and most of the summer building that house from scratch, board by board, doing most of the work themselves. After it was finished, they settled in with hardly any furniture. I know because I watched it being delivered. A sofa and chair, two twin beds, a table and four chairs. That was it.

It's almost like they ran out of money. Neither of them is a bit friendly, either. Made it quite clear they didn't want my company, even though he wolfed down those brownies I took over there last month as a welcome.

"Sam," I say as I pour out his second refill the next day, "you'd better look around inside the Gerards' place."

He's tossing the pill bottle from one hand to the other. "Just because you found this in their yard and just because you think "PER" means Roper doesn't mean your neighbors across the street are our burglars."

I like the "our" part. It's as though Sam considers me a kind of deputy. Which I like to think I am, considering he needs all the help he can get. "But what if they are? You want to solve the crime or just cruise around acting big and important?"

"Aw, Ellie, gimme a break. I'd have to get a search warrant. I'd have to have what they call "probable cause," which means—

"I know what it means."

"Well it'd take more than this here bottle to convince a judge your neighbors might be thieves."

"Suit yourself," I sniff. Men can be so contrary sometimes. For a moment, I consider going over there myself. I bet they've stashed a key somewhere in case they lock themselves out. But, no, I am not a snoop. Even though I provide Sam with his morning cup and an occasional home-cooked meal now and then, he'd probably throw me in jail if he caught me breaking and entering.

My problem's solved when the Gerards unexpectedly show up on the weekend.

"Miz Gerard," I call from the street. "Could I possibly borrow a cup of sugar? Wouldn't you know I'm plumb out and right in the middle of a peach pie."

"Come on in," she replies, gesturing toward the kitchen. Promising her at last half of the pie, I look quickly around the room, hoping I'll spot clues like the Ropers' Christmas tree or an extra television or something.

I spy the one comfortable chair and settle in for a friendly chat, but Mrs. G. seems to miss the signals. She walks straight to a canister on the counter and pours some sugar into my measuring cup, leveling it with a knife. As she hands me the cup, I put my hand to my forehead.

"Oh, does my head ever hurt! You ever get migraines? And wouldn't you know, I'm out of Motrin."

Mrs. G. gives me a cool look and an even frostier reply. "I don't keep aspirin in the house."

"Oh, that's all right," I reply, backing toward the door. "I'll just lie down for a while—that is, after I've got the pie in the oven."

My hearing must be getting worse because I back right into Mr. Gerard, coming through the front door as I'm going out. I nearly spill sugar all over his nice new carpet. He doesn't look happy to see me, so I get out of his way.

Sam tends to think I'm overly imaginative, so I decide I'm not going to tell him what I thought I overheard: Mr. G saying to his wife, "I thought I said we don't want company." This is followed by her saying, "She's gone, isn't she?" But, then again, my hearing probably isn't as good as it once was.

A few days go by, and we're strolling down the boardwalk under a large yellow moon when I finally tell Sam about my visit with the Gerards. He's more distressed that I've given them half the peach pie than anything else, even though I did save him the lion's share.

"That'll teach you to snoop around where you don't belong," he mutters.

"Well, I know you don't believe in woman's intuition, but there's something odd about that pill bottle lying there in the driveway and she doesn't even keep aspirin in the house. And, furthermore, the Gerards are distinctly antisocial."

Sam laughs. "Fortunately, not a crime."

"It's not natural."

"Lots of people come down here to get away from company," he reminds me. "The Gerards and a million other owners in Seabreeze Shores want to enjoy the peace and quiet, and if they don't want to socialize, that's their business."

Sam would not make a very good detective. Oh, he's all right as the town's only year-round policeman, but his curiosity quotient is sorely deficient.

"Why do you persist in suspecting them, anyway?" he asks, plopping down onto a bench near the boardwalk railing.

"Because they just put all this money into building their dream beach house—not to mention a whole lot of time and effort—and I bet they finished it without a cent left to furnish it. I bet they sat there in their beautiful empty house and watched carefully to see who leaves after Labor Day or after Columbus Day and who doesn't return the following weekend, and then, sometime during the middle of the week, they simply transferred everything from the Roper's house to theirs."

"Including the Christmas tree?" he asks, one eyebrow raised. And then he snorts. "They're not the type."

Oh, right. People, according to Sam, fall into three basic types. Owners like the Gerards are good types because they take care of their houses—at least most of them do—and they obey traffic signals and don't speed and generally cause no trouble. Renters like the kid next door are not so good. They have parties all night long and trash the places they're renting and run stop signs and generally act crazy and irresponsible—fortunately for only three months during the summer. Common folk are the ones that spell real trouble—or as real as it gets in Seabreeze Shores. They're the ones who live in the trailer parks and campgrounds inland from the ocean where the rent is cheap and life is mean and jobs are scarce, especially in the off season. Sam spends a lot of time and gasoline responding to accidental shootings or car wrecks or calls for help from poor trapped women who get beat up by their drunken husbands whenever payday rolls around and they've been celebrating with a few too many. Common folk, in other words, are the type.

To give him credit, though, Sam's not sure where the kid fits in. He's actually over thirty, and I think his name is Mike or Mark or something beginning with an M. The house he rents is really rundown, and his dogs—when he had them, that is—ran loose in the yard, barking their heads off all the livelong day. Let's call him Mike. He's been a lifeguard for at least as long as I've owned my place here, and that goes back about four or five years.

I've had my problems with Mike. I don't much care for loud hip-hop music that makes sleep impossible during the long summer nights. His yard is full of tall weeds—perfect territory for rats—and the kid does nothing to keep the house up, probably because he's only renting. Sam thinks he's a loser.

I was just about to sic Sam on the dog problem back a few months ago when both dogs turned up dead. Poisoned, it seems, and you could only suspect the whole neighborhood, me included, for all the aggravation their barking caused. Naturally, Mike was grief-stricken, and I did feel a bit sorry for him. The kid loved those two dogs. Used to go running up and down the beach with them. They'd go surfing, too, when he did. And then they both were killed.

I admit my motives weren't totally pure when I asked Mike if he was going to get another dog.

"Naw," he replied, shoving his hands into his pockets. "Learned my lesson."

Sam thinks if I stop feeding the kid, he'll get out of the rut he's in and find himself a "real" job. Sam's probably right.

"Look at that, Sam," I whisper, pointing down toward the far end of the boardwalk. Silhouetted against the moon—just like one of those posters from the movies—is a tall thin man with his arm around a raven-haired woman whose long legs and equally long hair remind me of a ballet dancer. Their heads are together while he whispers in her ear. Her hair falls away from her shoulders as she turns her face up to his, and I'm thinking, now, they'll kiss each other, but, instead, she shrugs off his arm, turns, and walks away.

The breeze carries his voice down to where we're sitting. "Aw, Joanie, don't get yerself all upset now. It can't be good for the baby."

She's wearing a baggy wool sweater over blue jeans, and maybe there's a bump beginning to show beneath that sweater, but where is her jacket? It's cold out here.

"You shouldn't of done that," she admonishes him. "This baby don't need no jailbird for a daddy."

"Joanie! Please!"

I nudge Sam in the ribs. "Go on now, arrest the guy."

Sam slides down on the bench, folding his arms across his belt. "She don't mean it."

"I mean it, Joe," she says, almost like she's answering Sam. She turns back to face the young man. "I suppose it's too late to undo what you done, but if you ever do it again, we're done."

"I won't. I promise, Joanie. I only did it 'cause—"

Just when I'm going to learn why he did whatever it was that would make him a jailbird, now she kisses him. They look long and silent into each other's eyes, and then they walk past us, his arm around her shoulder, and she doesn't seem to be resisting although I see tears on her face in the moonlight before she wipes them away. I watch them head toward the street, close now, like all is forgiven.

Just for curiosity's sake, I stand up to see where they're going. He's handing her up into the front seat of a dusty, beat-up pickup, and they head off inland.

I turn back to Sam. "Isn't that your class A exhibit of what you mean by common folk?"

The kid stops by on Wednesday to tell me he's heading south for a couple of weeks to visit his folks down in Raleigh for the holidays.

"You ever been over to the Gerards?" I ask him, pouring out a glass of lemonade.

"Nope. No reason to." He scratches the stubble on his chin—one of those pitiful excuses for a beard these young folk all seem to be sporting.

"Not very friendly, are they."

"I guess not," he says, eyeing the pill bottle that's still sitting there, unclaimed by Sam.

"Ever find out who poisoned your dogs? I ask.

He flinches, shaking his head, as though he's still grieving. "Guess I'll never know."

I've turned my back just once to wipe off the counter, and when I turn around again, the pill bottle has disappeared. The kid has swiped it right in front of me, and here I am biting my tongue and thinking fast and furious, what does he want with that? Does he have a headache? If so, why not ask for some aspirin, which, unlike the Gerards, I do keep in the house. But he's stronger and bigger than me, and I don't want to provoke anything, so I wait till the kid takes off and then call Sam.

"Why didn't he ask you for some aspirin?" he says.

"'Cause he's the one who burgled the Roper place. He took that bottle because it's evidence."

Sam doesn't say "hogwash," but I know he's thinking it. Instead, he says, "Did you ever taste any of that stuff?"

"Of course not. Clearly, it was some kind of prescription drug for one of the Ropers. You know, one of those drugs that kids steal from their parents these days? Oxy-something or other? It probably would have knocked me six ways from Saturday. Anyway, it still bothers me that the stuff is powder when the label clearly indicates tablets. Plus, you know I would never tamper with evidence."

"Good," he says, and hangs up.

Wouldn't you know, Sam is getting all the credit for busting the kid? Turns out, the powder in that pill bottle was the kind you sniff. The kid was supporting a habit by selling cocaine to common folks inland and even a few upstanding owners with large houses and private beaches north of town.

"Sam," I say, leaning across the table. "Remember when you told me the kid's dogs had been poisoned?"

"Yep."

"Did you know—that is, did anybody do an autops—"

"—Necropsy. And, yes, they did. The poor things OD'd on cocaine."

My jaw drops. "The kid poisoned his own dogs?"

"Umhmmm." He stirs another spoonful of sugar into his coffee. "Accidentally, of course. Seems he'd hide the cocaine at the bottom of those large bags of dried dog food. He's not saying diddly, of course, but I figure he must of forgot to put the dog food away one day, and while he was out, the dogs got into the bag and ate everything."

"Oh, boy. No wonder he was so upset!"

I'm remembering the kid telling me something about learning a lesson, but then another question pops up. "Why didn't you arrest him way back when the dogs died?"

"Oh, we wanted to." He tilts his chair back onto two legs, looking oh so pleased with himself. "But we knew he'd had plenty of time to hide the drugs. In fact, his new way of hiding the stuff turned out to be by putting it into used pill bottles."

"No!"

"Yep. Found a whole row of them on a shelf in his bedroom closet. At first, we thought he was peddling prescription stuff, but all of them were filled with coke. Turns out there weren't any four-legged critters tearing up the Ropers' trash bags—or any stuff the renters usually put out when their rentals are up. He wasn't picking up that scattered trash like they were paying him to do; he was scavenging."

Sam tells me he's very glad I had the sense not to taste the stuff in that bottle. I'm reminding him of the major role that I have played in this whole affair, but he's just sitting there, a secret little smile on his face, probably dreaming how he'll spend his Christmas bonus. Or is he imagining how loopy I might have been if I'd sampled the stuff?

One of these days, though, he'll have to come back down to earth and remember that he still has an unsolved crime on his hands. Oh, I know it's not as exciting as busting a drug dealer, but every day the trail that leads from the Roper place to wherever the stolen goods are is getting colder. And, okay. I probably did make a mistake with the Gerards. I guess they're not thieves, but they are definitely unnatural.

My suspicions have shifted elsewhere. Whoever it was that robbed the Ropers got themselves all the things they'd need to set up housekeeping—and even more, when you consider 'tis the season. I'm not telling Sam this time, even if that makes me what you call an accessory after the fact. If he finds the culprits using standard police methods, then I suppose justice will be served. But the Ropers have plenty of money. (I searched online for them, and they live in one of those huge houses in a gated community with a pool and a clubhouse.) They aren't going to suffer much.

I keep remembering a night on the boardwalk under a big round moon and how maybe at one of those low-rent places inland from the ocean there's a little house trailer full of secondhand sheets and towels and pots and pans and spices for the kitchen and toothpaste and toilet paper for the bathroom. Maybe there's a nice little Christmas tree, already decorated for the holidays, and a baby on the way and no money to make a decent home for it, and maybe desperate people do desperate things in the name of love.

*An old, boarded-up hotel inspired our next story, set in
Front Royal, Virginia. Old buildings cast long shadows
through time, and perhaps sometimes, every so often, those
shadows overlap others.*

*Ms Seabrooke is a prolific author of books for young
readers. Her most recent novel, "Cemetery Street" was an
Edgar finalist. This is her first mystery. We look forward
to reading more.*

Murder in the Middle of a Battlefield

by Brenda Seabrooke

It was providence, my friends Julia and Garrett joked, when I
lost my job at an ad agency in Rhode Island. They asked me to
paint walls and murals in the old hotel they were renovating in
Front Royal, Virginia in exchange for room and board while I
job-hunted. This was September. The painting would take me
through the winter. It was an offer I couldn't afford to refuse.

I packed my car, drove south, and then crossed the forks of the
Shenandoah River. On the corner of Main Street and Royal Avenue,
late afternoon sun broadsided the three-story brick hotel, built two
years after the Civil War. Its first guests had been lawyers trying cases
in the courthouse across the street, Julia explained. The hotel was first
called the Montview to entice people seeking fresh air in the surrounding Blue Ridge Mountains. Railroads brought commercial travelers

selling anvils, organs, and dry goods. The hotel was the Afton then, until Julia and Garrett changed it to the Battlefield Hotel.

"Hel-lo, it's the only hotel in America in the middle of an actual Civil War battlefield," Julia said. Fighting had raged through the town on May 23, 1862 as troops exchanged fire from house to house, until the Confederates under Stonewall Jackson captured most of the Maryland unit that had occupied the town for several months. "The battle is a big draw for Civil War buffs and vacationing families," she said.

The renovation had begun with the addition of green window shutters and white garden boxes planted with boxwood flanking the entrance. The first floor dining room, named the Front Royal Room, with enclosed porte-cochere, was a popular a restaurant. I was to paint Civil War soldiers, period houses and people but no battle scenes on the walls, nothing that involved killing.

"I can see the restaurant is doing well. It was full of lunchers when I arrived, but who will stay in the hotel besides Civil War buffs?" The town was not that big and though old and historic, it seemed more like a day trip destination to me.

"Front Royal's history is unique, but it has other charms. It's the canoeing capital of Virginia. Canoers come here to paddle the forks of the Shenandoah River. The north entrance to the Shenandoah National Park is here with hiking trails both in and out of the park. The famous Luray and Shenandoah Caverns, and the Appalachian Trail are nearby. People from Washington weekend out in the countryside. Lots of B & B's around, so we thought why not a hotel in the center of a battlefield?"

"You mean it was really fought right here on this very spot?"

Julia nodded. "Right where we're standing. The armies clashed in front of the courthouse, which was used as a Union hospital then, and on the hotel's lot."

It was agreed that I would paint the restaurant walls, but not during dining hours lest the fumes interfere with the cuisine. I found a book of Civil War uniforms in the Royal Oak Bookshop two blocks up Royal Avenue to use as a guide. I sent out resumes and worked on upstairs walls while I planned the murals.

The hotel lacked an elevator for now, so I used the back stairs alongside cabinets filled with kitchen equipment. My room, 201, was on the east and looked like an old commercial travelers' room with tweedy carpeting, white octagonal tiles in the bath, a veneered dresser-top burled with cigarette burns and water rings. The rest of the furniture wasn't much better, desk, nightstand, straight chair, metal double bed. Julia had added a wicker chair, ivy-printed comforter and a wicker lamp.

In the previous century, the hotel had declined into a home for the disconnected and forgotten. Even with thorough cleaning, 201 had an aura of loneliness, nights whiled away with cigarettes and Ripple. Paint and new carpet would remedy that. We planned to paint all the hotel furniture white and decorate with period touches, washbowls, mosquito netting, old photos and portraits.

The next day, as the last dinner customers left, I started faux-painting the plywood door to the front stairs, turning it into a latticed arbor gate. I hummed as I mixed colors for the red, pink, and white roses climbing the arch. If this worked out, maybe I could start a faux painting and mural business. I could make cards to put in the lobby.

By morning, the door was dry. Julia had set out bowls of coffee grounds to purify the air in the foyer. I gave the door a sniff test. Not a whiff of paint odor remained. Lunch customers commented on the door. Several touched it. "It looks so real," they said. "As if we could pick the roses."

Julia and Garrett were pleased. I pored over books in the Samuels Library all afternoon making notes about the town and people. Belle Boyd had been key to the Confederate victory. Out on a walk, she had discovered Jackson's troops nearby, and gave them information about the forces holding the town, assuring that it could be easily re-taken. Stonewall listened, and the rest is history. I'd had the impression she was homely but she was actually striking and stylish, attractive to the opposite sex, not to mention soldiers of either side. I decided I would depict her strolling south on Royal Avenue, and planned to transfer the designs to the walls for painting that night.

Sometimes events don't follow the program. Garrett got a call in mid-afternoon informing him that his father had had a stroke. He and Julia left for Florida. The staff and I managed dinner, then closed the restaurant until their return.

I didn't realize until I locked the doors that I would be alone in the hotel.

The back stairs creaked. Dim lighting caused shadows to lurk in corners. I imagined ghostly figures from long ago, hoop-skirted ladies and soldiers from the War, their long fingers reaching for me.

It's just a building, I told myself.

An old one, halfway into its second century, myself replied. No telling what went on here. Or what might remain from it. My footsteps sounded loud in the empty hotel.

Garrett and Julia had encouraged me to use their sitting room with the huge TV and other amenities, but I spent the night safely locked in my room sketching what I would paint tomorrow.

I closed the curtains and assembled my notes, pictures, drawing pad and pencils, and began with a belle in a hoop skirt on the lawn of Rose Hill, talking to soldiers. In the early years of the war, uniforms could not be distinguished on the battlefield because every unit had its own. Some Confederate soldiers wore blue, and some Union ones wore gray. Soldiers of both sides wore butternut. I painted them so that insignias didn't show. Blue, gray and butternut mingled on the lawn. If people wondered about it, they could ask and learn a little-known fact about that war. Later, uniforms were changed so the soldiers wouldn't shoot their own men.

I modeled the belle on myself, but gave her chestnut hair darker than mine and a rose-colored gown. I was almost in a trance as I worked. I didn't notice the stillness of the room, the unexplained chill, the sudden air current that sucked the curtains into the closed windows and belled them out again. I worked until long after midnight before I realized how sleepy I was and went to bed.

In the morning I reviewed the sketches but couldn't find them. I pawed through the loose sheets, paged through the pad several times and searched the notes folder. No belle. No horseman. No soldiers. No Rose Hill. What was going on?

Instead, appearing like spirit writing on the pages was a series of stick figure drawings. They seemed to be telling a story. I didn't know what to make of them. An icicle slid down my spine. Had someone substituted these sketches while I slept?

What reason could anybody have to do that? A rival restaurant? Hardly. Nobody but Julia and Garrett knew about the murals. Maybe I had mentioned them at the paint store but who would care?

I couldn't waste the whole day worrying about it. Julia and Garrett would expect results when they returned. I sketched free-hand on the wall the scene I thought I'd drawn last night. Again I used myself as model but gave the belle a heart-shaped face instead of my oval one. She probably would've been shorter than my 5'9" and would have had a tiny corseted waist.

As I worked, my mind worried over last night. I was sure I had sketched this scene on paper. Had I mislaid it somehow or in my sleep drawn these?

That was not possible. I clearly remembered working on the belle's rose skirt and thinking about the effect of light on it.

At noon I took a break and went upstairs. I stood in the doorway of 201, reluctant to enter. You slept here last night I told myself. No harm came to you. The room seemed ordinary with the coverlet thrown back to air the sheets. Nothing sinister here. Only sunlight pushed against the window curtains.

Reassured, I searched, but found nothing, no drawings anywhere in the room, nor in the bath.

After lunch I went to the library. "Are you that artist painting in the old hotel?" a woman asked me.

I nodded.

"I don't like old buildings myself," she said. "No old dust hanging around in cracks and corners for me. Or ghosts. That old hotel doesn't even have charm."

"It probably did in its day but it's been empty for a long time," the librarian offered.

"Is it haunted? Have you seen any ghosts?" the woman asked, her eyes turning avid.

"None," I said, "but I wondered if any murders had happened there."

"There was one," said the woman. "Let me see, it was about fifteen years ago. A man staying at the hotel murdered the manager there." Her fingers made air quotes around manager. "He was a salesman. She lived in the hotel and was no better than she should be, if you know what I mean."

. "Was it in the papers?'

"It will be on microfilm." The librarian strode briskly to the microfiche files and quickly produced a reel that she threaded on the viewer. "There you are."

I found what I was searching for, but hoped not to find. Carl Vinona, a salesman for the Woodhue Drug Company, staying in the hotel, had a date with Iris Grimes, a checker at Kratzer's Market. On the night of the murder, Cherie O'Phelan, the manager of the hotel lived in 201, my room.

Vinona was late picking her up, Grimes told police, so after getting off work, she changed and drove to the hotel. She used the back stairs but before she reached the second floor she observed Mr. Vinona exiting O'Phelan's room. He didn't see Grimes as she continued up the stairs. She knocked on his door, which was on the west side of the central stairs. He didn't answer for at least five minutes, Grimes remembered, because she was tired of standing in the hall and told him she was leaving. Vinona opened the door. He was not wearing a shirt. She was annoyed that he wasn't ready. They had a dinner reservation in Winchester.

Cherie O'Phelan was found dead of multiple stab wounds the next morning in room 201 by the chambermaid, Donia Daly. "She was laying there all covered with blood," the hysterical Daly told police. Grimes didn't come forward with her testimony until it was reported that she was seen leaving the hotel with Vinona.

"I don't believe he did it," Grimes insisted in an interview. "He was a nice man. We was gonna get married."

Carl Vinona denied any interest in O'Phelan. He had stayed originally at the Afton when all other hotels and motels were full. He liked it and continued to stay there on sales trips to the area. Vinona disputed the time Iris Grimes knocked on his door, saying he was sure it was at least five minutes after he had returned to his room from changing a light bulb for O'Phelan. He said he was never shirtless but had been ready to go out to dinner when he opened the door to Ms. Grimes.

Vinona's prints were found on the light bulb and on the wall switch. The doorknob had been wiped clean. No bloody clothes were ever found but Vinona had time to dispose of them after his dinner with Grimes.

The prosecutor contended Vinona stayed at the Afton because he fancied the manager. Vinona changed the light bulb for O'Phelan, who then rebuffed his advances. A lie detector test was inconclusive. Vinona was found guilty, denied appeal and now resided at the Keen Mountain Correctional Institute. The coroner believed the murder weapon to be a thin knife or a stiletto. It was never found.

I made a copy of the article. I knew what I had to do but I didn't want to do it. I drove to the first fast food place I came to and had an early supper of brain food—burger, fries, and vanilla shake. I chewed slowly. Then I went back to the hotel, brushed my teeth and changed. I didn't want to look too flashy or inconsequential for what I had to do. Black jeans, a chocolate vee-necked cotton sweater, medium silver hoops, black boots, a spritz of French Vanilla. Not too sober, casual, or gaudy.

. I was glad I'd had the forethought to hold the onions on my burger and had taken care to dress, when I was ushered into the Jackson Street police detective's office. Icy blue eyes under longish dark blond hair, a mile-wide bisected chin, Detective Thomas Riley wore jeans and a khaki shirt under a jacket.

"What can I do for you, Ms. um- ?"

I didn't want him to think I was one of these police groupies or a wacko job. "Zoe, please. I wish I were collecting for Girl Scout cookies. You'll think I'm a nut case for telling you this."

"Tell me." His eyes seemed to get bluer. Maybe he was trying not to laugh.

"I'm painting murals in the Front Royal Room." I pulled out the copy of the newspaper article. "Are you familiar with the Cherie O'Phelan murder case?"

If he was surprised, he didn't show it. He scanned the article. "I remember it."

I handed over the sketches, struck anew by how utterly lame my story would sound. I wished I hadn't come. I took a deep breath and explained why I was staying in the hotel alone. "I was sketching in my room last night, Rose Hill, belles, soldiers."

His eyebrow went up. The left one.

"I went to bed around midnight. This morning when I looked at my sketches, this was what I found. As you can see, these are not what I had worked on."

"You locked the door when you went to your room?"

"Yes."

"You didn't go out for any reason?"

"No."

"The door was still locked when you got up this morning?"

"Yes."

"Do you sleepwalk?"

"No. I mean I never have and my feet were clean."

He glanced through the sketches. "What do you think these are?"

"I don't know what to think. They appear to be sketches of a murder that occurred in room 201. I couldn't have drawn them. I didn't even know about the murder until today. I'm sure nobody came in my room. Even if someone did, who would take my sketches and leave these? This afternoon at the library I heard about the murder for the first time and read the account of it. The sketches coincide up to a point with the report but they seem to indicate a different murderer than the man convicted of it. In the first one a man is changing a light bulb for a woman. He leaves in the second sketch as another woman with dark hair watches from the stairs. The manager, Cherie O'Phelan apparently sees the woman but the man doesn't. In the third one the woman on the stairs goes to the door of 201."

I pointed at the figure. "Notice her raincoat has changed. It was beige, now it's rust and orange print. She must have turned it inside out. Cherie, the manager has opened the door and the other woman is entering. In the fourth panel, the woman raises something that looks like a knife. And that's all." My voice trailed off.

"You think this woman murdered the manager?"

"It looks that way in these drawings."

"Who do you think made the drawings, if you didn't?"

"I may have been the instrument of spirit drawing," I said in a small voice.

He looked at me. "Spirit drawing?"

I nodded. "Like spirit writing. Except drawing."

He didn't laugh. "Why didn't you draw what happened to O'Phelan?"

"I don't know why the pictures stop when they do. If the spirit of Cherie was drawing through me last night, maybe she didn't know what happened after that because she had just been killed."

He looked at the pages again. Then he looked at me without saying anything. I tried not to squirm like a kid in the principal's office.

"I assume you're trying to decide if I'm crazy or at least what my angle is. I'm not a medium. Nothing like this has ever happened to me before. At first I was furious when I saw that my sketches weren't there. All that work for nothing. Then I sort of got spooked."

"I can see that. May I keep these?"

I shrugged. I had no use for them. I stood up. I'd done what I came to do. What he did with the information was up to him.

"Are you related to Carl Vinona?" He remained seated as he drilled me with those blue eyes.

"No. I'd never heard of him before today. I hadn't even heard of the murder until a woman in the library mentioned it. I certainly wouldn't be staying in the hotel by myself if I had."

"One of those people is dead, one is in prison. If another person did the murder, he or she wouldn't want to bring it to anybody's attention. You're hardly in danger from any of them."

"That's true, but rooms can have auras."

"Does this one?"

"I'm not sure. Several times I thought I heard someone sigh but decided it was the wind or curtains or something."

He cleared his throat. "Ah – thanks for coming in. I'll look into the matter."

"Just being a conscientious citizen," I said then mentally kicked myself. How lame did that sound?

I'd done my civic duty. I went back to the hotel and changed into my work clothes. I pulled some tables together and laid out my notes and drawing materials in the Front Royal Room. I wouldn't draw in

201 anymore. I wanted to do Rose Hill next, but my fingers sketched a lute player that turned out to be a portrait of the detective.

I transferred him to the wall with the belle and then opened the cans of water-based paint, blue, the same color as his eyes, for the uniform. I'd started on the house when someone rapped sharply on the front door. I ignored it. This was after hours. It couldn't be anybody who needed to be here.

The rapping continued. Then, more ominous. "Open up, police!"

How did I know it was the police? It could be a perp saying that. I tiptoed to the front desk to use the restaurant phone.

"Ms. Fisher? It's Thomas Riley."

"If you're Detective Riley, tell me what I said I wished I were doing when I walked into your office."

He laughed through the door. "You said you wished you were collecting for Girl Scout cookies."

I opened the door. "It must be at least ten."

"Ten-twenty, to be precise. I couldn't get away sooner but I wanted to talk to you about these drawings." His gaze went beyond me to the dining room. "Are these the murals?"

He brushed past me to look at the belle. "Nice. You forgot your freckles." He nodded at her.

"She would have put sour milk on her nose at night to bleach them away." I kept the sprinkling across my nose covered but he detected them through the makeup.

Then he noticed the lute player. The eyebrow went up.

"Sorry about using you as a model. Maybe people won't notice."

"They'll notice." He didn't seem bothered to be the model for a possible Confederate lute player. A detective with a sense of humor. "Show me your room."

I just looked at him.

He smiled. "Sorry. That didn't come out right. The scene of the crime."

I started to the front stairs but he wanted to see the back ones. As we passed the table where I'd been working, he asked me to bring my sketch pad and pencils.

"You went a demonstration?"

"Call it curiosity."

He checked the long cabinet by the stairs where can openers and other tools of the restaurant trade were kept.

201 wasn't locked. "I didn't expect company." I twitched the duvet over the unmade bed and went to the desk. He sat in the other chair.

"Do whatever you did before." He nodded at my pad.

I opened it. "I'll draw the house." I could see it in my mind as I picked up a soft pencil and began sketching. He didn't say a word, just watched my moving fingers. I described everything I was drawing, the deep porch, the dogs under the steps, the flowers that would have been blooming that day.

"All right. I think you've been at it long enough," he said as the town clock struck midnight. I had no idea it was that late.

He scooped up the sketches and looked through them. I had numbered them. He asked me what each one was according to the number.

"The first one is the thumbnail sketch for the overall mural. The rest are enlargements of parts of the scene."

He went through them, taking his time. "That's what you think you have drawn?"

"Of course, it is." I was irritated. "It didn't work this time. Maybe it only worked last night and won't happen again. Or maybe it only works when I'm here by myself."

He studied the drawings, then me, as if trying to make up his mind about something.

I stared back at him. A five o'clock shadow was faintly visible. He caught my look and I felt myself turning red. I opened my mouth to say something to prevent more embarrassment. At the same time I noticed a chill in the room. Had I left a window open?

Over his shoulder a blob of pixels swirled in the bathroom doorway. My mouth stayed open. He followed my gaze in time to see the apparition of a woman forming. Neither of us moved. We couldn't have, even if a Komodo dragon had burst in, salivating for human flesh.

The pixels coalesced into a woman wearing a black negligee. Her peroxided hair was long and tousled as it might be from sleep.

Her arms reached out, beseeching. The apparition lasted less than a minute, but it seemed like hours. Then she broke into pixels that faded with the receding cold.

Riley looked at me. We were both standing. I was clutching his arm. I let go.

"How did you do that?" he asked.

"What?" My voice came out in a squeak. "Me? I didn't do anything. That scared me as much as you."

"I'm not scared," he said in a tough voice. He ran his hands over the walls.

"What are you doing?"

"I'm looking to see where a lens could have projected through a pinhole".

"If I arranged a haunting in this town, the ghost would be a Civil War soldier, not one that looked like she stepped off the cover of a Mickey Spillane paperback."

He didn't reply as he went over every inch of the room and bath. Then he picked up the sketches and again asked me what they were. Again I explained them to him. "Come on." He took my arm as if I might try to stay. No way would I stay in that room now.

Downstairs he asked for coffee. I made a quick pot while he waited, arms folded at the table.

"Cream? Sugar?"

"Black."

I brought the mugs of steaming coffee to the table and sat opposite him.

He held up my first sketch. "Describe what you see."

"The man exiting room 201." One by one he held up the sketches. They were identical to the ones I had drawn before.

"If you're doing this, I need to know how."

"I'm not. I mean I'm not doing it purposefully. Or even knowingly. I didn't do that apparition either."

"Okay, if you're not doing it, then we have to assume it's supernatural. Cherie has returned but why now after all these years?"

I didn't like the probable answer to that question. "You think I'm a medium? I'm not."

"I didn't imply that you were. Maybe it's your drawing. Her spirit is able to attach itself to your hand."

"I don't like that answer either."

"She doesn't intend to harm you. She's making use of your talent."

"All right." I didn't mind my drawings upgraded to talent.

"Why didn't she show us what happened to the murder weapon? Nothing was ever found." He asked this as if I had a pipeline to Cherie.

"I don't know. I can only guess but as I said before, maybe the shock of her murder shut down her perceptions. It's obvious that Iris was the murderer. Are you going to arrest her?"

"On what evidence?"

He had a point.

Riley thought awhile. He'd forgotten his coffee.

"Let's go back to the room. I want to check something." This time I trailed him up the stairs. I was in no hurry to go back.

He stopped in the doorway. "The furniture appears to be the same as in the sketches except for one chair. I couldn't find anything in the files about the room search. I assume it was thorough but I'll do it again even though the room has been cleaned hundreds, if not thousands of times since the murder and the carpeting replaced. Or not," he added looking at the interesting stains.

He checked the drawers for places of concealment. I was glad I hadn't unpacked and was still living out of suitcases except for what hung in the closet. He searched that next, then the bathroom, and the furniture. The bed was last. He pulled off the mattress, checked the metal headboard and footboard. They were both made of a single curved metal tube with smaller vertical tube posts between the arms of the U. He lifted the foot of the bed. One of the rollers fell off and something clanked. He hoisted the footboard higher and an object fell out of the leg.

We stared at it. "Get me some plastic bags, please."

I flew down the stairs and returned with a box of large-sized. He took one out and slid his hand in to retrieve the ice pick with rust stains on it. He dropped it in another bag and sealed it. "The murder weapon. That's why Cherie didn't show what happened to it in the drawings. She was dead when the murderer put it in the bed frame."

"Why didn't the murderer return it to the cabinets downstairs?"

"The murder happened at a busy time at the restaurant. She ran the risk of being seen."

"How did it rust like that in the post? Wasn't it sealed in there?"

"It's not rust." He looked at me. "Listen, will you be all right? I have a busy night ahead of me."

"I'm fine. I have to paint anyway. Nothing happens downstairs."

The rust proved to be Cherie's blood. The plastic handle held fifteen-year old prints but they weren't Carl Vinona's. They belonged to Iris Grimes who still lived in the area in her dilapidated childhood home with sagging porch, peeling paint and overgrown yard. Her prints were on file from the old case.

A few days later the police went to her house to bring her in for questioning, but before they could knock on the door, she burst through it wearing a cerise nightgown that looked like somebody had shredded it with a sharp instrument. She was a wreck, dark circles under her eyes, her dyed black hair tangled and dry as wadded paper. She ran screaming into the front yard. "Help! Police!"

In the interview, Riley determined that she hadn't slept since the night we saw Cherie's ghost. After Cherie appeared for us, she moved on to Iris's house, to materialize and point an accusing finger at Iris. "One time I could forget about, ya know, but she wouldn't leave. She kept coming back and coming back and coming back."

Iris confessed everything. She was relieved to be out of that house, free of the apparition and safe in jail. She had seen Carl leaving the manager's room, saw Cherie in that black negligee and thought she was after her man. "It was what I'd a done if it'd a been me, ya know?"

She believed that Carl would marry her, so she killed her supposed rival with an ice pick, she picked up downstairs. The murder was premeditated because she went back for it and turned her raincoat inside out to stab Cherie. She reversed it to hide the blood spatters when she went to Carl's door. During Vinona's trial she found out he was already married and had girlfriends in towns all over the South. "It was all for nothing," she said, over and over.

"It usually is," Riley told me later. "The reasons people murder other people are always stupid, except in self-defense, and they often project their own ideas onto others. Iris would have done what she suspected Cherie of doing, poaching her boyfriend. To her, that justified the murder."

On his release, Vinona sued and settled. He moved to Belize to write his story. His wife had divorced him when he was arrested. He didn't take any of his old girlfriends with him, though one or two prison pen pals may have followed him.

The spirit drawing and apparition were never mentioned in police reports or the news. Riley told a plausible story about finding the ice pick in the loose bed frame when it fell off its roller, and I asked him for help in getting it back. Iris pled guilty and was sentenced to twenty-five to life. She'll be over sixty when she gets out. "All I wanted was to be loved," she sobbed in an interview.

That may be all any of us want but most of us don't resort to murder.

The hotel and its murals were a success, leading to hotel bookings and commissions for me. I started a mural and faux painting business in the Shenandoah Valley with police work on the side. Thomas has solved four cold cases and one fresh one with my help. We're a good team. Nobody knows how we do it and we plan to keep our methods secret since they're not admissible in court.

America's heartland calls us next. A reporter eager for a killer story gets in over his head — the question quickly becomes, will he also lose it?

Mr. Hegenberger is releasing an avalanche of books over the twelve months, an even dozen, featuring several protagonists, settings, and eras. He has a great fondness in old movies, including silent films.

Unhappy Trails

By John Hegenberger

It was a single-story, brick-façade house, set back from the road with a gravel drive, surrounded by mature trees. When I got out of my car, climbed the three steps and rang the bell, I was greeted by the familiar yapping of two small dogs rushing the door. They kept it up for almost a half-minute before Dan came and let me in, deadpanning, "Wanna buy a dog?"

I smiled in spite of myself. Dan and I had been friends since we'd met in film class at The Ohio State University thirty years earlier.

He shook my hand strongly and said, "How's it, hero?" Five foot six inches, sandy receding hair, rimless bifocals, easy grin. "Want some coffee?"

The twin miniature Beagle pups were a pair of oxfords with twitching tails, sniffing and wetting my shoes with their noses. We all moved as a unit through the kitchen and into the rec room where Dan kept his currently favorite books, movies and pipes. I noticed a dozen or so Roy Rogers and Hopalong Cassidy DVDs stacked neatly beside the TV.

It was a warm day in late Autumn and I had come bearing a birthday gift.

The ex-chief of police and I shared a love of old movies and older detective stories. This year, I brought him a first edition of the movie version of Hammett's the Glass Key; the one with Alan Ladd and Veronica Lake on the dust jacket.

Taking the book out of the brown paper bag I had used as gift wrap, he nodded. "This is great, Scotty. I've always enjoyed it."

I nodded, too. "I went back and re-watched the 1942 version of the film. My favorite scene is where Ladd confronts a guy and they argue eye to eye. Then, instead of throwing a punch, Ladd merely kicks the guy in the shin, causing him to hop around on one leg while Ladd calmly walks away."

"That's one of my favorite bits, too," Dan chuckled. "Maybe they should have called the movie The Glass Knee."

"Ouch," I winced and fake-limped over to an easy chair. I continued to rub my knee as if in pain.

Dan watched and selected a pipe from a nearby rack. "Which reminds me, are you still going on those long walks in the park?"

I gazed out the window at a stand of pines across the lake. A couple of Canada geese flew overhead. "These days, being out on trail is my best remedy for clearing away stress from pounding the keyboard at the paper. You should try it," I advised. "In fact, something interesting happened while I was out at Slate Run Metro Park last week doing a 6-miler."

"Go ahead," Dan said, waving out the kitchen match and leaning back in his chair. "Spin me your usual rambling yarn."

I cleared my throat to get a running start. "Well, the terrain is heavily forested, see, with small open meadows carpeted with wild clover, topped with a cloud-flecked sky. The gravel and dirt trail slants between wooded cliffs, folding back to a burbling creek below."

"Sounds literate."

"Don't interrupt. I had trekked at a steady pace for close to two miles and came out of deep woods into an open prairie where park administrators have built a playground beside a small man-made lake. About twenty paces in front of me, a big, blocky guy with a thin mustache, wearing a dark blue jacket had two big dogs on separate leashes, walking them through the grass and wildflowers. They were milling around midway between me and the lake. I automatically switched course, of course."

"Too literate," he puffed.

"Okay, so I veered to my right to avoid them; you happy? But the dogs had seen me now or caught my scent and one of them broke from his leash and dashed top speed directly for me." I paused for dramatic effect and sipped strong coffee from a World's-Best-Police-Officer mug. "He probably weighed over 100 pounds, but came at me like an arrow. Sort of a cross between a wolf hound and a German shepherd with big teeth, burning eyes and red diamond patch of fur on his forehead."

"Not teeth," Dan said. "Fangs."

"Yeah, well, so I brought up my hiking staff to defend myself, while the guy in the blue jacket hollered and struggled to hold back the other excited dog. I tried to decide between standing my ground or running across the open field, when the guy yelled, 'Heal! Heal, Lucky!' And the dog stopped dead on command, but continued to growl and stare at me with determined hate."

"Lucky?"

"Yeah, apparently that's the dog's name. So the blocky guy caught up to Lucky and we all stood there breathing hard, men and dogs, just as a Park Ranger cruised by in his truck, making regular rounds."

Dan went "Hmmm".

I reached down and rubbed one of the pups behind the ear. Of course, the other one wanted it too. "Well, the blocky guy was restless, moving from foot to foot. He buried his tanned face deep in his beard and said, 'I'll give you $100 not to say anything to the Ranger.' The dogs stayed quiet and the Blocky Guy pulled a smartphone from his jacket pocket and held up in my direction.

"No real harm done, I thought, right? So I swallowed and waved to the passing truck and the Ranger waved back and Blocky waved back and the Ranger slowly drove down the road and out of sight.

"Blocky reached into his back pocket and pulled out a worn brown wallet, but I told him, 'Don't worry about it,' and walked back out of the field and into the woods. But the more I thought about it, the more I wondered why he would offer as much as $100, not to alert the park authorities.

"So I turned around and walked back to where I was still hidden by the brush and watched him load the dogs into the white van and slowly drive away.

"It all seemed perfectly normal, but what the heck, I made a note of the license plate: EA78NG. And that was that."

My coffee was cold. Dan picked up a pencil and wrote on the brown paper bag that I'd given him. "When was this again?"

"Last Monday afternoon, when it was cool and dry. Perfect weather for hiking."

"Is that why you came here today? To share your latest saga?"

"No," I protested. "I came here to celebrate your what eightieth birthday, Old Cop."

It was his turn to wince. "Sixty-sixth," he said. "You were at Slate Run Park, right? I wonder if you know that the next day there was an escape from the level three security facility near there."

"No kidding…"

"The Chief of Security is a friend and keeps me notified of events."

"No kidding…"

"The escapee has not been found. For some reason, the guard dogs couldn't track him."

"Can you check with your friend and see if they have a dog with a red diamond on its forehead?"

"Maybe tomorrow. Today's my birthday." He put down his pipe and came to his feet. "And I just happen to have a DVD of The Glass Key. You might get a kick out of it."

"Ouch," I winced again. "Sounds fun."

"Sounds dull," my editor said. "Besides, I need you back on the Political beat."

"But, he can get me inside, Andrea. And he even knows the Chief of Security."

She pushed a strand of hair from her face and squinted at me. "Sounds weak, too," she said, starting to walk away. "You've got better things to do."

"Come on," I followed. "We haven't published a prison tour in ages and we've never done a blog from behind bars before. It'll get us lots of comments and re-twits on our webpage."

I'd been with the Columbus Inquirer for over eleven years and watched it slowly shrink and go "social". I wasn't the best journalist on staff, but I was the most loyal to the traditions of a classic reporter.

Still, I'd gradually started to learn how to blog and hoot and post stories to our Facebook page.

She turned back to scowl at me. Must have forgotten to put her contacts in today. "I know that you know that it's not 're-twits', Scotty. And you're not going to be able to coast on your involvement in the Just Sweats murder forever."

"Still… I'd like to take a crack at it."

"You're like a dog with a bone. Once you get the scent…"

Dan drove us in his Ford 150 through the cool, grey morning past Grove City to the Bolton Correctional Institution.

I saw randomly stacked chunks of grey concrete with a white colonial façade entrance. Level 1 inmates had placed painted, white rocks along the drive. A high chain-link fence with three Yield signs rolled to the right on stubby wheels to let Dan's truck into the visitor's lot.

There were cameras mounted on the corners of the building and above the solid grey entrance door. Dan talked to the video screen and showed his creds. We were buzzed through the sally port double set of doors to a holding area. All very cold and official.

I emptied my pockets into a grey tub on a conveyor belt that lead to an x-ray machine, like the ones they have at the airport. A prison officer who looked like a linebacker bagged my stuff and waved a metal detector hoop up and down my arms, legs and torso.

The windowless room was brightly lit from a cascade of florescent panels overhead. The concrete walls gleamed with grey paint. More cameras high in every corner. Low 'locker-room' benches bolted to the polished grey and white tile floor. Intake holding rooms. All very official and cold.

The Desk Officer listened while Dan told him why we were there, and then made a call. Ten minutes later, we were greeted by Deputy of Operations, Jerry Wade who'd already been briefed of our visit. He shook Dan's hand and looked at me with an open expression. "You the reporter?"

"Journalist." I shook his warm hand. "Scott Robinson."

"And you think?" He let it hang there.

I glanced at Dan and then said, "I think I may know something about the guy who escaped last week."

Deputy Wade rattled off: "Bolton Correctional seeks to provide offenders of felony convictions within the State of Ohio a safe, efficient, humane and appropriately secure correctional…"

"Yeah, I saw that on your website."

I watched him study me. "You don't make friends very quickly, do you?"

There was nothing to say to that. But I went ahead anyway. "I've done my homework and the guy who got away was Omar Aldagon, who was in here for making threats against the federal government, according to the state attorney general's office. How exactly did he get away?"

Wade glared at me with a stare that was hard enough to crack diamonds. It wasn't my most shining hour. Dan quickly stepped in, saying, "Look, Jerry. What Mr. Robinson here means is that we think we know something about how Aldagon got away. But first, can you tell us how a he got beyond your confines?"

Wade addressed Dan, as if I'd faded away. "He hid up above the air ducts during the afternoon and got out when the gates were opened to receive a returning work crew. We tracked him, but couldn't run him to ground."

"Did you track him with the dogs?" Dan asked.

"Of course."

"Including Lucky?"

"Among others, yes."

"Who handles Lucky now?"

Wade considered. "That would be Officer Crandall."

"Blocky guy with an anemic mustache? We think that he tampered with the dog's training and that's why you couldn't track him."

I watched Wade process this. There were nests of wrinkles at the edges of his eyes and hard lines at the sides of his mouth. "How do you know Crandall?"

I answered by relating my encounter with Lucky and Company at the park.

The lines at his mouth got deeper and the muscles at his jaw swelled. "I cannot act without evidence, you understand," he said. "But I can take steps to ensure the security of the facility while we investigate." He stepped behind his desk and punched a button on his phone. "Have Officer Crandall put on unpaid leave immediately and escorted off the premises."

Cold. Official.

"Satisfied?"

I was impressed and a little embarrassed. "Do I still get the tour?"

On the drive back, Dan said, "I promised him that you wouldn't publish anything on this yet."

"What? Why?"

"I talked with Wade while you were being shown around. He kicked Crandall out, hoping to trail him and possibly lead them back to Aldagon."

He had seemed to jump on it pretty quickly.

Sunlight glared off Dan's glasses. "Wade says that lately Crandall has been ranting about how prison life is soft with free medical, dental, three squares and easy access to the Internet. Called it a bed and breakfast. He's even mentioned something about the Foundation Citizens."

"The right-wing supremacist group? They were involved with the shooting of a prison director in Colorado a few months ago."

"I know. You can see why Wade doesn't want you to print anything yet. Everything I'm telling you now is off the record."

"Yeah but, these Foundationers are essentially domestic terrorists. There was that backpack bomb with the fishing weights coated with rat poison in Spokane in 2011 and the gallon of napalm wired to a suburban home up in Cleveland the year before. Dan, you can't expect me to suppress this."

"You don't have any evidence," Dan said. "Just the story that I'm telling you now."

"Yeah but…"

"Yeah but, yourself, Scotty. I promised that you'd sit on it for a couple of days, so Wade and his people can work the problem. I did you a favor getting you inside. Don't make me go back on my word." The road ahead of us was clear, so he glanced my way. "And you need to work on improving your people skills and stop being such a loner."

I knew he was right, but I still made a sound in my throat like I'd swallowed a tack.

The next day, back in the office, I worked on an election year politics story about Alex Newton, state senate candidate from the heart of the heartland, who was scheduled to smile and wave during next week's OSU vs. Michigan football game. I knew him for being a firebrand lawyer with a head full of graying hair and a mouthful of expensive dental work. A pro at slapping babies and kissing backs. He was supported by several of the unions for his stance on the homeless problem and the Green party for being anti-fracking. Nobody really cared much about Newton, but politics and sports is what the news is all about, sometimes.

I'd saved a draft of the story on my laptop and went to get a fresh cup of Dark French Roast from the Gevalia machine in the break room. It had been awhile since I'd contributed to the Community Coffee Fund, so I folded a twenty and dropped it into the jar, when a local news story on the overhead TV monitor told the public that a car had gone off the road, through a guard rail and landed upside down at the bottom of Marblecliff quarry. The driver, one Edmond Crandall, had been crushed flat by the impact and "died instantly", if you could believe the local TV news nerds. They had no idea what the real story was. I wasn't sure I did either.

I called Dan about Crandall's death. He said the authorities were working on it and I should continue to hold my water. Damn.

That night, I dined alone on pinot grigio and frozen pizza, watched The Big Lombowski and took my headache off to bed. As I slipped into a restless sleep, I thought, Screw 'em, I'm taking myself out on trail tomorrow, so this dude can abide.

Wednesday was supposed to warm up fast into the high eighties. I decided to get an early start. Dressed in khakis, sturdy shoes, a denim shirt and my multi-pocketed, light-weight fishing vest, I pulled my rust bucket into the empty lot at Pickerington Ponds Metro Park. The lavender light was just spreading across the sky, diffusing the darkness, while the eastern horizon began to glow like the mouth of a furnace.

I had the place all to myself. It's one of the flattest and quietest parks in Central Ohio. The morning air was cool and smelled of damp earth. The trail was crushed gravel and wound through a collection of old farm pastures that had been combined and flooded to create a seventeen-acre wetlands with runoffs filled with cattails and shoulder-high tufts of wild grass. As I crunched along the winding path, my spirit lifted and my mind began to float free.

Being on trail is cathartic for me. I think about things I'd done wrong and the things I'd done right. Where I'd chosen correctly and where I'd gone wrong. I had chosen to follow the safe and successful route of being a general news reporter, instead of a novelist. As a result, it often felt like I'd given away my unique perspective, in exchange for the common man's POV; the universal man who gets a weekly paycheck, who reads the daily newspaper and then discards it.

But, whatever was lacking in my life——whatever I thought I'd lost——I always hoped that I'd find it hidden on trail. Something about being true to the basic principles or Curley's "One Thing" that could make me a better person. Dumb stuff, like that.

I hiked for over an hour, clearing my mind and looping along the trail that circled Arrowhead Marsh, watching the egrets stretch their wings in the sun, finally yo-yoing back to the public parking lot where a green SUV was now parked next to my car.

As I strolled nearer, two guys got out of the other car and one of them pointed a sweaty, stern face and gun at me, saying, "Keep quiet and give me your keys."

The rest of our conversation was even shorter and so was the trip, with me at gunpoint in my own passenger seat and the SUV following, until we all bounced up a long driveway to an old farm house with a dilapidated For Sale sign out at the highway in front of a 30-acre lot that hadn't been plowed for at least two years.

———•••———

Maybe it was the adrenalin from the danger, but I was pissed. I struggled to keep myself under control. They helped with their guns.

We parked next to the white van that they had used to transport the dogs and trudged up the three sagging steps to the front porch. "Bring him on in," I heard a voice call through the screen door.

Inside the house, stood a guy with stern brows and faint flame tattoos rising from under the collar of his open shirt. "Omar Aldagon," he said and stuck out his right hand for me to shake. When I reach for it, he slaps me hard. "Asshole."

The left side of my face stung and I felt hot with embarrassment. "Is that your official title?"

He tilted his head to the side, like a hound. His shoulders are narrow and he has stiff, black hair that no amount of grease seemed capable of flattening. He blew out a laugh and had his men turn out my pockets, leaving me with my comb, handkerchief, pen, pad, loose change and wallet. He took my phone and held it up. "These are a godsend." He hit me hard in the shoulder with his open hand. "That's how we found you."

They had traced me from a biometric scan app when my photo was taken in the park via Crandall's smartphone. And they had a contact with access to DMV info, who used some software to match the photo with the one on my driver's license. Nobody is off-the-grid any more. Technology can get to anyone.

I put it out there. "You murdered Crandall."

"Yes," Aldagon grinned with yellow teeth. "We didn't need that butt crack anymore, but we do need you."

"To do what?"

"To report the facts of the big story after the big event."

I noticed a bunch of candidate posters and flyers for Newton's campaign stacked up in the corners of the main room of the farm house. These guys appeared to be supporting Newton's political campaign for the state senate, but I knew they had something to do with the Foundation Citizens. So why do they want me to believe that they are part of Newton's support team?

Aldagon's lips were compressed; his neck muscles bunched. "You're going to be our guest here for a few days and when you wake up late Sunday, you'll be ready to tell our exclusive, inside story."

That sounded like I'd do well to bide my time until they let me go. But why Sunday? It slowly dawned on me that Aldagon's big event might have a political angle. He and the Foundationers intended to do something on Saturday and blame it on Newton, based on my reporting. They planned to use me to make people believe that Newton is responsible for… The words bomb and football game made an 80-point headline in my head.

———————————

They kept me locked in a windowless room and fed me microwaved Chicken Alfredo packs. The water bottles had already been opened. I figured that they were feeding me small portions of a sedative over time, so it would be easy to fully drug me unconscious on Friday, while they're setting up the "big event".

I've had experience during long hikes of going without food or water, so I scooped the food from the cardboard containers and piled it on the top shelf of an empty closet. I poured the water down a crack in the floor behind my squeaking bunk. I hoped the flies and ants didn't give me away.

By Friday, I was acting doped, which wasn't hard, since I hadn't eaten in days. I try to stay alert as Aldagon comes into the room with a syringe and stops.

There is a knock at the front door of the farm house. Faintly, I hear Dan's apologetic voice. His car broke down? No bars on his cell? Can he use the phone? He wrote the license plate number on the birthday wrapping.

Then, lots of other voices; all shouting. Thumping. Firing. "Show us your hands!"

Aldagon eyes looked like nails driven into his face. He yanks me out of the room, toward the back door, gun to my neck. "Okay, shithead. Move your ass."

I stumble and he pulls me up. We're face to face and it comes to me to kick him in the shin, just like Alan Ladd in The Glass Key. He yelps and automatically grabs for his leg.

Behind me, Dan yells, "Scotty, get down."

There's no way of knowing how many lives were saved that day. The Foundationers planned to set off several explosive devices at the packed football stadium, but they were stopped.

And with only one casualty.

"You do the best you can," Dan told me from his bed at the hospital. "And if things don't work out, you let them go." And then it was time for Dan to let go.

When I'm back out on trail again, I won't be alone. There'll be two yapping dogs with me, sniffing and searching forever for the Old Cop.

Ever enticing New Orleans is next on our itinerary. She's a city ancient and scarred by life, but as this story shows she's still a demmed fine woman.

After a career in interior design, Ms Hamilton is now engaged in writing stories and novels featuring Lizzie Christopher, an interior designer with a penchant for mysteries.

The Bride Word Gold
A New Orleans Wedding

By Margaret S. Hamilton

"Look, there's the streetcar, over there."

Nick grabbed Lizzie's hand as they dashed across Canal Street, and elbowed their way on a crowded St. Charles streetcar. They settled in a mahogany seat; Lizzie stroked the old brass fittings, then hung out the window with her camera, anxious to see everything.

"We take this all the way to your friend's house?" she asked, as the bell clanged and the streetcar rumbled forward.

"That's right, through the business district and down St. Charles Avenue. They live a few blocks from the streetcar line."

They passed restaurants and hotels, and then grand historic homes in pristine condition behind wrought iron fences. The live oak branches formed a tunnel overhead. "Look, I see Mardi Gras beads in the trees." Lizzie laughed.

"St. Charles is one of the parade routes. The beads hang in the trees all year."

Nick pulled the passenger signal cord; they exited the streetcar at the next stop, and walked down a side street. The sidewalks were buckled by tree roots, the gardens in lush bloom with crepe myrtle trees, flowering vines, and perennials. They approached a white house with a raised porch supported by columns, tall windows hung with lace curtains. Nick steered her up the driveway, through a gate, and into the backyard.

Plywood table tops mounted on sawhorses filled the patio, next to a huge pot sitting on an outdoor propane cooker. Coolers and washtubs filled with iced beer lined one side. Jazz blared from outdoor speakers.

Nick waved to a man holding an Abita beer and wearing a tee shirt emblazoned with "Bobby's Crawfish Boil,". "Hey Blue," Nick called, "We're here."

Blue wrapped his free arm around Nick. "Dog, it's about time you showed your sorry face in my city. How long's it been?"

"Since your wedding."

Lizzie stepped to one side and smiled. She and Nick, both widowed, were newly married. Nick had planned their honeymoon trip to include attending Bobby's son's wedding. Bobby enveloped her in a huge hug. "So you're the bride. Dog's a lucky guy."

"Dog? Blue? Maybe I shouldn't ask."

Nick laughed. "Blue and I were college roommates. He came north on an athletic scholarship, but preferred chasing girls and going the pre-med route to playing football. He never stopped talking about his blue tick coonhound, so I called him Blue. And he called me Dog because if he couldn't have his coonhound with him, he had me."

"That's right," Bobby said. "Coonhounds are intelligent, tenacious, and loyal, just like Dog." He whistled, and a black and white spotted dog ambled over and nosed Nick and Lizzie. "This here's Benny. He's a good boy." Blue massaged the dog's head and ears, then shooed him off. "Let's find Charlotte. She's been going steady with the bridesmaids all day and needs some adult conversation. Our sons helped me set up."

"It looks wonderful," Lizzie said. "I've never been to a crawfish boil."

Blue put his arm around her. "You're in for a real treat. And it's just family tonight, with Bubba's bride, Ceci, and her folks. They're real nice people; after five boys, Charlotte's excited to have a daughter-in-law."

Charlotte was an exquisite blond, groomed to perfection, wearing a simple lavender flowered cotton shift and sandals. "Lizzie, we're so happy that you and Dog could come to Bubba's wedding." Nick and Bobby faded away. She took Lizzie aside. "He's a quiet one, Dog is, but with a big heart. You can't go wrong with him."

Lizzie smiled. "He's a keeper, and I'm not going anywhere in life without him."

"That's good, Sugar. Now come with me. We've got a problem on our hands, and I suspect you might be just the person to solve it."

"Charlotte, you have a lovely home. It can't be about decorating." Lizzie managed an interior design shop in her small Ohio town.

"No, we got the place all cleaned and painted up for the wedding. Bubba's the first; I imagine we'll have more weddings in the next few years."

Charlotte guided her to a wrought-iron settee on the screened porch, cool under whirling ceiling fans. "We can have a quiet word right here." She poured Lizzie an iced tea, garnished with lemon and fresh mint.

"Something to do with the bridesmaids? Bobby mentioned that you spent the day with them."

Charlotte sighed as she pulled a brown manila envelope out of a magazine. "Bubba's bride got this in the mail today." She handed it to Lizzie.

The envelope contained a large color photo, produced on a computer printer. A young woman, her naked body covered in sinuous snake tattoos, her dark hair pulled in a bun, lay on top of a young man. The woman had a small blue fleur de lis tattoo on the nape of her neck. Only the man's curly brown hair showed in the photo, and one hairy arm.

Lizzie looked at Charlotte. "Is this Bubba and Ceci?"

"No, definitely not. Ceci doesn't have one tattoo on her beautiful body. Bubba swears it's not him in the photo. Besides, he's got fair skin and blond hair. I know my son, and this isn't him."

"No harm done. If it's not the bride or groom, who is it?"

"We think it's a girl Bubba knew growing up. Jewel. A nice girl despite her trashy name."

"And why would Jewel send a photo of her naked body to the bride?"

"That's what we don't understand," Charlotte exclaimed. "Bobby said you're a detective, solving all kinds of murders in your little town. I thought you might be able to solve this mystery."

Lizzie shook her head. "It appears to be a prank." She took a close look at the photo. "I'm not knowledgeable about digital editing, but I suspect this photo has been altered, maybe even by adding the male body." She sipped her tea, thinking. "Does Ceci feel threatened in some way?"

"She does. Ceci's just a bundle of nerves right now, especially with her food allergies. The bridesmaids aren't being as supportive as she would like; one of them, in particular, has been downright nasty. That Gabby, she's just a monster, consumed with jealousy that Ceci is marrying Bubba."

"What's on the schedule for tomorrow? Perhaps Ceci and Bubba could spend a quiet day together."

"Friends and relatives are pouring into town, with the rehearsal dinner tomorrow night. You and Dog will attend, won't you?" Charlotte was anxious and fretful.

"We'd be delighted to attend. I brought an extra dress, just in case."

"If you don't mind." Charlotte bit her lip. "No, that's a lot to ask."

"We're happy to help."

"Could you keep an eye on Ceci tomorrow? She and Bubba plan to spend the afternoon around the pool at the hotel. Then we'll walk over to the wedding venue for the rehearsal, before we get cleaned up for dinner."

"That's fine. Nick and I have plans for the morning. We could come over to the wedding hotel afterwards, and stay until everybody leaves for the rehearsal."

"Could you? That would relieve my mind so much. I'll be spending tomorrow dealing with the grandparents, and making sure the boys don't get too rowdy."

"Of course." Lizzie stood up and stretched. "I see corn and onions going in the pot. When will Bobby cook the crawfish?"

"First the potatoes, then the other vegetables. He puts them in coolers to keep warm while the crawfish cooks. He steams the crawfish in the ice chests for five minutes at the very end."

Charlotte picked up the iced tea tray. "I see Ceci and her parents have arrived. Why don't I introduce you and let her know you'll be keeping an eye on things tomorrow."

———◆———

Bobby and his sons set up folding chairs around the tables, and spread layers of newspaper on the plywood tops. He cooked sixty pounds of crawfish in batches, allowing each batch time to absorb extra seasoning before a final steaming. The boys dumped mounds of hot crawfish on the tables, passing platters of corn, mushrooms, and potatoes. Bobby gave Lizzie step-by-step instructions how to separate the tail from the head of each crawfish, then pull the meat from the shell. Dipping sauce was optional. Lizzie ate her first crawfish and gasped, gulping a glass of water. Bobby laughed in delight. "That's my secret seasoning. It really grabs you."

Darkness fell, the boys lit twinkling lights in the trees, and the music played on. Nick hugged Lizzie. "Happy?"

"Very happy. What a wonderful evening." She paused. "Just thinking about everything Charlotte told me. We have a date poolside tomorrow afternoon. Ceci feels the need for backup."

———◆———

Lizzie and Nick enjoyed a swim, then sat reading by the pool under an umbrella. Bobby's siblings remembered Nick and came by to visit. Lizzie hid behind over-sized dark glasses, under a sun hat, able to keep an ear tuned to the bridesmaids' idle chatter while pretending to focus on her magazine.

"Gabby, just get over it. Bubba's marrying Ceci. They've been together, more or less, since freshman year. Just because you got your claws into him when Ceci was out of town doesn't mean he belongs to you."

Gabby was trouble. Lizzie knew her kind: a toned, perfect body poised for the hunt, with a tanning bed tan and long red talons on her predatory hands. Her curly hair was cropped very short, her ear lobes studded with multiple piercings. Her skin would resemble alligator hide by the time she hit forty.

"I'm determined to get Bubba back. Ceci's a wimp. All she can think about is babies." Gabby snarled.

"In your dreams, girl. Be nice, paste on a smile, and get through the wedding. Ceci enjoys her teaching career, and isn't about to quit."

Gabby produced an evil smile. "I still have a surprise for Bubba and Ceci."

Lizzie looked at her magazine and sighed. Gabby was out to sabotage the wedding. Lizzie and Nick would be on protection detail until it was over. She still didn't know the identity of the tattooed woman in the photograph. Lizzie carefully checked the assembled young women draped around the pool. A few had subtle tattoos, but none had full-blown body art.

Lizzie explained her suspicions about Gabby to Charlotte at the rehearsal dinner. She and Nick would eat at the same table with Gabby that evening. Gabby didn't have an escort for the wedding, so Bobby's brothers were taking turns. "Nobody likes her," said Charlotte. "I don't understand why on earth Ceci included her in the wedding."

"Were they sorority sisters?" Lizzie asked.

Charlotte nodded.

"Have a chat with your boys before the party ends. I'm sure the young people will spend the rest of the night carousing in the Quarter. Nick and I need a good night's sleep."

On wedding day morning, Bobby rounded up his sons and Nick, and went for a long run along the river. Lizzie would be spending the day with Charlotte, Ceci's mother, and the bridesmaids, having her hair and makeup done. She assembled a stack of magazines, put on a button-down shirt and shorts, and reported to the bride's suite with freshly washed hair.

Ceci's sister, Lucy, cornered Lizzie on the balcony, closing the sliding glass door behind them. "Are you guarding Ceci?"

"Charlotte asked me to keep an eye on things. The photo of the tattooed woman upset her, as I'm sure it did Ceci."

Lucy nodded. "Ceci was shocked, but anybody could tell it was a fake." She grasped the balcony railing. "What's up with Gabby? Is she just being what my grandma would call a 'pill', or is she determined to sabotage the wedding?"

"I don't know. She's in a snit; she and Bubba had a fling a few years ago."

Lucy laughed. "They all had a fling with Bubba, passing him around the sorority like prime meat. By junior year, Bubba and Ceci were committed to each other, and they've been together ever since."

"What about you, Lucy? No competition from a younger sister?"

"I went out-of-state for college and didn't bother with a sorority. When I spend time with the bridesmaids, I realize what a smart decision I made."

"Any other suspects?"

"I'm keeping an eye out," Lucy said. "Thanks for helping us."

Lizzie's sewing skills were needed; she had a kit and scissors ready to snip off tags and labels, and stitch up rips and tears. Gabby refused to have her short hair styled, and requested what Lizzie considered stage makeup. Her ears were studded with a line of small pearls, diamond stars glittering in her earlobes. She spent the entire day checking her cell phone for text messages, growing angrier with every hour.

Nick and Bobby spent the day keeping a lid on the groomsmen; they left the hotel on foot ten minutes before the bride swept through the lobby, on her way to an air-conditioned limo. Lizzie tagged along with the other mothers. Despite Gabby's disgruntled disposition, everything seemed fine, the bridesmaids laughing as they posed for selfies.

Charlotte escorted Lizzie inside a brick nineteenth century warehouse, refurbished as a wedding venue. The ceiling fans whirled, round tables filled the space, decorated with tall glass vases spilling gold and purple flowers, combined with greenery to complete the Mardi Gras- themed arrangements. "Bubba and Ceci met during Carnival freshman year; Ceci celebrated their meeting with her wedding colors. She ordered commemorative strings of beads for the wedding guests."

"Now I understand," Lizzie exclaimed. "I didn't want to ask in front of the bridesmaids. The girls look lovely, and so do you." Charlotte wore pale lavender silk chiffon with a wrist corsage of orchids, and pearl drop earrings. Cool, immaculate, and chic.

She guided Lizzie to a table, the grandmothers dressed in pale pink and the grandfathers in black suits with neckties striped in Mardi Gras colors. They welcomed Lizzie, who admitted that she was giving her own bright blue wedding dress a second wearing, and showed off Nick's mother's sapphire ring. Bobby's mother remembered Nick with great fondness. "For a Yankee gal, you've done well for yourself. And there's nothing like a Louisiana honeymoon," she said with satisfaction.

Lizzie smiled, then excused herself for a quick visit to the restroom. "Don't wander off," Bobby's mother warned. "You two will be with us for the ceremony and reception. Dog's part of my family, and so are you."

The catering crew filled the restroom. They cleared a corner for Lizzie, who dabbed her face with a paper towel and touched up her lipstick.

"Hey, Jewel, how're you dealing with lover boy getting married?"

A tall, skinny, brunette stood in front of the sink, applying layers of mascara. Her hands and lower arms were covered with tattoos. Lizzie assumed her server's uniform covered most of her body art;

she wore black slacks. She pulled her long dark hair into a bun; Lizzie recognized her fleur de lis tattoo. Jewel frowned as she stuffed the mascara tube in her bag. "He's marrying his college honey. I hope she's worth it. All work and no play make Bubba a very horny guy." She smirked. "And that's what Jewel knows how to fix." She rolled her sleeves down and buttoned the cuffs. "Me and my magic tats get Bubba every time."

"Not your magic titties?" giggled one of the servers. Several of them laughed. Jewel glanced down at her flat chest and sighed. "I'll get back at the bride, don't you worry."

The catering supervisor edged her way into the restroom. "Listen up, I've got the final shift roster here. Most of you will be serving and cleaning up. Jewel, I need you in the back, unloading the catering vans and assembling food. And stay out of this restroom. You all use the one near the kitchen." The supervisor nodded to Lizzie, and shooed the girls out.

It sounds like Bubba had himself a fling while he was wooing Ceci, Lizzie thought. I wonder if Jewel's a sorority sister, too. She was sure Jewel was the tattooed woman in the photo; the tattoo on the nape of her neck matched the one in the photo. She threw a paper towel in the bin, noticing two empty bags of ground almonds. That's odd. Why would food trash be in this restroom? She grabbed the empty bags with a fresh paper towel, and stuffed them in her shoe bag. Lizzie checked the straps on her dancing shoes; Charlotte had told her to bring comfortable walking sandals for the end of the reception. She had no idea why. New Orleans certainly had its own unique wedding traditions.

Nick joined Lizzie as the grandparents negotiated the steps and lined up at the edge to the courtyard. The massive fountain was shut off; an electric violinist and drummer played jazz. The crowd found seats, humming and tapping their feet. Women waved fans in the late afternoon heat.

"Shouldn't we grab two seats?" Lizzie asked.

"Girl, you're kin, so you're with us," whispered one of the grand-mothers.

Lizzie smiled her thanks and held Nick's arm.

She enjoyed an unobstructed view of the wedding procession from an aisle seat. The bridesmaids wore solid purple or green dresses, their bouquets matching the reception flowers. The bride wore gold, embellished with purple and green beading, and carried a bouquet of purple flowers and peacock feathers. Ceci was radiant, her skin tanned to perfection, her dark hair pulled into a low bun. She glowed in a shaft of sunlight. The grandmothers were abuzz about her gown. In Lizzie's opinion, Bubba's smile as he greeted his bride told the whole story. Lizzie squeezed Nick's hand and dabbed her eyes.

"It's like getting married all over again," he murmured.

Lizzie kept an eye on the bridesmaids as the readings were intoned, vows stated, and rings exchanged. Gabby glowered, her face a thun-dercloud. The bride and groom were pronounced husband and wife, as the big fountain burst into full rushing flow. The music resumed, and the courtyard filled with happy conversation. Ceci and Bubba led the recessional, with the bridesmaids and groomsmen bunched behind them.

Gabby grabbed the arm of a young man with long hair tied back in a ponytail, wearing jeans with a purple shirt and Mardi Gras striped tie. "There you are. I didn't see you. Let's give the bride a big surprise."

She dragged the purple shirt by his necktie through the throng, elbowing her way to Ceci and Bubba. "My date finally turned up. He's a big fan of yours, Ceci."

Ceci looked at the guy, gasped, and crumpled on the ground. Bubba shouted, "Give her some air."

Lizzie grabbed Nick's hand and plunged into the crowd. Nick knelt down, checking Ceci's pulse. "She fainted, possibly from dehy-dration. Let's get her inside and cooled off." Bubba and Nick carried her inside and laid her on a couch in the manager's office. The bartender gave Lizzie paper towels and bottles of cold water. She gently dabbed Ceci's forehead, trying not to disturb her makeup.

"Bubba, does Ceci know the man in the purple shirt?" Lizzie asked.

"She sure does." He held Ceci's hand, caressing her cheek. "That's the guy who tried to assault her freshman year. He drugged her with rohypnol at a frat party. She was afraid to report it in case her parents found out and made her live at home."

"Did her sorority sisters know this?"

"Probably. No secrets between those girls."

"And do you suspect that Gabby invited him to the wedding, without informing Ceci's parents?"

"For sure," said Bubba. "Mama would have flagged the name if she'd seen it on the guest list. Gabby didn't have a plus one."

"We'll escort him off the premises," Lizzie said. "I guess we're stuck with Gabby for the reception. Any chance we can ask her to leave?"

Ceci's eyelids fluttered and she sat up. "No, Gabby... she needs to explain." She sipped her water. "Gabby tried to ruin my wedding by bringing that guy. I want to know why."

Lizzie handed her a paper towel, speaking in soothing, gentle tones. "Ceci, Bubba is your husband. Hold his hand, and you'll get through this. No one out there knows what happened. Just say it was dehydration and stay out of the heat. You're going to be fine. This is your day to shine."

Lizzie was angry. How dare Gabby do this at Ceci's wedding? She asked the manager to stand guard outside his office, giving the bride time to recover. She took Nick's hand. "Come on, let's get rid of the guy and Gabby too. Her behavior is unforgiveable."

She found Gabby in the crowd and grabbed her arm in a vise grip. "You owe Ceci and Bubba an apology. You can do it right now, and then you and your pal in the purple shirt can leave. The stunt you pulled is hateful and cruel."

Gabby burst into tears. "It's just a joke, I swear."

"Not the right answer." Lizzie grabbed Gabby's shoulders, and spoke, face to face. "Apologize, then leave. Now." She spit each word with machine-gun precision.

Nick spotted the guy at the outdoor bar. He walked up behind him, spoke in his ear, then pushed him towards the sidewalk gate, waving down a security guard.

Lizzie marched Gabby into the manager's office. She poked her in the back. "Speak your piece, young lady."

"Ceci, I… I don't know what I was thinking. I'm so sorry. Please forgive me for being so cruel and thoughtless."

Ceci took a swig of water. "I'm not in a forgiving mood. It's time for you to say goodbye."

Lizzie pulled Gabby back down the stairs and through the court-yard to the gate. "This bridesmaid is leaving," she told the security guard, "and not returning."

He nodded, and opened the gate, ushering her through.

Ceci's sister, Lucy, approached Lizzie. "Nice work. Don't worry, I've got the other girls doing damage control. Ceci fainted in the heat and needed to be inside where it's cool."

Lizzie hugged her. "Thanks for your help. The girl in the photo with the snake tattoos is working on the catering crew. I saw her in the restroom before the ceremony. I'm still keeping an eye on things. It's too much of a coincidence that she's working at this wedding."

Lizzie skirted the outdoor bar area, and glanced down the cobble-stone alley. Jewel stood next to a catering van, smoking a cigarette and glaring at the world. Lizzie wondered what mischief she had planned.

Many of Bobby's relatives remembered Nick, and were delighted to meet Lizzie. The reception proceeded on schedule, with a buffet line serving the best of New Orleans cuisine: gumbo, crawfish cakes, a mix of seafood, chicken with pasta, mango pork loins, and several kinds of potatoes. The guests swarmed the specialty food bar, ordering grits in combination with everything from shrimp and andouille to asparagus and a variety of cheeses.

Nick and Lizzie danced to a medley of music, from rock and roll to jazz tunes, then escaped to the courtyard for a breather. The grandparents joined them, laughing as they told stories of their own weddings. "There will be wedding cake," one of the grandmothers said. "But first, we're going to have some New Orleans bourbon bread pudding." She smacked her lips in anticipation.

Lizzie saw Jewel haul trays of desserts to serving tables, each goblet of bread pudding garnished with a mound of whipped cream and drizzled with bourbon sauce. Her mind flashed back to the empty bags of nuts in the restroom trash.

"Are ground almonds an ingredient in the bread pudding?" Lizzie asked.

"I hope not," said one of the grandmothers. "Ceci has a serious tree nut allergy. One swallow and she'll go into anaphylactic shock. Her mother told the catering crew months ago."

Lizzie jumped up. "Nick, we'll have to find Ceci and warn her not to eat anything, especially the bread pudding. After the catering crew cleared out of the restroom, I found empty bags of ground almonds in the trashcan. Hurry, somebody's still out to get her."

The bride and groom appeared at the top of the stairs, leaving the dance floor to enjoy their dessert in the courtyard. Nick and Lizzie raced over and explained the situation. Bubba turned white, then put his arm around Ceci, murmuring in her ear. Nick told the catering manager to put aside the two goblets of bread pudding decorated for the bride and groom, then call the police. Lizzie grabbed his hand, and pulled him towards the food preparation area. They watched Jewel prepare the last of the bread pudding goblets, then pick up a pair of rubber gloves and a trash bag. Jewel slipped behind the DJ at the edge of the dance floor, Lizzie and Nick following her. She knocked on the women's restroom door, calling out "Cleaning crew. Coming in."

Jewel waited for a group of guests to leave, then entered, Lizzie and Nick right behind her. Jewel snapped on the rubber gloves and dove into the trash cans, throwing used paper towels on the floor.

"Looking for something?" Lizzie asked. She crossed her arms and glared.

"Butt out and go away. Mind your own business."

"The bride's health is my business. Don't bother looking for the empty ground almond bags. I have them, ready to hand over to the police."

Jewel screamed in rage before charging towards the door. Lizzie stepped to one side, tripped her, then planted her foot on Jewel's back. "Are the police here yet?" Nick opened the door and motioned an officer into the restroom.

The police officer cuffed Jewel and pulled her up. "Time to take a ride down to the station, Sweet Cakes."

"I didn't do anything. I'm part of the catering crew." She wailed.

"You've been doing food preparation all evening," Lizzie said. "The bride has a life-threatening allergy to tree nuts; I found the empty bags of ground almonds in the trash when you and your crew were shooed out of the restroom."

"It wasn't me," she screamed, stamping her feet.

"The rest of the crew were servers, and you were assigned to food prep. I saw you decorating the bread puddings. The only reason you're here is to find the empty ground almond bags and cover your tracks. The catering crew isn't responsible for cleaning the restrooms."

Jewel, enraged, tried to kick Lizzie. She backed out of the restroom and joined Nick, breathing heavily.

"Come on, let's get you outside," Nick said.

"Did Ceci eat anything tonight?" Lizzie gasped.

Nick shook his head. "Thankfully not. Her grandmothers fed her some eggs and toast this afternoon. Her dress is so tight she was afraid to eat. All she's had is water, from a sealed bottle."

Lizzie sighed with relief. "We have no idea if the wedding cake or anything else is contaminated." She headed for the bride's changing room. "Come on, we have to make sure Ceci's going-away outfit isn't sabotaged."

Lizzie met Ceci's mother and sister in the changing room, intent on the same mission. They carefully pulled the short white lace dress out of a garment bag and shook it out. "It looks all right," Lizzie said with relief, checking that the zipper worked.

The door opened, and Samantha, one of the bridesmaids, entered, carrying two large fringed umbrellas, one black and one white, with ribbons in Mardi Gras colors twined around the handles.

"What are you doing in here?" asked Lizzie. "What are those umbrellas?"

"Those are for the Second Line parade at the end of the reception," Lucy said. "Let's see if they're damaged."

"Bad luck opening them inside," Lizzie said.

"Worse luck finding out they're ruined." Lucy replied. The umbrellas were in shreds. Samantha bolted for the door. Nick blocked her exit.

The policeman entered, escorting Jewel. "The patrol car is delayed, so we'll wait in here."

Jewel looked at Samantha and screamed. "It's all your fault. You've gotten me into a heap of trouble, and I'm telling the police everything."

Samantha shrieked, "Just shut up and don't say anything. They've got no proof."

Lizzie pulled the edited photo out of her bag. "Recognize anyone in this photo? You did a sloppy job. It's obvious that's not Bubba in the photo. He's blond." She looked at Samantha. "You've had it out for Ceci all along, haven't you? The silent sorority sister. Did you hire Jewel to contaminate the reception food with ground almonds, knowing that Ceci would have a severe allergic reaction?"

Samantha's face turned red. "It was always about Ceci. Perfect little Ceci. Bubba told me I was his woman, and then Ceci wormed her way into his heart. Bubba belongs to me, not her."

"Bubba and Ceci made up their own minds," Nick said. "And now they're married, and you're on your way to the police station to be charged."

Jewel wailed. "She paid me a hundred bucks. All I had to do was sprinkle the ground almonds in the bride's bread pudding. Honest. I didn't mean any harm. She didn't tell me the bride was allergic to nuts."

A police officer knocked on the door, entered, and had a short conversation with his fellow officer. He cuffed Samantha, and the two officers led the culprits away.

"Ceci's safe now. What a relief. But what are we going to do about the umbrellas?" Ceci's mother asked.

"I always have a spare pair in my van," the wedding planner announced from the doorway. "I'll put the decorative ribbons on them, and we'll get Ceci in here and changed for the Second Line. The band is due in thirty minutes."

Nick escorted Lizzie out to the courtyard, where the grannies waited in anticipation, anxious to hear every word. Lizzie drank a sealed bottle of cold water and gave them a detailed version of the evening's events as she changed into flat sandals. Nothing, she was amazed to learn, got past the grannies.

"Did you see Ceci's diamond butterfly earrings?" one of the grandmothers asked.

"I did, they're lovely."

"At one time Ceci wanted a little butterfly tattoo on her ankle. Bubba loathes tattoos, so he bought her a pair of beautiful earrings instead."

Bubba and Ceci appeared with their fringed umbrellas. They posed for photos with their grandparents, then Lizzie and Nick. "Dog, you're a good friend to our family," Bubba said, hugging him. "And that goes for you too, Miss Lizzie." They handed the umbrellas to Lizzie and Nick. "Let's get a photo of you newlyweds with the umbrellas."

Lizzie and Nick laughed and posed, then said good-bye to the grandparents.

"Don't forget your white hankies," one of the grannies cautioned.

"Hankies?" Lizzie asked. "To mop up our sweat and tears?"

"Neither, girl, to wave in the parade. Laissez les bons temps rouler." The grannies laughed as they shook their wedding beads.

Lizzie and Nick joined the parade behind the jazz band. They held hands and danced through the Quarter, waving their hankies.

Sin City itself, Las Vegas, draws us next, where fate is about to deal a tricky hand to a Thomas Gavel, on vacation with his family. Thomas is a bright young fellow, an expert at programming computers, and an avid poker player. Has he the skill to play in a far more deadly game?

The verisimilitude Mr. Terlecki brings to his writing is informed by over two decades of experience in the filed of developing video games.

Mess with the Bull, Get the Horn

By Michael Terlecki

My name is Thomas Gavel. I graduated from Stanford University at age twenty four with a Master's degree in Computer Science. I landed a job with "Big Slot Games"(BSG) as a software engineer making a six figure income. BSG is the world's largest manufacturer of slot machine games and it was my dream job. I married my college sweetheart Brittany, bought a brand new home outside of Sunnyvale, Ca. and have two wonderful children, Thomas Jr., four and Jessica, two.

Sounds like the perfect life, right? Well, three days ago I would have agreed with you. But, I'm sitting in an "interview" room of the Las Vegas Nevada police station, waiting for my second meeting of the day with a homicide detective. It seems I am a suspect in the possible murder of a local businessman, and according to the police, that is the least of my problems.

The 'businessman' in question was Guerrino Bianchi. A Las Vegas businessman with an Italian surname. I think you get the picture. Not only do the cops suspect I was involved with this man's death, they tell me he was connected to the Milano crime family.

"Do you know what they will do to you Mr. Gavel?" The detective said.

He went on to describe a ridiculous scenario in which Bianchi was blackmailing me for secrets about slot machine software. Then he offered me witness protection in exchange for my testimony against Bianchi's associates.

"It's the only way to ensure your family's safety." He said.

So, how did I get into this mess? I keep asking myself the same question. The simple answer is, I didn't. I mean I didn't go looking for trouble, it found me… Okay, I admit it, I may have made a few small errors in judgement along the way.

It started eight months ago when I decided to take a family vacation—to Las Vegas. Las Vegas was not our final stop, it was only one along the way. SeaWorld, Disneyland, Knott's Berry Farm and Universal Studios were our real destinations. We were doing the whole Southern California tour.

I had a good reason to stop in Vegas first as it's our company headquarters. By stopping here and attending a few staff meetings, I was able to write off part of the trip. With the money I saved, we were able to add Magic Mountain to our itinerary. The kids were thrilled.

In hindsight, Las Vegas was a horrible decision. My plan to save a few bucks had dire consequences.

We arrived on a Sunday afternoon and checked into the hotel. Our room was located on the fourth floor and the path from the front desk to the elevators took us past the casino. A giant Blazing Cherry slot machine, over eight feet tall and five feet wide stood near the entrance. I knew the machine well, since I had written the software.

The spin lever alone was three feet tall and looked like a colossal pink lollipop. At least that's what my children shouted as they broke free of our grasp and darted towards the machine.

"Daddy, daddy, can we spin the wheel, please!" They both yelled.

To the casual observer this may have been an adorable sight, but hotel security had a different opinion. Aside from the fact that children were not allowed in the casino, as an employee of BSG, I was prohibited from playing the machine. The company had strict rules and regulations about employees gambling on company made machines. If I won a huge jackpot and word got out that I was the one who programmed the machine, all hell would break loose. There would be cries of foul play and possibly a Gaming Commission investigation. It could shut a casino down for days and cost millions of dollars in lost revenue, not to mention the negative press and possibly my job.

Two burley men hustled over. They were easily over six foot two and loomed over me.

"I'm sorry Mr. Gavel, but children are not allowed on the casino floor. I'm going to have to ask you to leave immediately."

They were polite, but firm. It did not strike me as odd that the man knew my name, but it should have.

Strike One.

After dinner, we arranged for an in-room babysitter and Brittany and I headed down to the casino. My wife loves the one-armed bandits where I prefer games of skill. I reminded her which machines were off limits, company rules included immediate family members, and headed off in search of the poker room.

I am a regular at our local Native American Casinos, but this was my first time playing poker in Las Vegas and I did surprisingly well. Up three hundred dollars, I decided to call it a night. I found my wife donating her last twenty to a machine just outside the poker room. Combined, we were a hundred dollars ahead. Not bad for the first night.

After a day of me attending meetings and Brittany entertaining the kids at the pool, we made our way back to the casino. I was disappointed to find a private tournament in progress and no tables available, so I decided to play some black jack.

I was stopped on my way out of the poker room by a large man in a dark blue suit and tie. He looked to be part of the hotel staff and said that if I really wanted to play poker, he could arrange for me to join an offsite, private game. I asked what he meant by offsite and he pointed at the ceiling, indicating a room on one of the upper floors. I agreed.

Strike Two.

I told Brittany about the private game, gave her the room number and said I would be back in a couple hours.

I was escorted to a luxury suite on the fifth floor. The furniture had been removed and replaced with four poker tables. The dealers all wore black tuxedos, as did the bartender. A voluptuous blonde in a tight-fitting, gold-sequined dress, delivered drinks to the tables. Every table was full. The murmur of small talk and the sound of poker chips clacking filled the room. I stood and admired the opulence, wondering what I had done to deserve an invitation to such a prestigious event.

A tall, thin man with dark, slicked back hair and chiseled features approached. He also wore a tuxedo and spoke with a heavy New York accent. He introduced himself as Tony and said he was my host for the evening. He offered me a drink, explained the rules of the game and seated me at one of the tables.

The game was Texas hold'em, no-limit, twenty dollar ante. I had seen no-limit games on television, but I had never played in one. The pots could get very big and I was more than a little nervous. I only had a bankroll of three hundred dollars, but since the ante was twenty dollars, I could afford to look at a few hands.

An hour later my bankroll had swelled to $2000 and I was feeling pretty good about holding my own against these skilled players. I decided to celebrate with a cocktail.

Strike Three.

I can't say for sure what was in that drink, but shortly after finishing it, my analytical skills, along with my inhibitions went right out the window. In hindsight, it wasn't the only thing working against me.

I was dealt pocket aces and when a third ace came up on the flop along with a jack and a five, I was sitting pretty. Three of a kind was a good hand, but not great. When a second jack came up on the turn, my hand went from good to great. I had a full house, Aces over Jacks. There was a strong possibility somebody else was holding a jack, giving them 3-of-a-kind and probably feeling pretty damn good about their hand. Even if someone was holding a pair, two pair could not beat my full house.

I should mention, that when Tony seated me at the table he handed me five markers, each worth $10,000, for a total of $50,000 in house credit. I tried to give them back, insisting I would never use them since I couldn't afford it. Tony was equally insistent that I hang on to them. He said, "You never know."

Well, it turns out he did know. When I calculated my chances of winning at well over ninety percent—I went all-in. Not only did push my entire bankroll into the pot, I tossed in four of the markers as well. I had over forty thousand dollars riding on that one hand. I was shocked when two other players called my bet. The total pot was over $120,000. It was an incredible amount of money and I took a deep breath to calm nerves. Was I really playing in such an enormous hand?

The deal announced betting was over, the pot was right and dealt the river. It was the five of hearts. Two pair were now showing on the board, jacks and fives. The card didn't help or hurt my hand, but there was now a very good chance one of the other players had a full house as well. It didn't matter, there was no way their top three cards could beat my three Aces. My heart pounded in my chest so loud, I thought the other players could hear it. I was about to win a year's salary in one hand.

The dealer called for me to show my hand. I flipped over my cards and proudly announced. "Full house. Aces over jacks."

The player to my left cried, "Shit!", and tossed his cards face down into the center of the table.

There was one player left and only two possible hands that could beat me. If the law of statistics held true, I was about to walk away with the biggest win of my life.

"Come on buddy, let's see what you got." I said to myself.

The man cocked his head to one side, looked at me and smiled. "Sorry pal." He flipped over his cards and revealed a pair of jacks.

"No, no way!" I thought to myself. "This is unbelievable!" The son-of-a-bitch had four of a kind.

My stomach fell so hard, I nearly messed my pants. I stared in disbelief. How could this happen? What were the odds? Not only had I lost the pot and all my money, but I lost forty thousand dollars that wasn't even mine. Money I would need to pay back. Money I didn't have.

***

My guts churned and I thought I was going to throw up all over the table.

Tony walked over, placed a hand on my shoulder and nonchalantly said. "Tough break Mr. Gavel. What are the odds of that?"

He didn't need to tell me. I knew exactly what the odds were. Incredibly high-too high. The smug look on his face and the irony in his voice told me what I already knew. I was more than a victim of odds. I had been set up.

"Look at the bright side Mr. Gavel."

Bright side? What bright side? There was no bright side. And when my wife found out, it was going to get a whole lot darker.

"You still have one more marker and a chance to win your money back."

I had just been ripped off for forty thousand dollars, there was no way in hell I was going to give him a chance to make it fifty.

My knees wobbled as I stood up and said, "No thank you". I turned for the door, but before I took my first step, the large man who had escorted me up to the room stepped in front of me.

"Not so fast Mr. Gavel," Tony said. "There is a small piece of business we must take care of first."

***

He led me across the suite and through a set of double doors into a large office where a short, powerfully built man in his mid to late forties, wearing an expensive three-piece suit sat behind a desk. His hair was short and dark, which matched his eyes. He had a ruddy complexion and a nose that changed direction more than once.

"This is Mr. Bianchi," Tony said. "He will help you arrange a payment plan."

The man behind the desk flicked his head and Tony disappeared, closing the doors behind him. Bianchi motioned for me to sit. There was a single chair in front of his desk and I did as he asked. He leaned forward, placed his elbows on the desk and clasped his hands together. His arms were like small tree trunks. I thought the seams of his jacket were going to split at the shoulders.

"So, Mr. Gavel—Thomas is it? You owe me fifty gees. How you gonna pay me back?"

Fifty? Wait, it was only forty.

His voice was raspy with a thick Jersey accent. I swallowed hard. It felt like a dream, or more precisely, a nightmare. The Godfather theme played in my head. The truth was, I had no idea how I was going to pay him back, but he wasn't the kind of guy who accepted 'I don't know' for an answer.

My voice stammered. "I… I don't know Mr. Bianchi. I need to talk with my wife. I'm sure we can come up with some sort of payment plan."

"Do I look like a freaking bank Mr. Gavel." Only he didn't use the word freaking. "I'm a business man and the loans I make are short term-very short term. And the interest rate, well let's just say you won't like it."

He leaned back in the chair and crossed his arms across his thick chest. "And the penalty for non-payment, Mr. Gavel." He shook his head back and forth. "I don't even want to think about how bad that would be for you and your cute family."

My anger surged as he made the threat, but what could I do? At five ten, a hundred and sixty pounds, I certainly wasn't going to jump over the desk and kick his ass.

"I… I can take a second out on my house. I can pay you back. I promise."

He waved his giant paw like he was swatting away a fly.

"You mean the house you bought for half a million dollars and is now worth three hundred and fifty thousand? No thanks. I told you, I ain't no freaking bank."

How did he know how much I paid for my house? What else did he know about me?

"Here's what we are going to do Mr. Gavel. You are going to work for me."

Work for him?. What kind of work could I do for him? He was an organized crime boss and I was a software engineer

"You make slot machines for BSG and you are going to make me a very special machine. You are going to put one of those Easter Eggs or backdoor things into a game. One that will allow my associates to hit the jackpot whenever. Three or four good jackpots and your debt will be paid."

Technically what Bianchi was asking for wasn't an Easter Egg or a backdoor.

An Easter Egg is an inside joke, or harmless hidden message intentionally placed in a video game by the programmer. They are generally well hidden and difficult to find, hence the name.

A backdoor is some code left in a computer program that allows the original programmer to bypass normal security and gain access. It's like having a spare key to the house you just moved out of.

What Mr. Bianchi was actually asking for, was a cheat code.

Cheat codes are secret passwords left in a game by the programmer and cause the game to do unusual things. It could be as simple as adding an extra life or allowing the player to become invincible.

We use cheat codes all the time while developing our games. They are more like short cuts, so we can trigger a feature whenever we want. Punch in a code and hit the jackpot on the next spin, things like that. Without them, it would be nearly impossible to test a game. The cheat codes are removed before the game is sent to the customer.

I told him it wouldn't be that easy. The software is monitored by my company and thoroughly tested by the Gaming Commission. Even if we were able to get past them, the casinos had computers that kept a running average of every coin put into a machine and every coin paid out. If a machine paid out too much, too fast, the casino would notice and pull it off the floor.

Bianchi slammed his beefy hand on the desk causing me to flinch.

"I don't want to hear freaking excuses Mr. Gavel. You graduated from Stanford. That makes you a pretty smart guy. I'm sure you will figure something out. For your family's sake, I hope so. And as far as the casino's spotting my people winning, you let me worry about that."

I realized anything short of a "Yes sir" was going to get my legs broken or worse. I was about to say exactly that when I heard a beeping sound. It was coming from Bianchi's phone. He silenced the alarm, then opened his desk drawer and took out a prescription bottle. He popped one of the pills and set the bottle on the desk. I glanced at the label. Carbamazepine. The name meant nothing to me.

Bianchi stood up. "I trust we understand each other Mr. Gavel."

"Yes sir."

"Good. Then you are free to go." He waved a hand toward the door. "Go and enjoy the rest of your vacation. You never know how many more opportunities you'll have. Life is short. One of my associates will be in touch. He will monitor your progress."

My knees were still shaky, but I stood up and made a beeline for the door. Just as I got there, he called out to me and I turned around.

"One more thing Mr. Gavel. I have eyes and ears everywhere. So don't even think about going to the authorities. That would be very hazardous to your health. And, should you quit your job or get fired before this debt is paid…" He made a tsk, tsk noise out of the corner of his mouth and shook his head. "That would be very unfortunate."

On the elevator ride down, I evaluated my options. What the hell was I going to do? I could go straight to the police or maybe the FBI. Surely they could protect me. Then I remembered how many news articles and TV shows I had seen about witnesses against the mob. They had a way of disappearing or dying horrible deaths. I had visions of myself sinking to the bottom of San Francisco Bay with a 50 pound block of cement chained to my ankles and my wife and children right behind. Then I wondered if the mob had some code of ethics. They didn't kill woman and children, right?

I decided not to test that theory. My best option was to go along. I would do exactly as he said, at least for now.

———————

I made no mention of my losses or the meeting with Mr. Bianchi to my wife. I did my best to enjoy the rest of our vacation.

As Mr. Bianchi promised, every two weeks, Tony came by to check on me. It didn't take long to realize he had no idea what I was working on, only that it was a personal project for Mr. Bianchi.

I immediately began work on the cheat code. Naturally, I went through the four phases every programmer goes through when presented with a difficult task; Denial, Epiphany, Bargain and White Knight.

Denial. "Can't be done. Not now, not ever. Not by me, not by any programmer."

Epiphany. "I've been thinking about it and I have come up with a solution."

Bargain. "It's difficult, but I can do it. Only it's going to take twice as long as we originally estimated."

White Knight. "I'm done! Not only that, but because I'm a genius, I finished in half the time."

That is exactly what I did. Mr. Bianchi was right, I am a smart guy and I did figure out a solution. But it wasn't the solution he was expecting, or one he was going to like.

Getting my cheat codes past my supervisors and the internal software reviews would be easy. Can you say apathy? The casinos on the other hand, were a different story. Unlike my bosses, who were trying to spot problems before they happened, casinos were experts at spotting them after they did.

Casinos payrolls are filled with mathematicians, analysts and statisticians. They are the first line of defense. I wasn't kidding when I told Mr. Bianchi the casinos monitored every single machine. Those number crunchers knew exactly how much money each machine should pay out. The slightest deviation from the daily average would raise suspicions.

The second level of defense was what I liked to call, the Pinheads. These guys are programmers like me, but they've taken it to a whole new level. These guys graduated magna cum laude from The University of Geek, with a PhD in pattern spotting. They loved nothing more than to spend day after day pouring over slot machine history records analyzing every single spin and finding out what led up to the 'suspect' jackpot. If there was a pattern, and there always was, these guys would find it.

I had to prevent the numbers crunchers from recognizing that a machine was being manipulated. Unfortunately, a big part of not being detected depended on Bianchi and his associates. If they ran into a casino and started milking machines for thousands and thousands of dollars, the gig would be over in a hurry. I had no illusions that Bianchi would be able to control himself and I knew eventually he would get greedy. When he did, the number crunchers would notice. I couldn't control any of that. What had me even more concerned, was what happened after the number crunchers noticed.

If the aforementioned Pinheads were brought in and they identified a pattern, they next thing they would do, was start analyzing the source code. They would dig through my code like ants at a picnic. Looking at every line, trying to determine if the pattern was caused by an honest software bug, or was an inside job. That would spell disaster for me.

The first thing my cheat code needed to do, was to correctly identify that one of Bianchi's associates was sitting at the machine. After all, I didn't want just anybody triggering the cheat. This was usually accomplished by some sort of signal. The associate would need to tell the machine, "Hey, it's me. Time to payoff." Pressing the buttons on the machine in a predefined sequence was one such method. For example, the player would bet one credit, then two, then three, four and five. He might repeat this several times in a row. The software would be looking for this specific pattern and once it spotted it, two things would happen.

First, the machine would notify the player it recognized the pattern. This was usually done by flashing some graphics or playing a specific sound effect. Second, of course, the Jackpot would hit. The biggest drawback to this method was it generated a pattern. The Pinheads would easily recognize that the player pressed a specific set of buttons right before the jackpot paid off and I would be busted. I needed a better way.

The solution I came up with was ingenious. (Phase 2, Epiphany at work.) Instead of the player signaling the machine, I would have the machine signal the player. The easiest way to do this would have been to have the machine stop on a certain set of symbols, for example Cherry, Cherry, Cherry, then Bar, Bar, Bar. There could be many such sequences and the player would need to watch for these sequences to come up in the correct order.

This idea had the same problem I mentioned earlier, it generated a pattern. If the Pinheads evaluated the history file, they would easily find the pattern. I had to find a signal which was not recorded in the history file. All games recorded the amount bet, the symbols that came up and the amount won. What it did not record were incidental things that happened prior to the spin. And this, is what I exploited. My stroke of genius was simple, the only way to prevent a pattern from being detected—was not to generate one.

After two weeks of hard work, I had finished my cheat code. The name of my game was "Snorting Bull". It featured a large, angry looking bull, with a gold ring in its nose. The bull snorted billows of smoke from his nostrils. The smoke was nothing more than fancy special effects and because it played no part in the actual outcome of the game, it was not recorded in the history file.

When a machine was sitting idle or between player spins, it is customary to play animations, sound effects or little graphical movies to entice players. It was during this idle state that my cheat code signaled the player. There were two parts to the signal. The first was the bull snorting smoke, the second was a glint of light that flickered off the tip of the bull's horn. You've probably seen this type of effect in cartoons. It is generally used to show that something was razor sharp, like a knife. In this case, it was the tip of the horn.

Bianchi's associate would need to pay close attention to these special effects and specifically what order they occurred in. I had programmed in a very specific pattern. Left nostril, right nostril, both nostrils, left horn tip, right horn tip and then a loud roar. When this pattern played, the player had exactly two seconds to bet one credit and spin the reels. The next time the pattern occurred, the player had to bet two credits and so on until they reached five credits—the maximum bet on the machine. If the player missed the two-second window or failed to bet the correct amount, the cheat code was cancelled and the whole sequence had to be started over again.

Because these graphic patterns were displayed at completely random intervals, not even I had any idea of when they were going to occur or how many spins it might take. It could take anywhere from two minutes to two hours. That was the brilliance of the scheme—there was no pattern.

Two months later the machine had passed all testing and was approved by the Gaming Commission. The cheat code had gone completely undetected. A few weeks after that, the machine was on casino floors.

I contacted Mr. Bianchi and told him the project was complete. He arranged a meeting at his office in Las Vegas. I asked him to please have one of the "Snorting Bull" machines present so I could show him how the cheat worked. That brings us full circle and back to where I started my story.

I arrived two nights ago and had a meeting scheduled with Mr. Bianchi yesterday morning. Naturally, Tony and his bodyguards were present, but they were asked to wait outside. Bianchi had a "Snorting Bull" machine sitting in his office just as I had requested. I explained the basics of how the cheat code worked. I could tell he was suitably impressed, if not a bit confused.

"Seems pretty freaking complicated Mr. Gavel."

He really liked that word, "freaking".

I agreed the scheme was complex, but told him it had to be that way or we would get caught. I assured him, with a little training and practice, his associates would pick up the signals in no time.

I moved on to a live demonstration. I sat down at the machine and walked him through the sequences. I showed him what each of the signals looked like. First, the smoke from the nostrils, then the tip of the horns flickering. It took a while, but eventually he picked it up. I showed him everything except the final step. I was very careful not to trigger the Jackpot. I needed to make sure he was the one who initiated the final spin.

When I finished my presentation, we swapped seats. He sat down at the machine and I stood behind and watched. It took nearly thirty minutes, but he successfully navigated through the first four sequences. All that was left was the final Jackpot.

My heart pounded as I waited for the secret signal to show itself one last time. They say 13 is an unlucky number. I'm not sure if that's true or not, but for Bianchi, it most certainly was. Exactly 13 spins later, the nostrils snorted, the horns shimmered and the bull roared. Mr. Bianchi increased his bet to five credits and pressed the spin button.

The Jackpot hit, bells went off, the beacon on top of the machine started spinning. The room was bathed in an alternating red and white glow. The strips of light that ran down the sides of the machine pulsated rapidly, keeping perfect time with the fast paced, Spanish Bullfighting music that blared from the Dolby sound system. The word "JACKPOT" appeared on the screen in giant letters and flashed on and off. Fireworks exploded behind it. Chase lights ran around the edges of the winning symbols blinking on and off and changing color from red to blue to yellow then green. It was a total sensory overload.

Within moments Bianchi began to convulse. His shoulders twitched and his head bobbed up and down violently. His whole body shook uncontrollably. Then he lost his balance and listed hard to the left. He toppled off the stool landing hard with a loud thud. It was like watching a giant tree fall. He rolled over on the floor and looked up at me pleading for help. A white frothy substance formed on his lips. He continued writhing on the floor looking like someone who had been hit with a stun gun. While drool oozed from his mouth, he reached an arm out in desperation and grabbed my pant leg. He stretched the other arm up reaching toward my face.

I'm not sure he knew what had happened, or why. But when I stepped back and slapped his arm away, I think he understood. I fought the urge to kick him in the ribs. One for each of my kids and one for my wife. Instead, I just smiled down at him and watched as he gasped for air and his face turned blue. Finally his eyes rolled up in his head and his body jerked spasmodically before going limp. I calmly stepped over his body, opened the machine, reset it and deleted the log files. When I was sure it too late, then, and only then, did I rush to the door and frantically call for help.

Paramedics arrived within minutes and furiously worked on the big man, but it was too late. Guerrino Bianchi was dead. The police showed up and asked lots of questions. They took my statement and since there were no signs of foul play, I was released.

I thought it was over, but last night two homicide detectives paid a visit to my hotel room. They had a lot more questions about why I was in Las Vegas, why I was meeting with Bianchi and the circumstances surrounding his death. I don't think they bought my story about giving him a private demonstration of our new machine. They questioned my company's logic in sending a programmer to do salesperson's job. Speaking of my company, I was certainly going to have some explaining to do when I got back to work, assuming I still had a job. But right now, none of that mattered. My wife and children were safe and that was all I cared about.

The detectives told me the frothing at the mouth and asphyxiation were possible signs of poisoning and until the medical examiner had a chance to run some toxicology tests, I was not allowed to leave town.

This morning the lead detective called and told me to come down to the station for some follow up questioning. After another hour of trying to poke holes in my statement and explaining all the benefits of the witness protection program, he was called out of the room. He returned a few minutes later and announced.

"Well Mr. Gavel, it looks like it's your lucky day."

"How's that?" I asked.

"The coroner says there was no poison. Apparently, Mr. Bianchi suffered an epileptic seizure and died from asphyxiation. The bastard choked on his own vomit. You would think a guy with his condition would know better and stay away from flashing lights. Between you and me, it couldn't have happened to a nicer guy. Anyway, the official cause of death is being ruled natural causes. You are free to go."

I thanked the detective and stood up to leave. He held the door open for me.

"One more thing Mr. Gavel, sorry about the whole witness protection thing. We thought… Well, let's just say we thought something else was going on here."

I arrived home later that evening to find my wife sitting at the kitchen table crying. I rushed over to her.

"What's the matter, sweetie? Are the kids alright."

"Why didn't you tell me Thomas? What didn't you tell me what was going on?"

My heart sank. Somehow she had found out. Despite my best efforts to keep everything a secret, she still found out. She knew everything. She knew about Bianchi, about the cheat code and about the fifty thousand dollars I used to owe. I didn't know what to say or do. I just stood there looking guilty. My fears were allayed when she unfolded a glossy piece of paper she was holding and set it on the table. It looked like a page torn from a magazine. It wasn't. It was a brochure for Carbamazepine, a drug used for treating epilepsy.

She stood, threw her arms around me and hugged tight. "Why didn't you tell you had epilepsy."

I hugged her back then gently brushed the tears from her face and kissed her forehead. "I don't honey, but I recently knew someone who did."

An angry biker with a gun is only one of the challenges facing Prior Howard Avila, the leader of a small monastery in the American Southwest. Threaded throughout this story is an engrossing discourse on morality and free will.

Mr. Bull has had considerable success with his writing, with stories published in a wide variety of publications. He is a practicing psychologist and lives in Kansas City.

Wrestling with the Noontime Demon

by Warren Bull

Prior Howard Avila tried to ignore the clock on the wall, knowing if he looked again he would feel discouraged that so little time had passed since his last look. The second hand of the clock moved so slowly it seemed to struggle through thick sludge to make any progress at all. Simplicity and order, hallmarks of the Benedictine monastic life had fled Avila's mind, leaving it full of gloomy thoughts and images.

A major reason for his unease leaned forward in his chair while droning on about his faith. Brad Jenkins had recently completed his postulancy. He had progressed to become a Novice. He now wore a habit and participated fully in monastic life. Avila had contemplated opposing Jenkins' advancement, but he could never quite formulate a coherent spiritual reason for his opposition. God had done wondrous things with the most unlikely people; Avila himself, for example.

The young man's constant grubby appearance, uncombed hair, and acne scars did not disqualify him. Even his enormous size, which made Avila feel crowded when the two of them were together in a room, could not be held against Jenkins. On the other hand, Jenkins' constant talking might. Jenkins repetitively shared the wonder of his conversion experience with men and women who had committed themselves to God long ago. Silence was highly valued in the community because in silence it was easier to experience the presence of the Almighty.

More than two years earlier Jenkins had picked up a flimsy pamphlet from the floor while standing in line at the checkout of the local Piggly Wiggly. The words inside, although ungrammatical and misspelled, introduced Jenkins to the need for salvation and the joy of belief. A door opened in his life. Jenkins was no longer a discontented, antisocial person who doubted the reason for his existence. In Avila's most secret thoughts he considered Jenkins had gone from a sufferer to a carrier.

On the off chance Jenkins had changed topics, Avila listened to Jenkins for a moment.

"… not because we earn or deserve forgiveness…"

Avila retreated into his thoughts again. He could have arranged for another member of the community to spend time with Jenkins, vacuuming the entrance hall, washing the display cases of desert rocks in the gift shop, and putting out new informational brochures for visitors. But if Jenkins was going to proceed on the path before him, becoming a monk would be the next step in his spiritual advance. Then Avila would have to deal with him for many years to come. Avila prayed fervently for greater patience and tolerance with all of God's children and especially for help with this particular thorn in his flesh. Avila strove to see and welcome Christ in Jenkins, but so far his efforts has been in vain.

The men heard voices from approaching visitors. Four women walked toward them. The Prior recognized three of them as they were frequent visitors. He did not know the fourth woman who hung back from the other three. She looked gaunt. Her eyelids drooped as if she was half asleep. Her complexion was pallid.

"Welcome, it's good to see you again Mary Catherine, Teresa and Bernadette," said Avila. "You are our first visitors of the day. I don't believe I've met your friend."

"I'm Elizabeth Bishop," said the woman as she stepped forward. "My friends told me about this place and about them being Oblates. I needed some refuge from the shambles of my life and I was curious."

"I hope God will grant you peace," said Avila. "Your friends live in the world and yet they seek to follow the wisdom and example of Saint Benedict as a way of being dedicated to the Almighty. They live bravely. I admire them for that."

"I thought monasteries were for people who wanted to escape from the world."

"You know, that's interesting. The original Benedict started as a hermit. Over the years he attracted so many followers that he became Abbot of a monastery out of concern for those who came to learn from him. Later for the same reason he could not avoid becoming head of a holy order. He wrote a book about how the order should do things. We still look to his book as authoritative. I'm sure establishing a religious order was the farthest thing from what he had in mind for himself when he set off into the wilderness alone. We have a saying, 'If you want to hear God laugh, tell Him your plans.'"

"So you didn't plan to become head of a monastery?"

"Oh, heavens no. In my prayers I frequently remind God how utterly unqualified I am to be Prior. So far I'm still Prior."

Avila looked at the other women.

"But here I am chattering away, keeping you from getting settled in. How unlike a Benedictine. Ms. Bishop, your friends can fill you in about our ways of doing things. As you no doubt know, we are located just outside Big Bend National Park. People who appreciate the desert landscape vacation there. If you step outside I want to caution you to stay close to the monastery. We are in a high-elevation desert. Distances can be deceptive. More cacti exist in the Chihuahuan Desert than in any other region of the world. Rattlesnakes are common. Mountain lions, black bears and other predators live here, too. The heat can be so oppressive that it's hard to think about anything else. The landscape looks similar in all directions so stay where you can see the buildings. If you lose sight of the building, stop moving and start shouting so we can find you. "

"The altitude has an effect too," said Jenkins.

"Thank you for reminding me, Brother Jenkins," said Avila. "You are correct. People unaccustomed to the altitude tire easily. The altitude, dehydration, plus the heat can cause confusion. Please forgive me for not introducing you to our visitors before. Ladies, this is Brother Brad Jenkins who recently became a Novice here."

Mary Catherine commented. "The Prior has never lost a visitor."

"Yes," said Avila. "And I don't want any of you to be the first. Every year people traveling through the desert get disoriented. Some of them die. Undocumented people from Mexico looking for work are especially at risk. Smugglers sometimes drop them off in the middle of this massive arid landscape without directions or sufficient water. The desert goes from blistering hot during the day to downright shivering cold at night. You can still feel the chill this early in the morning. That is enough of the negative. Although the desert looks barren to many people, it's possible to come to recognize the beauty in all of God's creations. Anyway, as I was saying, I hope you find the weekend here beneficial. Brother Brad, will you please escort them to their rooms?"

"Can I talk to you later, Prior?"

"Certainly, Ms. Bishop. My duties as Prior are not overwhelming. I don't plan to leave here."

Ten minutes later, Avila was talking with an older monk, Brother Michael, when he heard a thumping noise and a muffled cry at the front door.

"Good heavens, what is that?" asked Brother Michael.

"Trouble," said Avila. "It may have followed our new visitor here. You know the building and grounds better than anyone else. Would you please find Ms. Bishop and escort her somewhere to hide where she won't be found?"

"I know just the place."

"Don't tell me where," said Avila. "I want to be able to honestly say 'I don't know where she is.'" He hurried toward the sounds.

In the entrance hall he found a man dressed like a biker bouncing Brother Brad against a wall. The back of his black leather vest proclaimed, "Don't Mess With Texas" in bold lettering. Avila noticed it did not have a Hells Angels patch on it.

Avila swallowed and then addressed the man. "What's the problem here?"

"This dress-wearing wimp claims he doesn't know where my wife is." He gripped Brother Brad's habit and lifted him off the floor.

"Who are you looking for?"

The stranger turned his attention to the Prior. "My wife, Lizzie Parker. He claims he never heard of her."

"I don't know anyone by that name either," said the Prior. "Is it possible she uses another name?"

The stranger opened his hands. Brother Brad collapsed to the floor.

"It's the only name she should use. That or Mrs. Alan Parker. Since the divorce, she's started to use her maiden name, Elizabeth Bishop."

"You know it's entirely possible that Brother Brad told you the truth if you asked him about your wife or Lizzie Parker," said Avila.

"Oh, sorry. He's big enough that I thought he might put up a fight, but he didn't," said Parker. "That's Lizzie for you, getting another man in trouble by just showing up."

"Bother Brad, you didn't fight. Well done. I'm proud of you. Go to the infirmary and get yourself looked at."

"But you'll be in here alone with him," said Jenkins.

"Mr. Parker, do you intend to be violent toward me?" asked Avila.

"Nope. I promise."

"Do you always keep your promises?" ask Avila.

"Yep."

"There, you see? I'll be fine. Go on now, Brother."

Jenkins stood up, wincing. He staggered for two steps before getting his balance and walking away.

"Now, are you going to tell me you don't know my wife?" asked Parker.

"You obviously know she's here," said Avila. "I don't know her exact whereabouts right now."

"I believe that," said Parker. "I don't know if you would tell me if you knew."

"An interesting ethical question. May I ask about your intentions toward the lady?"

"She's no lady no matter what airs she puts on. I know how the church feels about divorce. I'm her first and only true husband. I've come to take her home."

"Yes, well it appears she disagrees with that. Would you force her to accompany you?"

"As head to the household, that is my right. I would."

"May I ask how?"

"I don't expect much opposition from men wearing skirts. And if her so-called friends interfere, I came prepared."

Parker reached under his vest and pulled out a pistol. "I see by the expression on your face you don't approve. This is just a tool."

"Even if I concede that, what is it a tool for? You can't paint with a hammer. You can't drill holes with a paintbrush. That tool only kills and injures. Who do you intend to kill or injure here?"

"This here is a persuader. It will persuade you and yours from interfering with me and mine."

"And if your wife refuses to go with you, what then? If you use the weapon on your wife, you will lose her life and eventually your own."

"Maybe that would not be such a terrible idea. I'd go out like one of the old gunslingers."

"You'd go out like a coward and fool," said Avila. "I don't know of a single gunfighter who killed himself. You would be just another poor slob who failed at living his life. Life is a gift from God. It's not our place to squander it away, attractive as that seems to us sometimes."

"You're pretty ballsy for a little old man in a dress," said Parker. "But I don't believe in your God. So there."

"Bah, you don't even know my God. You probably don't believe in the crotchety old bastard with a long white beard in the sky. The one who never wants anybody to have any fun. The one who keeps a log of every sinful thought and act you've ever had. Guess what?"

Avila lowered his voice and leaned toward Parker. "I don't believe in him either."

Parker shook his head. "Nice try, old man. You nearly had me going there. Someday I'll come back to listen to you preach. Today, I aim to find my wife. You lead the way."

"Well, I tried. I'll hold to you to that promise. My God never gives up. As to your wife, I don't know where she is. You tell me which way to head."

The Prior led the way following Parker's directions. Parker followed close behind. Avila told everyone he met to relax and not to interfere with the search. Increasingly frustrated as the search continued unsuccessfully, Parker kicked open the doors to the last few rooms he had not already searched.

"Where could she be?" asked Parker. He glanced through a window. He slapped his forehead.

"She's out there. That where we go next."

"I would advise against going far into the desert," said the monk. "It's easy to get lost. The combination of heat, altitude and dehydration can be extremely disorienting. The plants and animals are certainly dangerous."

"So am I. You don't want me to go there. Therefore it is exactly the place I want to go. It's the only place you have objected to."

"I don't want you to get hurt," said Avila.

"You're concerned about me? Why?"

"I don't agree with what you're doing. It's wrong. But, of course I'm concerned about you. Why wouldn't I be? You are a valued, cherished child of God. Uh, I mean my God, not the one you don't believe in. That one doesn't give a damn, but it doesn't matter since, as we both agree, he doesn't exist."

"I'm going out there."

"Oh, all right, let's get broad-brimmed hats and water bottles."

"I don't need them."

"I do. I am the Prior and therefore I am not allowed the impetuousness of youth. Come with me while I prepare because I will not go out otherwise."

Parker pulled out his pistol again. He pointed it at the monk. "I think you're stalling."

"Put that thing away. It could go off and hurt somebody. If you're worried about stalling, stop arguing with me and come along."

"I like you, little monk, but nobody tells Alan Parker what to do." His complexion reddened. Parker kept the gun centered on the Prior.

"Do you see how limited the weapon is?" asked Avila. "It's not persuasive with me."

"Shut up. You know I could kill you."

"You could have killed me any time," said Avila. You could have rid the world of one annoying little man. How would that help you find your wife?"

Parker's hand holding the gun started to shake. His face grew redder.

"Shooting me in anger increases your problems tenfold. You'd have to stop searching and hide. Eventually the authorities would find you. Unless you plan to kill everyone in the monastery, there would be a raft of witnesses to your crime. Did you bring enough bullets to kill everyone?"

Parker gritted his teeth. Avila walked toward the pistol. He stopped a few inches away from it. "You can't miss at this range. If you came here to kill someone, and I think maybe you did, kill me and get it over with."

"You don't know how tempting it is."

Monks who had been watching, pulled Avila away. They restrained Avila while Parker regained control of his emotions.

"You don't know how close you came to meeting your God, little man," said Parker. "Get your hat and water bottle. We're going outside."

Avila shrugged off comments from the other monks that he had been reckless. He put on a hat, drank his fill of water, and filled up a water bottle. Then he returned to where Parker was waiting.

"Don't say a word about what I need to do," warned Parker.

When they opened the door, the desert smelled like dust with exotic overtones. The arid air blew over the men, stealing moisture from exposed flesh.

"Look there's a path here," said Parker, pointing at the ground.

"An animal trail probably," said Avila.

"Is this what you didn't want me to see?"

"I've been with you since you arrived," said the Prior. "I didn't hide your wife. As I told you, I don't know where she is. I haven't lied to you."

Parker did not reply. He started forward along the faint marks on the ground.

"I'm not telling you what to do," said the monk. "But I strongly suggest we stay within easy view of the monastery. It's easy to get turned around and lose your way."

Avila took a swig of from his water bottle.

Following the faint marks took them through a meandering arroyo and over some hills. Shortly after that the marks disappeared.

"They covered their tracks," said Parker.

"Or the wind blew them away," said Avila. "Or the ground has more rocks and less dirt here. "

"We'll move in a widening circle from here. We should be able to find the tracks again."

The men circled area, but found no evidence of tracks. Parker was looking so intently at the ground to one side that he did not notice a cholla cactus until his leg brushed against it.

"Ow!"

Spines tore through his jeans, leaving bloody scratches.

"Let me see," said Avila. He looked the injury over. "It's not as bad as it looks but we should go back to get it treated. Wait, that's a suggestion, not an order."

Parker sighed. "Okay. You win."

"I assure you I was not trying to win anything. When I suggested we stay inside, I was concerned about the hostile environment out here," said the Prior.

"Wasn't I being hostile enough inside?"

"I preferred the known hostility over the unknown. Which way do we head?"

Parker turned in a slow circle. "I don't recognize anything. Let's retrace our footsteps in the dust."

That proved to be no easier than following the tracks, which had faded out.

"Do you have any water left?" asked Parker.

"Just a little. I suggest you drink it all."

Parker swallowed what remained in a single gulp. "Now what?"

"We can stay where we are and yell," said Avila. "They'll be listening for us at the monastery."

"This is humiliating," said Parker.

The men yelled and stopped to listen for a response. Nothing. They yelled twice more. Parker pulled out his gun.

"They probably called the cops," said Parker.

"How will that help if the police come? You'll be outgunned. Are you hoping for suicide by police? If you consider your own death unimportant, does it matter to you how much your death will weigh on the mind of the officer who has to kill you?"

"I've heard quite enough from you on that topic," said Parker. "Ow."

Avila's first impression was that Parker had stepped too near another cactus. He was surprised to see Parker shaking the hand that used to hold the weapon. The gun was gone. In another moment police officers surrounded them. The police handcuffed Parker and read him his rights.

"Come see me when you get out," said Avila to Parker. "You promised. My God isn't done with you yet."

"How did the cops get to us so quickly?" asked Parker.

"I told you I was concerned for you," said Avila. "I even warned you that the heat, altitude, and dehydration could be disorienting. Despite all the ground we covered, I made sure the monastery was never farther away than over the next hill."

Parker lunged toward the Prior, but the restraints allowed him only minimal movement. The police officers led him away.

Avila turned toward Brother Brad and Brother Michael.

"Who threw whatever it was that disarmed Parker?"

Brother Brad blushed.

"Well done. Were you a pitcher as a youth?" asked Avila.

"No. I used to throw bricks through store windows. Now I have to find the geode I threw in order to return it to the gift shop. And it wasn't well done. I was aiming at his head." Jenkins walked into the desert.

"Where was Ms. Bishop?" Avila asked Michael.

"I immediately drove her to the nearest police station and returned with the police."

Avila nodded. "You totally ignored my instructions. You did well."

"You did not," said Brother Michael. "You baited a man with a gun. You pressured him over and over again. You practically begged him to shoot you."

"Well… he might have shot someone else. I just focused his attention on me," said the Prior

"You said when your depression influenced your duties as Prior, you would see a doctor about it," said Brother Michael. "Even if you think your death would be unimportant, which is almost blasphemy, did you think about how seeing you die might harm those who were watching?"

He shook his head. "I did not," Avila said.

"You seem to believe that Mr. Parker might come to see the light someday," said Brother Michael.

"He's not as bad as he appears at first glance. He is redeemable," said Avila.

"I agree completely," said Brother Michael. "So tell me, did you consider how committing murder would affect his self-image? How would it change the way he is seen by others? And just exactly how would a long time in prison or years on death row help him find God?"

Tears came into Avila's eyes.

"Father Andrews is here to hear confessions any of us might want," said Brother Michael. I took the liberty of setting up an appointment for you with a psychiatrist the order has used before. Brother Howard, there is no shame in asking for help. You know as well as I do that anyone can become depressed. I don't believe you will miss fighting your depression."

I won't," said the Prior. "It will be a relief to stop wrestling with the noontime demon."

Door County, Wisconsin is our next destination. A young, independent PI follows a case from her Chicago haunts to a summer vacation paradise – in early spring. She's on the trail of an old, and perhaps deadly secret.

Ms Moss knows Door County well, through numerous trips and stays, and she brings that familiarity to her story. This editor can attest to this, as Door Country and Washington Island were our summer destinations, too.

The Letter B

By Bern Sy Moss

I finished making the coffee and headed from the kitchen to my desk where I occupied myself by staring out the big window facing Archer Avenue. The sun was shining through it, as best it could, and I decided the window probably hadn't been washed in the hundred or more years since the building was constructed. I supposed the floor was shiny with varnish at one time, but the finish was long gone and brown stained wood stared up at me. Sometimes on hot, humid Chicago nights, the smells from Joe's tavern downstairs seeped up through those floorboards and the smell of booze and cigarettes mixed with the mustiness of old wood and grime in my flat. I wondered what secrets those stains might tell if they could. At different times, the building had been a bookie joint, a brothel, a little speakeasy, tucked away in an inconspicuous storefront apartment building, like so many that lined Archer Avenue.

My flat consisted of three rooms; a bedroom, a tiny kitchen, and a living room that faced Archer and opened off the front stairway to the second floor. I used the living room as my sparsely furnished office. That's where I sat now, waiting, hoping for clients that didn't come except for the few Joe sent up. Those guys who didn't trust their significant others, wanted me to stake out the wives, tail the girlfriends and report their every cheating move. For the most part nobody was doing anything worth reporting and if those guys stayed home at night, instead of hanging out in Joe's, they wouldn't have any need for me. Maybe they figured that out for themselves because Joe seemed to be running out of suspicious boyfriends and husbands. That business seemed to be as dried up as yesterday's coffee in the bottom of my cup. I got up to wash the cup and get some coffee.

The street level door slammed and brought me to attention. I could hear someone coming up. The creaking of the old wood steps, music to my ears as long it was a client, and not Joe looking for the rent money. I wasn't ready for that conversation.

"Where can I find Frankie Rizzo?" he asked as he walked into my office.

He was short and stocky. His clothes said "not a lot of money". He eyed me in the way an eagle does, severe and untrusting.

"I'm Frankie," I said. "How can I help you, Mister?"

"Randell Murphy, I work for your grandfather at the restaurant. He gave me your card. Said you could help and you did good work."

I was surprised. Grandpa Angelo made it clear he wasn't pleased with my career choice. He constantly berated me with, "Nice girls aren't detectives and detectives aren't nice girls." Lately, he threw in, "you're my only grandchild. Come work for me. I'll pay you good and then you can get out of that damn, rat-trap flat, already."

Randell added, "And Angelo said you work cheap."

Oh, there you go, Grandpa. That's more like it.

I stood and stretched my arm over the desk to shake his hand. It was thick and clammy. "Have a seat. What kind of help do you need?" I asked wondering what else my grandfather told him.

"You're so young," he said. "I didn't think you'd be so young. How long have you been doing this?" he wanted to know.

"I look much younger than I am and I have lots of experience doing this kind of work," I lied.

"I need some detective stuff," he said. "I can't pay much," he continued and seemed comfortable saying this as he looked around my unpretentious office.

"Specifically, what do you want me to do?" I asked.

He ran his fingers through his black curly hair, took a deep breathe and said, "My mother died last year and I need to sell the house so I started cleaning it out and I found this in one of the drawers."

He slid a picture post card over the desk toward me. I picked it up. The picture depicted a ferry on a lake and a Victorian home on a bluff in the background. I turned it over and read the description in the corner. Apparently, the ferry was going through Port des Morts, the strait between the peninsula and Washington Island, in Door County, Wisconsin passing by Hemingway Guest House in the distance.

Someone had written, "I'm coming to get him in a few months. He's mine and you can't stop me." It was signed with a large letter B and addressed to Elizabeth Murphy on South Richmond Avenue in Chicago. The date was almost obliterated by a brownish stain, but I could make out that it was sent twenty-five years ago.

"And what is it you want me to do? I asked.

"There's this too." He pushed a photocopy of a birth certificate at me. The age of the child described would have been twenty-seven now, about the same age as the man sitting across from me. The birth mother was Elizabeth Murphy age sixteen.

"This is your birth certificate?" I asked.

He nodded and pointed a stubby finger at the age of the mother and said, "My mother was thirty-two when I was born."

"You must have noticed the discrepancy before," I said.

"My mother said it was a mistake, the hospital put in the wrong age. I believed her. It didn't seem to make any difference before, but it does now."

"Why now?"

"Look where I was born. My mother never talked about ever being in Door County, I never thought about that until I found the postcard."

The certificate said the child was born in Sturgeon Bay, Wisconsin, father unknown.

"You didn't know your father?" I asked.

"No, just me and my mother. That's the way it's always been."

"What exactly do you want me to do Mr. Murphy?"

"I want you to go to Door County and find this "B". I want to know if she is my mother. Like I said, I can't pay a lot, but your grandfather said you work cheap."

Oh, that word again.

The wheels in my head were turning now. Was this a real case or was my grandfather setting me up for a fall? Maybe, this was a test. If I failed, there would be no end to the ridicule Angelo would lavish upon me and he would know if I failed, maybe that's why Randell Murphy was sitting in front of me.

If there was one thing Angelo Rizzo and I had in common, it was tenacity, so I planned to see this to the end no matter who was really paying for it. Even though I was suspicious, I knew not accepting this case would immediately label me as a failure in my grandfather's eyes.

As I stared into space and thought over my predicament, Randell started drumming his fingers nervously on my desk.

"Maybe, "B" is your father," I said.

"I hadn't thought about that," he said.

We discussed just how cheaply Mr. Murphy could obtain my services. We came to an agreement; he signed a contract and was on his way.

I woke early the next morning, packing only a tote for a two or three day stay, expecting to be driving five to six hours, less if my lead foot took over. The April rains were pummeling the big window in my office, the wind banging hard against it as I left.

Not long after I crossed the state line, I stopped at a visitor's center. It was one way to familiarize myself with the area. I had limited knowledge of Door County, a peninsula jutting out from Wisconsin, surrounded by Green Bay and Lake Michigan. I perused the numerous pamphlets exhorting the wondrous attractions Wisconsin offered. I was only interested in those in Door County.

I wanted to get there before noon. I already knew the locations of the constabulary offices, sheriff and police. That's where I planned to start. I was worrying though. Would anybody remember a sixteen year old from twenty-five years ago, if there were one? All I had to go on was the letter "B".

The rain stopped by the time I reached the sheriff's office, a two-story brick building with floor to ceiling windows. I parked my car in the parking lot and walked to the front entrance slapped by a cold wind as I went.

A counter separated visitors from the law enforcers. I stood and waited until a deputy appeared. I handed him my card.

He introduced himself as Deputy Tim Avery and said. "Please follow me." He led me down a hallway to small office. The deputy sat behind the desk in the office and I sat across. He studied my card for a few seconds and then asked, "How can I be of service, Miss Rizzo."

I liked his looks, so neat, so pressed. His eyes were kind, but the set of his jaw seemed to say, mess with me and you'll be sorry. I did not intend to mess with him.

I explained what brought me to Door County and asked if the name Elizabeth Murphy from twenty-five years ago meant anything to him.

"Wow, twenty-five years ago. I was just dreaming about being a cop at that time. Still in grammar school, matter of fact," he said. "You know, unless you hit the right person to ask or this Murphy did something to make the news, well, you may just hit a dead end."

"I know," I said.

"I'll tell you what I can do. I'll ask around here if anybody knows any Murphys or about any Murphys and I'll have Meg contact the various police stations to see if they have anything. Check back with me tomorrow."

He got up and shook my hand signaling we were done.

As I started to leave he said, "I'm sure glad you checked in with us, Miss Rizzo, and would you be carrying? If you are I'd really like you to leave it with us until you're ready to go back to Chicago."

I reached in my purse, pulled out my Smith-Wesson and laid it on his desk.

"You won't need that here. Worst thing that happens here is somebody runs a stop sign. So, be careful at those stop signs." He smiled, turned toward his computer and started typing.

I decided not to waste any time, especially since Randell Murphy was paying for it, and headed to the main library. I checked the Internet, before I left Chicago, for any reference to an Elizabeth Murphy with ties to Door County. I got no results. I now planned to check the twenty-five year old news items and obituaries on the library's microfilm reader for any mention of the name Murphy. The local telephone directory might be helpful, too.

The library was not far from the Sheriff's office, a formidable brick building with two-story white columns. There was no Elizabeth Murphy listed in the phone directory, but she could have married or had an unlisted cell phone. I then searched through the old newspapers on microfilm. I started with 1988, the year Randell Murphy was born, scanning through the articles and obits. And then there it was: Elizabeth Murphy Missing. Her employer, Sally Hemingway reported that she had not shown up for work for several days. The eighteen year old was last seen leaving Chuck's Roadhouse on Highway 42 two days ago. If anyone has any knowledge of Miss Murphy's whereabouts, please contact Deputy Ted Smith in Sturgeon Bay.

The article was dated March 8, 1990. I made a copy of it. On June 6, 1990, another article mentioned that she was still missing.

Highway 42 was the main artery that connected every place I needed to find with every other on the peninsula. It stretched from one end of Door County to the other. I headed north on 42 looking for Chuck's Roadhouse. The librarian said to watch for it after I passed through Ellison Bay. I found it easy enough. A large sign near the road read:

Chuck's Roadhouse

Best Burgers in the County

The bar was a two story building covered with white vinyl siding, some of it loose and blowing in the wind. Several windows on the first floor, shaped like portholes, faced the front parking lot; more parking spaces were on each side of the building. Arms like an octopus stretched out from the second floor, LED lighting on the ends.

I parked on the side of the building and walked around to the front, the wind having no more respect for me than the siding, shoving and slapping me around.

The inside of Chuck's smelled like my apartment on those hot humid Chicago nights. Booze and cigarettes. I felt right at home. The place was almost empty except for the bartender and a few guys at the bar watching highlights from the last Green Bay Packers and Chicago Bears game on a large screen TV. The bar was a large oval that dominated the center of the room, part of it anchored to the back wall, the liquor and the refrigerators in the middle. A few tables for four were scattered in the space remaining.

The bartender turned and looked in my direction. "Hello there," he said.

"Hi," I said as I approached him. I dug into my purse, found my business card and handed it to him.

"A PI," he said. "Wouldn't have guessed it. You look more like a…" he hesitated. "More like a college student, I guess."

I slid onto one of the bar stools near where he was standing and said, "I have a client that is looking for Elizabeth Murphy. I understand she went missing about twenty-five years ago. Do you know if she ever turned up?"

"Beth, you must mean Beth. That's what everyone called her. Nope, she was never found."

"Beth, "I repeated and then said, "I understand she was last seen here. Is that right?"

"Sure is. She was sitting right where you are now."

"You remember exactly where she was sitting?"

"All the regulars have their favorite places to sit."

"She was a regular?"

"A couple nights a week. Usually came in with George, They were engaged."

I dug into my purse again and produced a pen and my notebook. "Was he here on that night, the last night?"

"Sitting right there." He pointed to the stool to my right. "And they were really going at it."

"Going at it?"

"Big argument."

"So, what happened? Could you hear what they were arguing about?"

"Yeah, I wasn't trying to listen, but this is where I kind of hang out when I'm not serving, so I did hear some of it. She kept telling George it would be all right. That the three of them would live happily ever after just like in the movies. Told him he needed to give it a chance. George wasn't buying it. Said she should have told him before not spring it on him two weeks before the wedding. He also said something about what other secrets did she have. Finally, he just got up and told her he was done with her and the wedding was off."

"You wouldn't know George's last name and where I could find him, would you?"

"Sure. Garrison. Fisherman at Gills Rock. Just stay on 42 and you'll find it."

"So, he just got up and left. What did she do?"

"She sat there for a few minutes and then she ran out the door. After him, I guess."

"You were serving her liquor? She was eighteen. Wasn't she under legal age?"

He looked at me and said nothing taking time to organize his thoughts. "She always came in with George. He's my age so that makes him about forty back then. I guess I looked at him as, I don't know, maybe, a guardian, adult supervision."

"George was forty then and she was eighteen. She could have been his daughter," I said.

"Beth liked older men."

"How do you know that?"

He didn't answer at first. He just wiped at the bar top and shook his head. He finally said, "Rumors. Just rumors."

"And that was it. Nothing else you can tell me about that night?"

"Oh, yeah. One more thing, the deputy, Deputy Ted Smith. When she ran out, he got up and said he better make sure they don't kill each other in my parking lot and he took off after them. I guess he heard them arguing too."

"Where was he sitting?"

"Over there in the corner near the washrooms."

"So, they all left at about the same time and none of them came back?"

"The deputy came back. Said they were gone when he got out there. I think he went into the washroom came out and sat back down. His beer was still there, almost a full glass, when he went out to the parking lot. I left it in case he did come back. He sat for little while, downed it and took off."

"Did the deputy come in often?"

"Just about every night. Always sat there by the washroom."

"Anybody else in the bar?"

"Yeah, four or five guys came for the ice fishing. They were over there," he said nodding toward a corner table. They were working on a good drunk. It was their last night. I think they were staying at the motel next door. Warnings out that the ice wasn't safe, starting to crack and melt, so they were going home. They probably didn't even notice what was going on at the bar."

"Interesting. You seem to remember a lot after all these years."

"Right after she went missing I had to tell the Sheriff what happened, then the newspaper people, everybody and anybody was asking. I told the story so many times it's impossible for me to forget it."

"Anything else? Maybe something that was different. Something that normally doesn't happen."

He looked at me for a few seconds then he whispered, "Do you believe in ghosts?"

"I've never seen one, but I don't discount that usual things can happen. What did you see?"

"I didn't see anything," he kept his voice low. "It was the perfume. Beth's perfume. She always wore this one kind, smelled like lilies of the valley. Sometimes it was really too much, like it was that night." He stopped and looked into space as if he was trying to remember something he had not told over and over.

"Go on," I said.

Well, it started that night. It happened every night for a few nights, but it gradually faded away. I started to think that it was her ghost and she was trying to tell me something."

"Did you ever tell this to anyone else?"

"No." He was still whispering. "Didn't want people here to think I'm crazy. I got a business to run. But you, you're here today and gone tomorrow."

I nodded then asked, "How do I find the Hemingway Guest House?"

"Just follow Highway 42 to Port des Morts, then north. Can't miss it, big Victorian."

"Port des Morts," I repeated.

"Death's Door," he said.

As I opened the door to leave, I heard him say, "When you get done looking for Beth, come back and have a burger on the house. Best in the county."

———————

Hemingway Guest House wasn't hard to find. It was the kind of place I dreamed about when the city got to be too much for me. It was what I saw in my mind's eye when I meditated. I wanted so bad to stay here tonight, but knew the meager fee I settled for would only allow me to stay at the motel I passed on my way up here.

I parked in the small parking lot that was tastefully bordered with a row of arborvitae to block it from the view of the veranda and the guesthouse.

As I started up the walk, I could see someone standing on the veranda.

"Hello," she said.

"Hello," I said back.

"Are you planning to stay the night? The guest house is closed for a few more weeks."

I reached the veranda by then, found my card and handed it to her.

"Oh, a private investigator. I'm Sally Hemingway. I own Hemingway Guest House. What would you be investigating Miss Rizzo?" she said.

"I have a client that's looking for Elizabeth Murphy. I believe she may have worked for you at one time."

"Yes, Beth did work for me. What interest does this client have in her?"

"He thinks she may be his mother."

"Oh. Come sit with me Miss Rizzo."

She led me around the veranda to some rattan chairs facing the lake. The wind was now a gentle breeze, and the sun warm, making the porch a comfortable place to sit.

She nodded in the direction of the lake, "Porte des Morts," she said.

I knew from a brochure it was where Green Bay meets the waters of Lake Michigan, the strait between the Door County Peninsula and Washington Island.

"I'll be right back," she said.

When she returned, she was carrying a tray with two glasses of iced tea and some pictures. She handed me one of the glasses. She settled in the chair next to me and handed me one of the pictures.

"Beth when she first came here in 1988." She said. She handed me another. "And this was taken the day she disappeared."

Beth looked so fragile, easily broken, tall and thin with reddish blonde hair. Smiling in both pictures, she looked happy. I studied the pictures and could see no resemblance to short, stocky Randell Murphy with his black curly hair, but then we don't always look like our parents.

"It is possible that there could be a child, Beth's child," Sally said.

The rattan chair she chose was a rocker and she began to slowly rock as she poured out Beth's secret.

"Beth's mother brought her to me in 1988. Beth was sixteen. Her mother said she couldn't control her and she didn't approve of her friends. Her mother and I grew up together, lived next door to each other in Chicago. I put Beth to work here and we got along just fine. I didn't see Beth as a wild teenager, more like child desperately looking for someone to care about her. I thought things were going well, but after Beth had been here only a few months I found out she was expecting. She begged me not to call her mother and I didn't. When it was time, I drove her to the hospital in Sturgeon Bay. I didn't know what to do and finally decided to call her mother. Elizabeth, her mother, came. She said she was taking the baby home with her and Beth should stay here with me. In fact, she told Beth never to come home again. I presumed she was putting the baby up for adoption.

"The thing is, winter here can be a very private time for some of us. There are those who just sort of hibernate until spring. I'm one of them. It's the tourists and the ice fisherman that seem to love the winter and all it has to offer. I usually close after the fall foliage is no longer an attraction and reopen in time for the cherry blossoms. So no one here knew, except me, about her condition. No one around here knew about the baby. Beth was different after the baby was born. She seemed to grow up over night and she wanted to get her baby back. When George asked her to marry, it was the opportunity she was waiting for. She could give her baby a home and a father. She told me she was going to tell George that night, the night she disappeared."

She stopped rocking and rested her head on the back of the chair.

"Did she tell you who the father was?"

"No."

"Did her mother know when she went missing?"

"Yes, I called her. I barely gave her any details before she abruptly hung up. I heard a small child in the background, calling mommy. I guessed she didn't put the child up for adoption."

"No, she didn't. He thought Elizabeth was his mother until he found this."

I handed her the postcard.

"Did you know Elizabeth died a year ago?" I asked.

"No." She read the postcard and handed it back to me. "She never contacted me after I told her that Beth was missing. Never, not even for an update. And I never called her again. You can keep the photos. Give them to her son."

"What do you think happened to her?" I asked.

"I hoped she went home to Chicago and made peace with her mother."

"Do you know if anyone checked with her mother?""

"I don't think there was much of an investigation. No one seemed to care what happened to her."

We sat quietly for a while watching the ferry for Washington Island go by.

"It's called "Death Door" because it's so dangerous. So many ships are down there. But there are beautiful things here too. Come back when the cherry trees are blossoming," she said.

"I think I will, and maybe take one of those trolley tours," I said.

"Yes, the lighthouses and the wineries. In fact Door County is often called the Cape Cod of the Midwest," she said.

I decided she was trying to distance herself from the memories she felt were best forgotten. I thanked her for her help and got up to leave.

Back in my car, I scribbled down the gist of our conversation and then drove back to Highway 42 and the motel, the one next to Chuck's.

It was clean. It was basic. It was all I needed. A place to kick off my shoes, peruse my notes, and think. Instead, I sat on the bed and went through the brochures from the visitor's center. The idea of coming back on my time was taking hold. Dedication to the job made me put the brochures down and pick up my notes.

I read and reread them. I planned to call Deputy Avery first thing the next morning to find out if he had anything for me. The last thing I did was look at the copy of the newspaper clipping. It really didn't tell much more than the fact that Beth was missing. Inadvertently captured in the copy were a few other articles: a weather forecast, which included a warning about the instability of the ice, the schedule of the ferry between the peninsula and Washington Island and another about a car stolen on the same night Beth disappeared, Deputy Smith's car.

Exhausted, I fell asleep trying to piece the puzzle together and thinking I needed to talk to Ted Smith and George Garrison.

I awoke the next morning later than I planned, still dressed. I didn't make it back to Chuck's last night for the burger he promised and I was starving. After a quick shower, I dressed in fresh clothes and decided the snack bars in my tote would have to suffice for breakfast.

Deputy Avery picked up the phone on the first ring.

"Good morning, Deputy. It's Frankie Rizzo. Have you got anything for me?"

"Yes, matter of fact, I do. It seems Elizabeth, also known as Beth, Murphy went missing back in 1990 and never found. She was last seen at Chuck's, a bar and grill off Highway 42. Everybody that was there was questioned extensively, but she was never found."

"Who handled the case?"

"Looks like it was Deputy Ted Smith."

"He was there that night. Shouldn't someone else have handled it?"

"Maybe, but what's done is done. Smitty's report seems to indicate that she left with someone. George Garrison vehemently denied it was him."

"I'd like to talk to the deputy. How can I find him?"

"He's retired. Must be close to eighty by now. Look, I haven't seen him in awhile. He lives near Gills Rock. I'll meet you there about two."

Before we hung up he gave me the directions to Smitty's place and I asked him to bring the report.

I had enough time to talk to George Garrison before my scheduled meeting with the deputy, so, I started out for Gills Rock.

Chuck had mentioned George was a fisherman so I headed to the dock at Gills Rock and started to ask around if anyone knew him and where I could find him.

Most of the men didn't want to talk to me when they read my card stating I was a private investigator. Finally, one told me George was out on the boat and wasn't expected back for some time.

"What time would that be?" I asked. But the curtain of silence had fallen again. He walked away and I got no answer.

Now, I had some time to kill. A nearby café, where I could get a coffee, a sweet roll and a talkative waitress, was what I needed. I drove to the one I passed a few miles back outside of Gills Rock on 42.

Carol's Café was neat, homey and crowded with patrons. I walked up to the counter and took a seat. A waitress, a teenager, to young to know anything about Beth, asked for my order.

"Decaf coffee and a pecan roll if you have any," I said as my hope for a source who gushed out the gossip, especially the old stuff, faded away.

"You're the PI aren't you?" the waitress said as she put my coffee and roll down."

"How did you know?"

"She waved towards the tables. Everybody's talk'n about you being here and asking lots of questions."

Nothing ventured, nothing gained, I thought. I leaned over the counter and whispered, "Is there something you want to tell me?"

"Nope," she said and headed over to another customer for his order.

I took my time. I had run out of places to go and when finally I could drink no more coffee and the sweet roll was long gone, I took off for Smitty's. I would get there early, but like I said, I had no place else to go. I planned to come back and talk to George later if Smitty didn't have the answers I needed.

⁎⁎⁎

Smitty's place was a tiny ranch house in a cookie cutter subdivision. I parked one down from his house by a weedy vacant lot. I reread the article about his stolen car and I found it interesting that the stolen car was inside a fence.

The other properties on the block were without fencing and numerous cars sat on driveways. If that were true twenty-five years ago, they were more accessible to theft than Smitty's car. Still someone stole his car. The article describe the car as a 1980 green Ford with numerous rust spots and stated that Smitty thought his dog must have been drugged otherwise the thief could not have made off with the car.

I wondered if this was the same fence. It looked old enough to be it, a chain link, standing six feet high and surrounding the property. A hyper German Shepard, which I assumed was not the same dog, ran the perimeter of it patrolling constantly. A car I guessed to be Smitty's, was inside the fence.

Interesting, I thought.

I didn't see Deputy Avery pull up behind me, but heard the tap on my window. I pressed the unlock button and he got in and sat in the passenger seat.

"Here's the report. Do you want to read it now or after you talk to Smitty? he asked.

"I'll read it now," I said.

I scanned it noting much of it was verbatim as Chuck told me except one part. Chuck said the deputy went outside, returned and said everyone was gone by the time he got out to the parking lot. The report said the deputy saw Beth get into a car, but couldn't describe it.

"Hummm," I said.

"Are you ready to go in?" Deputy Avery asked.

"Let's do it," I said.

Since duct tape covered the doorbell, Avery knocked. No one came to the door so he knocked harder and called, "Smitty, it's me, Tim. Open the door."

A disheveled Smitty opened the door. Most of his gray hair was pulled back into a ponytail. Wearing dirty sweats and smelling as if he hadn't showered since 1990, he supported himself against the doorframe. His eyes shifted back and forth from Avery to me.

"Can we come in?" the deputy asked.

"Sure. Sure. The housekeeper hasn't been around in a long time, so don't mind the mess," Smitty said as he opened the door wider for us. "Sit down if you can find someplace. Been meaning to clean up. Just can't seem to find the time."

"Smitty, this is Miss Rizzo. She's investigating the disappearance of Beth Murphy. Do you remember her?" Avery asked.

Smitty slowly nodded.

"Miss Rizzo has some questions."

The couch and chair in the living room were covered with everything imaginable from old pizza boxes to newspapers and much more. Smitty sat in a recliner, the only place possible to sit. Beer cans and prescription bottles littered a small table next to the recliner. I leaned against a wall and the deputy stood only a few feet from the door.

"Do you remember Beth?" I asked.

"She's dead," he answered.

"I know. And I think you know who did it, don't you? What happened that night?"

"It's all in the report," Smitty said. He crossed his arms against his chest, leaned forward and started rocking back and forth.

"No, it's not all in the report. You lied in the report. Let me tell you what I think happened and you can tell me if I'm wrong," I said. "You went out to the parking lot and you killed Beth. Her perfume rubbed onto your jacket. That's why Chuck kept smelling her perfume. It wasn't her ghost that kept coming back, it was you. She's in the car isn't she? Where is she? Where's the car, Smitty?"

He jumped up from the recliner and lunged at me shoving me hard and pinning me against the wall.

"She deserved it. She liked other older men, what was wrong with me?" he screamed at me his spittle hitting me in the face.

"Smitty, maybe I should read you your rights," Avery said.

"Don't need to. The doc already told me I only have a few more weeks, maybe a month or two at best." He sat and started rocking again.

"Tell us what happened to Beth," I said.

He kept rocking and said, "She started to come to Chuck's with Garrison. Someone told me she was engaged to him. Figures, I thought. Everyone knew she liked older men. Then that night, George broke it off and left. I was going to move over to where she was sitting, but she ran out the door too. I thought that maybe she might still be in the parking lot and she was. She said she was trying to call Sally Hemingway to come pick her up and she needed some change. There was a phone on the bar's outside wall. That was before cell phones, when phones were in booths or on the walls. I told her I'd give her a ride and started to pull her to my car. She kept pulling away and started to scream and I hit her to shut her up. I guess I hit her too hard she fell back and hit her head on one of the rocks that lined the parking lot. Chuck always kept the lot lit up bright like noon when it was midnight. I could see her eyes; they were open, just staring at me. I knew she was dead. I picked her up and put her in the back seat of my car and I picked up the rock she hit her head on, the one with the blood on it, and put it in the car too. Then I went back to the bar to finish my beer." He stopped.

"Where is she?" Avery asked.

"I knew I had to get rid of her body. It was while I was drinking my beer the idea came to me. I could hear the guys who came for the ice fishing talking. They were going home because the ice was getting unstable. Not safe to fish anymore. They gave me the idea.

"I drove to the water and put the car in drive, put the rock on the gas pedal and sent it out. I could hear the ice cracking as it went. The moonlight reflected really good off the ice that night and I could see it got out pretty far before it sank and nobody's found it so far. I guess it's forty feet or more down in Green Bay. The next day I reported the car stolen. And yeah, I lied in the report about her getting into a car. I didn't want anybody snooping around the parking lot. I was afraid they might find some evidence, so I said she got in a car and left."

"I'll have to take you in, Smitty," Avery said.

"Need my meds," Smitty said as he pulled a plastic grocery bag from the mess on the couch and put the prescription bottles into it.

Avery took him by the arm and led it to the door. I followed. "Sick, old man," he said as he helped Smitty get into his cruiser.

"And a murderer," I said.

We separated. Avery took Smitty back with him and I headed to Chuck's, wondering if Angelo would see things differently now. Because of my investigative work, Randell would now know Beth was his real mother. I doubted they'd find her body, but at least he would know her murderer would be punished.

See Angelo, nice girls can be detectives.

Chuck was still holding up the bar as he had done for way more years than I existed.

"Back for the burger?" he asked.

"Can't pass up the best in the county," I said.

He went to place the order and I texted Randell Murphy. I told him to watch the news that night and that I would fill in the details when I got back to Chicago. I also, made a request of him.

Chuck came back with one huge burger with cheese, of course, dripping down the sides of it.

"I don't know if I'll be able to put my mouth around that," I said as my phone indicated I just received a message. It was from Randell.

"Gotta, have a beer with that," Chuck said as he put one next to my burger. "You are legal, aren't you?" he said and smiled.

It was the first time I had seen him smile and two deep dimples suddenly appeared.

"Got something to tell you, Chuck." I proceeded to tell him about Smitty. Then I couldn't help myself, I asked, "Chuck, were you having an affair with Beth?"

"Hell no, I was forty and married then. She was just a kid."

I turned my phone to show him the selfie Randell just sent. In it, he was smiling and deep dimples dented his cheeks.

Chuck ran his fingers through his still mostly, black, curly hair. "He's my kid isn't he?"

"I don't know, Chuck, is he?"

Yeah, sometimes we don't look like our parents and sometimes we do.

A man may disappear, vanishing totally from the lives of others, never be heard from again — and yet time has a way of catching up with anyone, regardless of how well they are hidden.

Mr. Cozine is well and widely published. His work has appeared in Ellery Queen's Mystery Magazine, Alfred Hitchcock's Mystery Magazine, Mysterical-E, Sherlock Holmes Magazine, and Woman's World. His story, "A Private Hanging" was a finalist for the Derringer award

Where Have You Gone?

by Herschel Cozine

The disappearance of Jeff Lisbon is still a topic of conversation wherever people gather. It seemed incredible at the time that someone as famous as he could simply vanish without a trace. Sure, it happens now and then. Take Jimmy Hoffa, for example. But this case was different. There wasn't any rational explanation for Lisbon to "take a ride". He wasn't in that line of work. Ask any baseball fan, and he will tell you about Jeff Lisbon. He was one of the greats. He broke into the Major Leagues in 1954, when ballplayers were still playing for the love of the game and not because they could make millions just for hitting .200.

Jeff played first base for the old Philadelphia Jaguars. They weren't much of a team, usually finishing in the lower division, if not dead last. But people went to the park anyway, just to watch Jeff hit the ball.

He never disappointed them. In his rookie year he led the league in home runs and batting average. He was a shoo-in for rookie of the year. His batting average and home run production improved over the next three years until, at the age of twenty-six he was already a legend. He was being compared to Ruth and Gehrig. The press carried stories about him almost every day during the season, predicting he would be baseball's first .400 hitter since Ted Williams.

Defensively he was no slouch either. He won the gold glove in his second year. And he fielded with a flair that delighted the fans. One of his fielding habits became legendary in the short time he was in the majors. Whenever the third out was made at first base, Jeff didn't roll the ball to the pitcher's mound or toss it to the umpire as most first basemen do. Instead he would take the ball out of his glove, carefully set it on the first base sack, then trot off the field. It was a little thing, but fans loved it.

In the fourth year, something happened. It started out well enough. Jeff hit ten homers in April, and was batting a heady .397. Fans were flocking to the park to watch him play. Remarkably, the team itself was doing well, holding on to first place through the first two months of the season.

Then Jeff disappeared. He failed to show up for a Sunday afternoon game against Detroit, and hadn't told a soul. Joe Grimes, the manager, dodged the sportswriters' questions after the game, saying he had had no communication with Jeff, but was certain there was a perfectly good explanation for his absence. After all, he had never done anything like this before. He could always be counted on to be at the park on time. But you could tell that Grimes was as puzzled as anyone, and a little upset with his star player.

When Jeff didn't show up for the Monday game either, rumors began to fly. He was in jail. He was sick. He was drying out in a drunk farm. None of these made sense to me. Jeff was not a drinker. His teammates used to razz him about his teetotaling ways. And he was not one to get into trouble with the law. He was a mother's dream, a role model for any youngster.

The truth was that Jeff was a loner. He seldom socialized with the other players off the field. Most of the time you could find him in his hotel room reading, watching TV, or listening to his pocket transistor radio through his earphones.

That left sickness. But surely he would let someone know if he was sick.

Another ominous rumor made the rounds. He had met with foul play. As much as I hated this theory, it was the only one with any credibility. Someone had kidnapped, or worse yet, killed Jeff Lisbon.

The team owners hired top investigators to look into Jeff's disappearance. The local police were also involved, giving more than their share of attention to the case. They went over Jeff's apartment with a fine-tooth comb. They interrogated friends and neighbors. Nothing.

Jeff was an only child, whose parents were dead, having been killed in an automobile accident a few years before. The neighbors in the town where he went to school knew very little about him. He was a hometown hero to them, but not one they got to know. Nobody was sure where Jeff was from originally, as the town where he grew up was not the town where he was born. His bio in the Baseball Yearbook listed his place of birth as Indiana. But there was no record of it in the State office. This, of course, was given a lot of play in the papers. He was being likened to Joe Hardy of "Damn Yankees", and more than a few people actually believed he had made a pact with the Devil.

There were countless false leads, phony extortion demands, anonymous tips. Every lead was carefully followed.

Days ran into weeks, with no word from Jeff. The team fell apart, sinking into fifth place by the end of June. By the end of July the Jaguars slid into the cellar, eighteen games out of first place.

During the off-season, the press started up again with speculations about the fate of Jeff Lisbon. The supermarket tabloids ran headlines that claimed all sorts of wild things about him.

LISBON CAPTURED BY SPACE ALIENS

JEFF LISBON FOUND IN MENTAL HOME IN MIAMI

And one of the most outrageous headlines:

JEFF LISBON HAS SEX CHANGE OPERATION IN BRAZIL

Headlines and rumors to the contrary, nobody knew what happened to Lisbon. It was a mystery that was grist for the mill, and helped liven up the sports page on a slow news day. But it was a tragic loss to the world of baseball in general and to the Philadelphia Jaguars in particular.

I often wondered since then what happened to Lisbon. I was convinced in my own mind that he had been killed, perhaps by the criminal element, perhaps by accident, maybe by a jealous woman or demented fan. But he couldn't be alive without somebody spotting him. I was sure of that.

In the early spring of 1995 I changed my mind. It was a Saturday morning, unusually balmy in New England for that time of the year. I decided to take a drive up into Maine and cruise the magnificent coastline. There would be no crowd, and the ocean was certain to have a calming effect on me. It always did. The furthest thing from my mind was Jeff Lisbon. I had been a senior in high school at the time of his disappearance. A few years later I hooked on with a newspaper in New Hampshire, eventually working my way up to my present position of editor.

I stopped about mid-morning in the small fishing village of Kennebunkport to stretch my legs and get a cup of coffee. As I climbed out of my car I noticed a group of young men playing a game of ball. Having nothing better to do with my time, I strolled over to the park and took a seat in the dilapidated bleachers on the first base line. No one paid much attention to me. There were no other spectators. The game was progressing in a casual, friendly way, and it was obvious that the players were there for the fun of it.

My attention was drawn to the first baseman for one side. He looked vaguely familiar. His sandy hair, disheveled by the wind and the activity, hung around his eyes. He was tall, lanky, but well coordinated. He fielded the ball with a grace and confidence that is unusual for an amateur.

But when he recorded the last out of the inning I sat up straight, mouth open, and stared. He took the ball, turned, and placed it in the middle of the first base sack!

Maybe it was my imagination, but I suddenly saw a distinct likeness between this young man and Jeff Lisbon. This man was about Jeff's age when Jeff disappeared. It was entirely possible that he was Jeff's son. Of course, Jeff wasn't married at the time. But if he were still alive he would probably be married by now, with children of his own. A son this age was entirely possible.

The game finally ended, and the players broke up, some toward their cars, others to the coffee shop. The young man I had my eye on was sitting on the player's bench removing his cleats. I walked over to him.

"Nice playing," I said.

He looked at me, smiled slightly and nodded. "Thanks."

"What's your name?" I asked.

He tied a shoelace, sat back and studied me through deep blue eyes. "Who wants to know?"

I laughed. "George Ferris." I held out my hand. He shook it tentatively, his eyes never leaving my face.

"Mitch," he said simply.

I sat there trying to think of a tactful way to broach the subject. Finally, deciding the direct approach would be the most effective, I said, "I was a great admirer of your father. He was one of the best."

Mitch looked up sharply, then picked up his glove and stuck it in his pocket. "I don't know what you're talking about," he said.

Years of working as a reporter had trained me to listen for nuances and inflections in people's voices when they talk. Often this will tell a reporter more than the words themselves. When that happens, the reporter must follow his instincts. In this case I sensed a reply that was a little too quick, too practiced. It wasn't the first time, I knew, that this young man had been in this situation. I was certain that Mitch was who I thought he was.

"You're Jeff Lisbon's son. I can see him in every move you make." I watched his face for a reaction, but there was none. He only squinted at me, gave me a bemused smile, then leaned down and tied the other shoe.

"Jeff Lisbon?" he said. "You mean the ballplayer who disappeared?" He laughed softly. "That's a good one." He shook his head and laughed again.

"Come on, Mitch," I said. "You walk like him. You move like him. You even have the habit of putting the ball on the first base sack like he used to do."

"Hey," he said. "I wasn't even born when he was playing ball."

"But you know who he is?" I said.

"Sure. I've heard of him. Who hasn't? But I don't know anything about him. He's just another name." He started to walk away. I put my hand on his shoulder.

"Mitch, listen to me. It's important that I know. If you're Lisbon's son, the whole world will want to hear your story."

He turned and looked me straight in the eye. "Are you a reporter?"

"I'm a baseball fan," I said. "Particularly, I was a great fan of your fa—Jeff Lisbon."

"Yeah," he replied. "I guess he was quite a ballplayer." He picked up his jacket and threw it over his shoulder. "But he's not my father. Sorry."

"But what about that gimmick with the ball on first base?" I asked.

"So what?" he said. "Lisbon didn't have a patent on it. It's a habit I picked up in high school. A lot of kids did it."

I had to agree that it was once in fashion, a tribute of sorts to Jeff. But it died out in the seventies, before Mitch was old enough to be playing baseball. I hadn't seen it done in several years.

"Listen, Mitch, I've got to know. I won't tell a soul. I promise. But..."

"I said I was sorry," he said. "I don't mean to be rude, but you're making it hard for me." His eyes glinted like steel and his jaw set firmly. The defiant stare made me take a step back. He balled his hand into a fist, then relaxed it and turned away. He opened the car door and slid behind the wheel.

I watched him drive away, cursing myself for not getting his last name.

From that day on, Jeff Lisbon became an obsession with me. I haunted the ballpark where I first saw Mitch, hoping to see him again. But he never returned. His teammates knew nothing about him. He was just a guy that showed up now and then and played ball with them. Yes, he was good. Very good. But he was a loner. He had no friends on the team. They didn't even know where he lived.

Back at the newspaper office, I visited the "morgue" and looked up editions of 1957, when the story first broke. I don't know what I expected to find, but as it turned out, I learned little that I didn't already know.

The first mention of Lisbon occurred in the Monday edition, June 10, 1957. At the time, there was no real story to report. He had simply failed to show for the Tiger game. All the story rated was a one line blurb in the capsule box of Page 1, referring the reader to the sports page. The rest of the front page concerned itself with stories about an upcoming presidential trip, an earthquake in Greece, and the killing of a bigwig crime boss in Detroit on Saturday night.

The next edition gave the story a front page spread, and by midweek Lisbon dominated the front page. But none of the stories were of any help. The human interest background, quotes from teammates and coaches, and the usual platitudes about his ability and his value to the game of baseball were there. But I knew no more about Jeff Lisbon's mysterious disappearance than I did before I started reading.

Lisbon's roommate on the road had been Spuds Denigan, a second string outfielder for the Jaguars. He became famous overnight because of Lisbon's disappearance, and had spent more time answering questions than playing baseball. I learned from Jake Fortner, our sportswriter at the paper, that Spuds was now a coach for the Fort Lauderdale Leopards, a minor league team in Florida. I decided to pay him a call.

I caught up with Spuds at the Leopard's ballpark. He hadn't changed much from his playing days. His blonde crew-cut had become a shaggy gray, and he had a paunch. But he was in remarkably good shape for a man his age.

I introduced myself and extended my hand. He shook it absently, never taking his eyes off of the players that were shagging fly balls in the outfield. But when I told him why I was there, he turned and eyed me with amusement.

"You can't be serious," he said. "Lisbon disappeared almost forty years ago. Since then I've talked to every reporter in the country. I've said all there is to say on the subject."

"I understand," I replied. "But I would appreciate it if you would talk to me about it. I'll pay you for your time."

Spuds snorted and spat a wad of tobacco juice towards third base. "Hell," he said. "There's nothin' I can tell you that hasn't been in the papers. And that you can get for free. Why would you want to pay me?" He spat again and grunted.

I ignored his protests. "You were Lisbon's roomie?" I asked.

"Yeah."

"How well did you know him?"

Spuds shook his head sadly. "Not at all, my friend," he said. "Lisbon didn't let anybody get too close to him."

"He was unfriendly?"

"No. I wouldn't say that. He was just quiet. Kept to himself. Never socialized, or even talked much." Spuds grinned. "He was a real loner. It's hard to believe that he was the same guy that was such a sensation on the ballfield." He smiled ruefully. "If I had his talent…"

"Did you see him on the night he disappeared?" I asked.

"Hell, I answered that one a million times," Spuds said. "Yeah. I saw him. He was just leaving the hotel room when I got back from dinner. I told him that me and some of the boys were going out to raise a little hell and asked him to come along. He refused, of course. I knew he would, but I asked him anyway, out of courtesy, mostly."

"Did he say where he was going?"

"No. But then I didn't ask. He seldom went anywhere at night though. Particularly before a game."

"There was nothing he said or did that was unusual, then? He didn't act nervous or strangely?"

"No. Other than going out the night before a game. But I didn't think much about it. It was none of my business." He took off his cap and scratched his forehead. "It seems to me that he only went out at night when he was in Detroit."

"What do you make of that?" I asked.

Spuds shook his head. "Nothin'. Maybe he had a girl stashed somewhere. I don't know. He didn't seem the type, but as I said, I didn't know Lisbon. None of us did."

"Did you ever meet his parents?"

"Never. In fact, I'm not sure the Lisbon's were his real parents. He may have been adopted."

"Oh?" I said, suddenly interested. "I don't remember ever reading about that. Did you tell that to the police?"

"Probably not. They never asked. Besides, I can't be sure. It's a hunch more than anything. They were already dead when Lisbon joined the team."

"Did he ever talk about them?"

"Lisbon never talked about much of anything. But I remember one time, when I asked about his father, he got red in the face and clammed up, even quieter than he usually was."

"Why, do you suppose?"

Spuds shrugged. "Dunno. I figured maybe he didn't get along with his old man when he was alive and he was feeling guilty about it. I never brought the subject up again."

"Interesting," I said.

Spuds nodded. "Mebbe," he said. "But what good is it to you?"

"None, I guess. But it's the only new thing I've heard in close to forty years."

Spuds chuckled. "I guess you can hardly expect to get any startling new information after all this time."

I nodded in agreement, thanked him, and left.

A month went by. It was early May when I finally got a break that led me to the object of my search. I had spent the morning in Wells, a town about ten miles south of Kennebunkport. It is a seacoast town dedicated to fishing. But its charm and scenic beauty makes it a popular tourist attraction. It was too early in the season for the tourists, and many of the shops and restaurants were not yet open. On this spring day, however, several were being painted and patched in anticipation of the coming summer and the influx of tourists.

I strolled along the deserted streets that rambled through the complex of shops and restaurants that made up a seaside area known as Perkins Cove. I stopped to watch a young man on a ladder putting the finishing touches to a sign above the door of a gift shop. I recognized him as the baseball player from Kennebunkport.

Remembering our last encounter, I decided against approaching him directly. Instead, I waited until he had finished painting and drove away. As a precaution I jotted down the license plate number of his truck. Then I climbed the steps of the store and went inside.

An older man was standing toward the back of the room with a clipboard and pencil taking inventory. He looked at me, then back to the shelves.

"We're closed," he said.

"I'm not here to buy anything," I answered. "But I would like to know if you could tell me who your sign painter is."

The man lowered his clipboard and studied me. "Why do you want to know?"

"He does good work," I said. "I may want to use him to do some painting for me."

The man nodded. "He's a freelancer," he said. "Guy by the name of Mitch Jeffries."

I suppressed a smile as I caught the last name. Jeffries. Jeff. Coincidence? I thought not.

"Where can I get in touch with him?"

"He lives in Ogunquit. Got his address here if you want." He crossed over to the desk at the rear of the room. He ruffled through a sheaf of papers, picked one up and handed it to me.

I thanked him and left, feeling a sense of anticipation as I made the short drive to Ogunquit.

It took a little help from one of the residents to direct me to the street I was looking for. But I finally found it, and turned down the tree-lined road on the edge of town in a middle class, quiet neighborhood.

I found Mitch's house easily enough. But my attention was drawn to the house next door to it. On the mailbox at the head of the driveway was the name, "Jeffries".

I guessed that this house was the one I was looking for, the home of Jeff Lisbon. It was a simple white house, with shutters drawn and drapes pulled. But the smartly groomed lawn and bright array of flowers was evidence that whoever lived there enjoyed keeping a house and yard. My heart raced excitedly as I climbed the steps. I pressed the bell and heard the chimes sound from somewhere deep inside.

For several seconds there was no sound. I was about to press the bell again when the front door opened slowly and a woman's face appeared in the doorway.

"Mrs. Jeffries?" I said.

She nodded.

"I would like to speak with your husband if I may. Is he home?"

"Who are you?" she said in a voice so soft I could hardly hear.

"I am a friend. A concerned friend."

She brushed a stray hair from her eye, studying me all the while. Finally, she said, "I never saw you before. I know all of Peter's friends." She started to close the door. I pushed an arm against it.

"Of course," I said. "I never met your husband personally. But I know him. So do a million other fans who used to watch him play ball."

The spark of fear that flashed in her eyes was fleeting. She covered it quickly. "I'm afraid you're mistaken," she said. "My husband is a fisherman."

I barely heard her answer, as my attention was drawn to the man in the hall behind her. He stepped forward and put his hand on the woman's shoulder. "It's all right, Charlotte," he said. "I'll handle this." He turned to me. "What is this all about?"

I studied his face. I could see no resemblance to the young Jeff Lisbon except around the eyes. But he was about the right age and height. He was in his mid sixties and stood an inch or two over six feet. Plastic surgery could account for the facial features.

"You're Jeff Lisbon," I said.

He frowned. "I don't understand," he said. "My name is Peter Jeffries."

I shook my head. "I met your son, Mitch, a few months ago. Watching him play ball took me back almost forty years. I know who you are."

"You're mistaken," he said.

I stepped back, never letting my eyes leave his face. "Mr. Jeffries," I said, "I apologize for invading your privacy. But I can't leave until I know why you did what you did." I waited for him to answer, but he stood there silently, returning my stare.

"I am the editor of the Concord Journal," I said. "I am sitting on the sports story of the century. You will be paid well for your story. I'd be willing to..."

He held up his hand. "There is no story," he said. "I am not who you think I am. Now, would you please excuse us?" He reached for the door and started to pull it shut. But I stood firm.

"Look," I said. "I could bring the entire world to your house by the end of the week if I chose. Neither of us want that. But I'm a newsman, and you are news."

He started to protest, but I went on. "If you cooperate with me, I promise I won't reveal your whereabouts. You have my word on that."

Mrs. Jeffries started toward me. "Please leave us alone," she said. "We're just ordinary people who mind our own business. All we want is our privacy." Her eyes were swimming with tears, and mirrored a desperation that frightened me.

A lot has been written about the lack of compassion that a reporter has when he is on the verge of a major news story. We are trained to go for the jugular, and not worry about the toes we step on or the privacy we invade. Sadly, this may be true a lot of the time. But I was suddenly confronted with my conscience and my sense of fair play. Looking at Mrs. Jeffries, hearing the desperation in her voice, sensing the fear, I hesitated. In my profession, hesitation is fatal.

I stepped back. "Please forgive me," I said. "Try to understand that Jeff Lisbon was a hero to millions. I was one of his fans—maybe his greatest fan. To this day the world wonders what happened. They deserve to know the answer."

Mrs. Jeffries was crying softly. Her husband put his arm around her, looking at me all the while. "Please go," he said.

I paused with my hand on the door. I pulled a business card from my pocket and handed it to Jeffries.

"If you are who I think you are, and you want to square your account with your fans, please call me. Anytime. Day or night."

I turned and left. As I nosed the car away from the curb, Jeffries came out of the house and waved me over. I stopped and rolled the window down.

"Mister Ferris," he said, "you seem like a decent sort. You won't make up a lot of stories and cause my wife and me grief because you think I'm some famous baseball player, will you?"

I watched his face as his expression went from worried to pleading. Then I shook my head. "As far as I'm concerned, there is no story."

Jeffries let an audible sigh escape. He extended his hand and I shook it. "Thank you," he said. "I certainly am grateful to you."

He stepped back. I pulled away from the curb slowly, watching him in the rearview mirror as I drove away. He stood, tall and erect, his arm around his wife. Together they went into the house.

I never told anyone about my meeting with Peter Jeffries, or Jeff Lisbon, if indeed he was who I thought he was. I did, after all, make him a promise. But it wasn't easy. I was sitting on the biggest story of my career; one that any reporter would give his soul to write. I knew I was right about Jeffries. But I had no hard proof, and furthermore, I had made a rash promise in a moment of weakness. I wrestled with the problem, cursing myself for letting my heart rule my head. And I was more curious than ever. What had happened to cause Lisbon to do what he did? And why, to this day, is he so afraid?

A year went by. I had put the meeting with Jeff Lisbon out of my mind, as much as one can, considering its importance. I had been away from my office for two weeks, attending a news editors' conference in New York. When the conference was over I took a brief vacation, telling myself that after a week in New York it was needed.

The letter was waiting for me when I returned. It was a small envelope, addressed in a feminine hand, with tiny loops and delicate lines. There was no return address, but the postmark was Portland, Maine. I opened it slowly.

A clipping fluttered out of the envelope and settled on the desk. I picked it up and read it. It was a brief accounting of a boating accident, which claimed the lives of Peter Jeffries and his son, Mitch. I sat back shocked at the news. Several minutes went by before I noticed that the envelope contained a note. It was from Mrs. Jeffries, and said simply, "Peter told me to get in touch with you. Please come see me at your convenience." It was signed, "Charlotte Jeffries."

I wasted no time getting up to see Mrs. Jeffries. It was only a two-hour drive from the office to her house in Maine. I knocked gently on the door, and she answered it immediately. With a soft smile, she invited me into the house.

"I was so sorry to hear about Mitch and your husband," I said. "Please accept my condolences." I held out a small bouquet of flowers. She thanked me, took them and put them in a vase, which she set on the table. I remembered her as a small woman, but in her grief she seemed smaller still, and vulnerable. Her eyes were red but dry. Her tiny shoulders were held square, and she faced me with a dignity that masked a world of hurt.

"Thank you for coming," she said.

She studied my face, as if looking for strength, or trust, or for some assurance that everything was going to be all right. Finally she sat down in the overstuffed chair. I took the chair across from her. A few awkward minutes went by while Mrs. Jeffries composed herself. Then, with a sudden resolve, she spoke.

"You were right about Peter," she said simply.

Although her words didn't surprise me, I felt a surge of excitement. She looked at the floor, her hands clasped together in her lap.

"He gave up so much, you know," she went on. "He had everything going for him." She shook her head. "It's all so sad. So very sad."

"Why did he run away?" I asked. "What terrible thing happened to make him do what he did? After all these years, the world still wants to know."

Charlotte Jeffries leaned forward. For several minutes the room was quiet except for the muffled whir of the air conditioner. When she looked up from the table her eyes were swimming with tears.

"You're a newspaperman," she said. "I'm sure you know all the stories surrounding my husband's disappearance. Do you remember the day he disappeared?"

"As if it were yesterday," I replied.

"Then you must know about Johnny Geller."

The name rang a bell. "Geller," I said out loud. "Johnny Geller. Why is that name familiar to me?"

"Johnny Geller," she said, "was a mobster. He was a gang boss who worked out of Detroit."

Suddenly I remembered. On the front page of the paper I studied when looking up Lisbon's disappearance was a story about the killing of a mob leader. His name was Geller.

"Yes," I told Mrs. Jeffries. "I know who Geller is—or was. But what does he have to do with all this?"

"My husband," she said in a voice so low that I had to strain to hear, "was with Geller when he was killed."

I sat up straight. Jeff Lisbon was the last person anyone would suspect of fraternizing with the likes of Johnny Geller. "Why?" I said. "What business would Jeff have with Geller?"

"Peter," she said, then caught herself. "Jeff saw the whole thing. The men who killed Geller tried to kill Jeff as well. He had no choice but to do what he did. His life was in danger, and he certainly had no chance to survive if he were to continue to play ball. He would be an easy target every time he walked out onto the field."

"Why didn't he go to the police?"

Charlotte shook her head. "What could they do?" she said. "They couldn't protect him twenty-four hours a day. Jeff Lisbon was a household name. He was always in the public eye. There was no way the police or anyone could protect him if someone wanted to kill him." A note of urgency crept into her voice. "And these thugs wanted Jeff dead. They would stop at nothing to kill him."

"How did he get away from these people?" I asked.

"Jeff was very athletic, of course. He escaped down an alley and vaulted over the wall. The men who were after him were not very good at that sort of thing. He was lucky."

I nodded agreement. Not many people live to tell about getting away from the mob. "Where did he go?"

"He went into Canada. He took on a new identity. He had plastic surgery so no one would recognize him. After a few years he met me and we were married. It was only after we had been married awhile that he told me who he was. I knew little about baseball, but I had heard of him."

"Was he in danger after you met him?"

"All of the time," Mrs. Jeffries said. "The mob has everything it takes to find someone if they want him badly enough. They have better resources than any law enforcement agency. We lived in constant fear of being discovered. We moved often, always a step ahead of them. We finally settled here in Maine where people tend to their own business. No one here recognized him. People left us alone." She pulled at her sleeve. "Then you found us. I was so afraid that you would write about him and give us away."

"It's quite incredible that I should find him when the mob couldn't. Mitch used the ball on first base gimmick which Jeff was so famous for."

"Yes," she said. "He told us. He hadn't done that for years. But he got careless." She smiled wanly. "Such a simple thing, but so important. Mitch was devastated."

I shifted in my chair. "I am sorry if I caused you any grief," I said.

She reached her hand out and placed it on mine. "Mister Ferris, you were so kind and understanding. We both knew that you knew who he really was. It was truly generous of you to do what you did. That's why Jeff wanted me to talk to you, to tell you the truth after all these years. We were both very grateful, and he felt he owed you."

"Mrs. Jeffries," I said. "I don't understand why Jeff Lisbon would be consorting with the likes of Johnny Geller. Jeff was above reproach in his personal life. Dealing with the underworld is not something anyone would expect of him."

Charlotte Jeffries lowered her eyes and sighed. "It was also against the rules. Jeff knew that. And he knew he could be barred from baseball for life if he was caught." She looked up. "But he wasn't doing anything wrong." Her voice quavered and tears filled her eyes again.

I waited for her to regain her composure. She folded and unfolded her hands and dabbed at her eyes with the corner of her handkerchief. "Forgive me," she said at last. "But I find this very difficult to talk about."

"I understand," I replied. "I hate to put you through this. But it is important that I know why Jeff was seeing Johnny Geller. It simply makes no sense. If, as you say, he was doing nothing wrong, then what possible reason could he have for jeopardizing his career as he did?"

Mrs. Jeffries took a deep breath and stood up. She turned and looked out of the window, her back to me as she spoke. "Mister Ferris," she said, "Johnny Geller was Jeff's father."

I had prepared myself to hear almost any wild story about Jeff Lisbon. But Mrs. Jeffries' statement, delivered softly and simply, hit me with the force of a locomotive.

"I...I don't believe it," I stammered.

"I know how ridiculous it sounds," she said. "I didn't believe it either. I didn't want to. I still have difficulty accepting it. But it's true."

I started to say something, then sat back and waited for Mrs. Jeffries to go on.

"Jeff's real mother was one of Geller's girlfriends. She put him up for adoption shortly after he was born. With Geller's money and influence, it was done without records or paperwork. There is no way anyone can trace Jeff's birth to Geller."

"When did Jeff find out who his real father was?"

"He learned it as a child. His real mother wrote and told him. It was a spiteful thing to do, but she had a falling out with Geller, and this was her way of getting even with him." She brushed her hand over her face. "It hurt Jeff far more than it hurt Geller."

"Did Jeff see his father often?"

"Whenever he was in Detroit," she said. "In spite of Johnny Geller's occupation, Jeff developed a respect for him, and a re-served kind of love that a son has for his father. And Johnny respected Jeff as a son and as a ballplayer."

"So his meeting with Geller that night was simply that of a son visiting his father. Nothing illegal?"

Mrs. Jeffries nodded.

"And because of it he sacrificed a career and a life that he obviously loved." I was talking more to myself than to her. "What a waste."

"Jeff never stopped loving the Jaguars and baseball. There were so many times when he wanted to go back and take his chances. He would be doing what he loved to do most, even if it cost him his life. But by then we were married and had Mitch. So he no longer had just himself to think about."

"But after so many years. Surely the mob…"

Charlotte Jeffries smiled ruefully. "They never give up, Mister Ferris," she said. "Jeff knew that. As long as he was alive they would want to kill him. He knew too much, or so they thought. After all, his father was a big man in the mob."

I nodded, all the while cursing Johnny Geller, the mob, and Jeff Lisbon himself for robbing the baseball world of one of its greatest stars.

We talked well into the night, my tape recorder capturing her every word. Finally she rose from the couch, smiled wistfully and cradled her arms across her chest. "So, you have your story, Mister Ferris. Peter won't rest in his grave until the world knows the truth. I know you'll be fair and tell the story the way it should be told."

"Will you be all right?" I asked.

"I have money saved. I have friends."

"If I can ever do anything for you, please ask."

She took my hand in hers. "Thank you."

I watched her with a growing admiration of her inner strength and determination. Jeff Lisbon had chosen well. Reluctantly I stepped outside and into the soft summer night. I left her standing in the doorway, her small figure silhouetted against the light.

The drive back to Concord was a lonely one, filled with poignant thoughts about a young athlete who set the world on fire, only to have it taken from him in a tragic fleeting moment. If only the Jaguars were playing somewhere else that day. If only the assassins had waited one more day. If only…

"Oh, hell," I said out loud.

Startled by my own voice, I shifted in my seat and sped through the night. Life is full of "if onlys". And no one, not even the Jeff Lisbons of the world, can escape them.

I wrote the story without revealing Mrs. Jeffries' whereabouts. I owed her that. She would be hounded for the rest of her life if anyone knew where she was. She had given me enough records and journals that I didn't need her to vouch for the story.

Naturally, I received many awards, including the Pulitzer Prize. But none of them seemed important to me. It isn't the kind of story one enjoys writing. Strangely enough, I gained a great deal of satisfaction out of a relatively mundane event that occurred this fall. The Philadelphia Jaguars, the doormat of the American League for all these years, won the pennant. They went on to take the World Series in five games. I know Jeff would have liked that.

About This Book

The typeface in this book is Garamond and Helvetica (for the headings). It was laid out using Adobe InDesign software and converted to PDF for uploading to the printing facility.

About Darkhouse Books

Darkhouse Books is dedicated to publishing entertaining fiction, primarily in the mystery and science fiction field. Darkhouse Books is located in Niles, California, an inadvertently-preserved, 120 year old, one-sided, railtown, forty miles from San Francisco. Further information may be obtained by visiting our website at www.darkhousebooks.com.